EMBATTLED HOME

BY

J.M. MADDEN

Print Edition

Cover by Viola Estrella

ACKNOWLEDGEMENTS

Ever incredible hubby gets top billing, simply for his unwavering support. I love you dearly babe.

Donna and Robyn, I can't imagine where I would be without you guys. Seriously. I love you both.

Madden Militia, you ladies ROCK! Thank you for loving my men as much as I do!

To my beta readers for this book – Mayas, Sandie, Andrea, Anima, you really gave great input. Thank you very much!

Mary, you are a rock star. Thank you for restraining the Comma Queen!

And to our military stationed around the globe. Thank you, thank you, thank you! I know you don't get recognized for what you do nearly enough, but hopefully more voices will join mine.

Chapter One

CHAD WENT FROM reclining in his seat, debating whether or not to take off, to hyper aware as he heard a crash of glass and a muffled sound from inside. His gaze snapped to the little white house with black shutters he'd been watching for the past couple months, but everything was dark. What the hell had he heard?

He'd been sitting here for five hours, waiting for the woman's supposed indiscretions to show up, and all had been quiet. The little girl had gone to bed several hours ago, just like clockwork. Lora O'Neil, formerly Malone, had then puttered around the house, picking up toys and re-locking windows and doors.

She had locked the windows and doors four times now.

Fumbling the door handle with his bad hand, he jumped out of the car and started to cross the suburban street, the hairs on his neck prickling. He circled her gray minivan and paused. Nothing moved. It was after midnight on a Tuesday and every normal person in this quiet Denver suburb was in bed. The woman had been the only one moving around. She'd been pacing constantly.

For a second, he debated what to do. If he went up to the house to investigate, he ran the chance of being exposed. The woman never slept for long stretches and as restless as she'd been there was a very good chance she was still up.

The decision was taken out of his hands when he heard a second crash from inside the house, followed by a woman's muffled scream. Adrenalin surged as he took off running. The front had been clear for the past several minutes, so he circled the house to the back door.

"Oh, shit," he grunted as he leapt the pile of glass that used to be her sliding glass door. Inside the house, things were upturned everywhere. Dark black potting soil littered the bright white carpet.

The ceiling fan was swinging as if it had just been hit. His heart pounded as he saw a smear of blood on the opposite wall.

A thump from somewhere down the hallway guided his feet. What the hell was going on?

A second smear of blood told him he was in the right area as he cleared the doorway to the master bedroom. For several heartbeats in time he couldn't believe what he saw.

His client, the well-to-do, likable Mr. Derek Malone was beating the woman Chad had been hired to watch. Her left eye was already purple and swelling shut. Blood had begun to run down her forehead from a cut at her hairline. Derek had his hand clamped so tightly over her mouth he was pushing her head down into the mattress. Her clenched fists were beating at his head ineffectually, and Derek laughed as he reached for his fly with his other hand.

Chad was overcome with a violent fury.

Lunging forward, he slammed his right fist into the side of Derek Malone's face. The jerk never saw it coming. The force of the punch knocked the ass off the bed and against the wall, dazing him for a moment. When Derek looked up and saw Chad standing over him, he sneered.

"Get out of here, gimp. This doesn't concern you. It's between me and my wife."

"Ex-wife, asshole," the woman croaked from the bed, levering herself up. Chad was dismayed to see she was holding her right wrist, and her lip was split on the right side.

Chad's inattention cost him. Derek leapt up and sucker punched him in the right kidney, then tried a roundhouse to the jaw, but Chad jerked back just in time. Doubling his own fist, he smashed it up into pretty boy's nose, breaking it instantly. Blood gushed, and Derek crumpled back to the floor, his hands trying to staunch the flow.

"You son-of-a-bitch," he garbled. "You're fired."

Chad barked out a laugh and pulled his cellphone from his pocket. "Too late, dude. I already quit. LNF is off the case."

Dialing 911, he requested a squad car and ambulance.

"No siren," the woman pleaded. Nodding, Chad passed on the

request and hung up. She was sitting up now, and Chad felt like shit. She was obviously in pain, hunched over and cradling her stomach and wrist. Occasionally she wiped away tears that coursed down her cheeks. At one point she found the blood on her head and sighed as she rubbed it away from her fingertips. Her whole demeanor screamed misery. It broke Chad's heart to watch her.

Derek, on the other hand, ran his mouth non-stop. Chad fought the urge to punch him again just to shut him up. When he started to berate the woman for being weak and asking for what he had done to her, Chad had had enough. Jerking Malone up by the collar, he frog-marched the shorter man out to the demolished living room to wait for the cops. He glanced at the woman before he cleared the doorway. "Will you be okay here alone for a few minutes?"

She nodded her head, wincing.

Within minutes, Denver P.D. arrived on scene. Chad flashed his state investigator's license and explained what had happened. Derek denied everything, of course, and told them he wanted his lawyer. They escorted him out in handcuffs, protesting the entire way.

The ambulance team had already disappeared into the back bedroom, and he found himself drawn back that way. The woman was blinking into a penlight beam with her one good eye and the paramedic was asking her questions. She looked up at Chad for a brief moment, and there was such desolation in her face that he almost stepped forward to console her. But he stopped when she looked away. It wasn't really his place to console her. Hell, he had been hired to gather evidence *against* her. Derek had retained the agency because he feared for his daughter's welfare, saying that Lora was subjecting the girl to unsavory characters.

So far, the only unsavory character he had seen her with was Derek.

Chad had collected no evidence the entire time he had been watching them. Lora kept her head down and watched everything warily. She hustled her daughter to and from the minivan and very rarely let her play outside. When she did go anywhere, it was to a nondescript house in Arvada where she would stay for several hours then leave. Chad had been unable to find out what was in the house, only that it was owned by a corporation. The only other person he had seen at the house had been an elderly black woman, no relation to Lora Malone.

Derek had said that he believed she had a boyfriend, and that she was partying at all hours, leaving her daughter to fend for herself. Derek's mother had also come forward with 'incriminating' evidence. Chad had a feeling now it had all been fabricated.

Chad had seen no evidence of any of it in the six weeks he'd been watching her.

"Is my mommy okay?"

Glancing down, Chad realized the little girl had come out of her own room, and was now peering into her mother's room. Shadowed green eyes widened when she saw the people grouped around the bed.

"Mommy?" her little voice quivered in fear.

"I'm okay, honey, just had an accident. Can you go to your room please?"

Chad's heart clenched when the woman smiled brightly for her little daughter. That had to hurt like a bitch with that split lip, but she didn't flinch at all. She was more concerned about reassuring her child.

Reaching down with his good hand, he turned the little girl's shoulders away from the doorway.

"Come on, sweets. Why don't you show me your room?"

Hanging her head, little Mercedes Malone trudged back into her bedroom. She dragged a stuffed animal with her by one ear. Chad realized it was supposed to be a dog, although it was about six different pastel colors. It was obviously well-loved.

Mercedes was supposedly six years old, but even to his inexperienced eye, the little one seemed tiny for her age. Climbing onto the twin bed, the little girl sat cross-legged in her pink and purple Dora PJs, not looking at Chad. Rumpled blond hair, so similar to her mother's, shaded her face.

"This is my room," she said quietly. "Is my mom okay?"

Chad looked at her in the illumination from the pale blue night-light, debating how much to tell her. "I think she will be, but she has to go get checked by the doctors right now."

She blinked at him, and he frowned at the knowledge he could see in her eyes.

"She's had accidents before. But only when Derek's around."

It took everything Chad had not to flinch.

"Were you in an accident?" she whispered. "Is that why your arm is like that?"

He blinked at the shift in topic and looked down at the combat-modified appendage. "Yes, I was. Several years ago."

She nodded and lay down on her mattress, pulling the comforter over top of herself.

"Can't the doctors fix it?" she whispered.

He shook his head and looked at the bookcase beside him, desperate for a distraction. "Hey, this looks good."

He pulled out a white book with a little girl having tea with a group of stuffed animals on the front.

"Oh, that's my favorite," she sighed.

"Your mom must love you very much then, because you have a bunch of these books."

Chad realized that was the incontrovertible truth too. He had logged many man-hours watching Lora O'Neil, and he had never seen her raise her voice, let alone a hand, to the child. Quite the contrary, actually. The child seemed to have every toy a kid would need, and her room was outfitted with nice furniture. Many times he had watched Lora snatch the little girl up in her arms and give her big, tickling smooches, with Mercedes wiggling and giggling. He had only ever seen a mother who loved her child. Certainly not a woman endangering her daughter with her irresponsible lifestyle.

Chad had seen men approach Lora, attracted by her classic blond good looks. And he had seen them be shot down, one after another. Those unique forest green eyes would darken with contempt before she forced a smile, shook her head and turned away. It was a little depressing watching her go through as many men as she had, because he had to admit, she appealed to him as well.

Damn it.

He needed to call Duncan and let him know what was going on.

Chad began reading the book. It only took a few minutes for the little girl to slip back into sleep. Covering her a little tighter with the comforter, Chad replaced the book on the shelf and left the room.

In the other bedroom, Lora was arguing with the ambulance workers.

"I'm not going to the hospital. I can't."

"Ma'am, you probably have a concussion. I also believe you have cracked bones in your face. Judging by the swelling in your wrist, it could be broken too." The gray haired technician was obviously going over the same argument again. "You have to be seen by somebody."

Lora shook her head obstinately, even though it looked like it hurt. "I can't leave. I can't leave my daughter."

Chad fought with his sickening guilt. If he had been just a few seconds quicker, she never would have been hurt at all.

"I'll stay with her."

He didn't even realize he had spoken until she whipped a venomous glare on him.

"Oh, really? And snoop through my house and gather evidence on me? I heard what you guys said to each other."

"Then you heard me quit, too…" he told her quietly.

She frowned, trying to make sense of his actions. Chad gave her a hard look.

"You need to go to the hospital. If for no other reason than to have documentation when you take him to court."

Raising a bloody hand to her head, she shielded her eyes for several long moments, obviously weighing her options. When she eventually looked up at Chad, determination lined her face. "I'll call a neighbor to come over and sit with her. You don't need to. I'll go to the hospital in a bit, after the neighbor gets here."

The gray haired paramedic immediately started shaking his head. "Ma'am, you need to go now. With the swelling on your face, you probably have a concussion under there, which can lead to swelling and bleeding and eventually death. You need to be checked out by the doctors as soon as possible."

She seemed to understand the medic's warnings, because her shoulders slumped in defeat. "Okay, but not until she gets here."

Chad crossed behind the medic and picked up the cordless phone from the floor. One-handed, he pushed a button to silence the 'disconnected line' beeping and handed the receiver to her. "Call her now. I'll wait until she gets here so you can go."

The ex-Mrs. Malone was normally a beautiful woman. He had seen the professional photos and candid family shots the Malones had supplied, but right now she was a mess. Her blond hair was bedraggled and dirty, blood was streaked across her face, and her left eye was so swollen it would be days before it was back to normal. But she had a bearing to her that was indomitable. Her t-shirt was ripped at the collar and hanging down over one breast, but she sat on the edge of the bed as if she were wearing an evening gown. It was impressive, her courage.

Holding the cordless in front of her face awkwardly, she punched in several numbers. Whoever she called answered quickly and asked very few questions, because she clicked the off button within less than a minute.

"Heather will be here in about twenty minutes." Pointing a chipped-nailed finger at the nightstand, she motioned to a tablet and pen on one corner. "Write your name, cell phone number and who you work for on that paper, please. And your boss's contact number so I can call to confirm who you are."

Chad bent over the nightstand and wrote the requested information down. Then he wrote Duncan's cell phone number. What a cluster this night had turned out to be, and he still had to talk to his partner and explain what had gone down.

Even though it was after midnight Duncan apparently answered on the first ring, because the woman asked him questions like she was an attorney, one right after another. His partner seemed to answer everything to her satisfaction, because she handed the receiver to him. "Okay, you check out. He wants to talk to you."

Chad took the handset from her and motioned to the paramedic to get her on the gurney, because she looked ready to fall over on the bed.

"Yeah, Dunc?"

"What the fuck is going on over there? It was a simple surveillance op, gather info and that's it. No contact. What the hell happened?"

Stepping out of the room to give the medics room to carry her out, Chad leaned against a wall in the hallway. Lowering his voice so he wouldn't be overheard, he filled his partner in on the details. Duncan was quiet until he finished.

"Okay, Chad. I should have known you wouldn't go off like that without a reason. Is she going to be all right?"

"Yeah, I think so. She's pretty beat up. I'm glad I got here when I did though, because he was about to remind her of his conjugal rights."

"Shit," Duncan said softly.

"Yep." Chad stepped to the living room to watch as they hoisted Lora O'Neil into the waiting ambulance. Her eyes were closed and her head was tipped back against the cushion as if she were asleep. Chad would almost bet she would not allow herself to pass out. That was one strong woman.

Duncan was still speaking on the other end of the line and Chad had to look away from Lora. "What? Oh, yeah, I'm going to stay with the little girl until her friend gets here to watch her."

Leaning past the doorjamb, he peeked inside the girl's room. She was a lump under the covers, sleeping deeply. Chad nodded into the phone, following his boss's conversation even though he studied the child. "I will. I know. I know. Okay, see you tomorrow."

He stood in that doorway and watched the little one breathe. Twenty minutes later, a woman knocked softly on the front door before letting herself in. She showed him her identification. It matched up with what Lora had said to expect, so he let himself out the door.

LORA WAS IN a haze of pain. There was nothing on her that didn't hurt. And it seemed like the doctors were prodding every single injury just to grade her pain. 'So looking at this pain scale, how would you rate your discomfort?' She'd finally gone off on them. "It fucking hurts," she screamed.

The doctor had looked at her as if *she* were the one being unreasonable. After that, everything floated away on a cloud of pain medication. She didn't feel her sprained wrist being wrapped, and she didn't feel the needle in her scalp as they sewed in stitches. The light over the bed was a blinding source of aggravation, and it was a relief when they draped her face in the blue cloth in preparation of fixing her head. It shielded her eyes, and allowed her to rest for just a few minutes.

One of the nurses came in with a clipboard, asking if she had been the victim of sexual assault. Then didn't seem to believe her when she told her no. When she asked the same question for the third time, Lora finally just rolled over on her side and ignored the woman. She seemed to get the hint.

Sometime later, a Denver Police officer arrived to question her about the assault. Lora went through every detail she remembered, then told the woman about the voicemails she had been receiving on her phone. Mostly just hang-ups, but Derek had called yesterday to wish her happy anniversary, even though they had been divorced for two years. Lora had known then he would be coming after her.

No, he hadn't raped her this time.

The officer kept referring to the notes in her notepad, as if she already had a statement from somebody. Oh, yeah, the tall guy. Duh. He stayed until the squad had taken her away. He had apparently talked to the cops and told them what he had seen, too.

She didn't know what to think about him. Relief and appreciation that he had gotten Derek off her, but she was still royally pissed too. He'd been following her for weeks. Her paranoia had served her well when she'd spotted him at her work parking lot one day, and recognized him later on sitting down from the house when she went home. Had he actually thought she wouldn't see him? He followed her everywhere. Sometimes in different vehicles, but always about the same distance away.

What was up with that arm? It stuck out. Even in the midst of her own crises, she remembered cringing in shared pain for him. It looked like he had been burned or something. The flesh was eaten away, and the bones looked kind of warped, like the healing skin was pulling them into unnatural shapes. It looked painful. The scars spread all the way up his neck to his hairline behind his ear. There were a few scars on his face too, but they were just pale white lines, like they had happened several years ago.

It wasn't any business of hers though. She certainly had no reason to be worrying about his pain when she had plenty of her own.

The doctor, too young to have very much experience, admitted her. Lora had expected that and called the sitter to let her know. Truth be known, she dreaded letting her daughter see her this way. Mercy remembered hearing loud voices during the divorce, after Derek had found her, but Lora had carefully made up her face to cover any bruising she incurred. Between the shiner and the cut on her head and the bulky wrap on her arm, she was going to have a lot of explaining to do to her little girl.

They moved her to a quiet room on the fifth floor and finally dimmed the lights before leaving her alone. Lora tried to sleep, but the scene from her house kept replaying in her head. When she did doze off, she would snap awake at the slightest noise from outside in the hallway.

When there finally was a knock at her door, it was almost a relief to have a reason to sit up and be aware. "Come in."

The private investigator stuck his head inside and gave her a slight smile. "Mind if I step in for a minute, ma'am?"

All the anger of the night came rushing back. "Why? Do you need more pictures? Does he want proof of what he did?"

The man shook his head and held out both hands as he stepped into the room. "No camera, I promise. And your ex didn't send me here. I came on my own."

"Why?" she snapped.

"I just wanted to check on you. I feel sick for letting you get hurt."

Lora took a moment to scan his somber face, and all she could see was truth in his vivid blue eyes. At least she thought he was being truthful. She wasn't a great judge of character recently. "I'm fine. It wasn't your fault."

He scrubbed a long hand over his short, walnut colored hair. "It was, though. I'd been there for hours, long past when I should have been off-duty, but something didn't feel right. I could tell you were nervous by the way you were acting and I should have been more aware."

Lora was torn. He seemed like a decent guy, just hired to do a job, but she was royally pissed he'd been watching her like that. "Well, I'm fine. I appreciate your stepping in when you did. Don't feel guilty about it. We're done."

For several long seconds he stared at her before glancing at the floor. When he looked back up, there was a determined look on his face. "Don't worry about our investigation. We are officially off the case. I talked to my partner and if there's anything you need us to do, please let us know." He fished a business card out of his wallet and stepped close enough to the bed to set it on the rolling table. "I called the jail. Derek will at least be kept for the night because they smelled alcohol on his breath, but it's up to the judge what happens in the morning."

Lora's insides tensed up when he stepped close, but she didn't let him see that. She stared at him as hard as she could with her good eye and left the card where it lay. "I don't believe I'll need your services."

Frowning, he turned away and crossed to the door. "That's fine, ma'am, but if he bothers you, let us know."

Lora didn't respond to his slow drawl and he walked out the door. She had a glimpse of scuffed gray cowboy boots before he disappeared.

Panic raced through her and she suddenly felt all vulnerable again. Her stomach shivered with fear, and she felt very alone sitting on the big bed. Slipping down off the mattress, she tried to drag the big recliner they kept for visitors over to the door with her good hand. It took her a while, but she eventually got it wedged underneath the handle. The nurses wouldn't appreciate it, but she would hear a person coming for several seconds. It would give her some time if she needed it.

After tugging on the locked window and crawling into bed, Lora finally allowed herself to relax. Emotions started to swamp her. Unfortunately, that also allowed the tears to come. *Five minutes, damn it, to cry. Then you're done.*

Chad's heart ached in his chest when he heard the woman crying softly in the room. It tugged at his emotions, getting him choked up. He wanted to go back in and pull her into his arms and rock her until she stopped being fearful. The door was blockaded though. And even if he made it in, she certainly wouldn't want his attention.

He gritted his teeth in frustration as he leaned against the wall. Lora O'Neil seemed to be a woman with heart, willing to fight for her child. Over the weeks he'd been watching her, Chad had found himself admiring her for her vigilance with their safety. The girl wasn't out of her sight at all, and the people that watched her seemed just as devoted. Lora worked at the local high school as a secretary, never missing a day or breaking her routine. It was why she'd been so easy to follow. He knew where she was going to be at all times. The only aberration was on Wednesdays, when she went to the big white house in Arvada. She would stay a few hours, then head home. Saturday mornings she took the girl to one of the parks in the city and then went grocery shopping.

The little girl would be worried when her mother wasn't there to cook her breakfast in the morning.

Walking down the hall, he talked to the nurse on duty. He was granted a little leeway with information when he flashed his investigator's badge. Lora would be released the next day at 11 o'clock, as long as the doctor thought she was able. Chad promised to be back then and headed out the door.

Chapter Two

AT TEN-THIRTY THE next morning, Chad waited outside Lora's room. The smell of the antiseptic fumes had hit him as soon as he'd walked in the front door, making him pause as emotions tried to swamp him. It had taken serious effort to make his legs move and remind himself who he was here for. Not for one of his guys. Not for him. Lora.

Nurses had been bustling in and out and he was sure one of them had told her he was there. He made it a point to smile congenially at everybody that went in, in spite of their leery looks. They knew what Lora had been admitted for, but they didn't know what her ex looked like.

Chad understood their hesitation. And appreciated it. There was no way to prove he wasn't her ex unless they asked Lora outright.

So he cooled his heels, waiting till he thought she would be getting ready to go. At quarter till, he knocked on her door and stepped in.

Lora's injuries didn't look any better in the light of day. Her unswollen eye narrowed in on him sharply. "Why are you here? I thought you understood I didn't need your help."

Chad shrugged, trying not to be put off by her demeanor. Honestly, he couldn't blame her for feeling bitchy. If he were in her position he would feel that way too. It wasn't like she had oodles of help.

"I do. I just thought I'd give you a ride home so we could talk about a few things."

Pushing to her feet, she grabbed the railing of the bed to steady herself. "I really don't think we have anything to talk about."

Chad hated to be the bearer of bad news. "Derek bonded out this morning."

A frantic look passed through her eyes before she straightened her spine. "Good for him. I need to get home."

He stepped forward one step. "I know you do. My car is right in front."

The hesitation was obvious on her face. She wanted to get home to be with her daughter, but she wasn't sure if she could trust him or not.

"Have you called for a ride yet?"

She pursed her lips, but winced when the split puckered. "No," she admitted. "I thought the security guard could call me a cab."

Chad held out a plastic Wal-Mart bag. "I got you a pair of sweats. I didn't think the squad grabbed anything for you on the way out the door."

For a long moment, Lora just stood and stared at the swinging gray bag in his hand as if it were a snake. "Lora, you don't want to have to walk into the house in the bloody gown you left in."

She frowned. "I think they may have thrown the thing away in the emergency room. There wasn't much left to it. One of the nurses was going to find me a pair of scrubs or something."

He set the bag on the end of the bed within her reach. "Now you don't have to wear somebody else's clothes."

She glanced at him from beneath her dark lashes. The purpling around her left eye was complete, although some of the swelling had receded, and Chad fought to keep the anger off his face. She'd been through so much and if he had only moved quicker, she wouldn't be here at all.

She reached out and took the bag. "I'll pay you back when we get to the house."

Chad nodded once. If she wanted to pay her way, that was fine. "I'll wait outside for you."

Within just a few minutes, a nurse arrived with her discharge paperwork. Then an orderly arrived and parked a wheelchair outside her room, knocking. Lora appeared in the pink sweats. Chad was impressed with himself. They fit her perfectly. She'd also put on the flimsy little tennis shoes he'd gotten her, but he could tell by the way she shuffled that they didn't fit her correctly.

She eyed the wheelchair belligerently. "I can walk."

The orderly smiled tightly. He'd heard this argument before. "Ma'am, it's hospital policy. I have to wheel you out."

Chad could feel the tension rise in the hallway as she shifted from foot to foot.

"I don't want to sit in the chair."

The orderly glowered. Lora shifted subtly back toward the room.

"Ma'am, I have to wheel you out. It's policy."

Fear skittered across Lora's face and he suddenly realized it wasn't the chair she was objecting to. It was having the big orderly behind her where she couldn't see him.

Chad shuffled forward, wincing slightly. "Mind if I push the chair? My hip's bothering me today. Must be some cold weather moving in."

The orderly looked him up and down, resting lightly on his left arm before meeting his eyes. "Iraq?"

Chad smiled tightly.

The man nodded once and released the chair handles. Chad moved in behind the wheelchair and met Lora's eyes. She didn't look much more accepting of him pushing the chair, but she stepped forward and sat down anyway, placing her feet on the foot rests.

That small glimmer of trust touched him greatly. The poor woman had been through hell, partially brought on by his actions. He wanted to reach out and rest a hand on her shoulder, but he knew for a fact that would send her screaming in the other direction.

Shoving off, he made sure to favor one side to keep his story believable. The orderly walked ahead of them, pushing the elevator button and triggering the automatic doors for their passage. At the parking loop in front of the hospital, he opened the door of his Chevy for Lora and stepped back. As quickly as she could manage, she slid into the seat and shut the door.

Chad turned the chair over to the orderly and thanked the man, shaking his hand, then circled the hood to get in.

Lora had already fastened her seat belt, but she turned her head to look at him. "Thank you for doing that. I didn't want him behind me."

The words were gritted out, as if they'd seriously hurt her pride to say. Chad nodded once, and tried not to make a big deal of it. "I thought not. You're welcome."

They didn't say anything as he pulled out of the hospital lot and turned away from downtown, heading toward her little subdivision.

He glanced at her as they got onto the freeway heading east. "Do you have a place you can stay for a while? Family or something?"

She shook her head. "I don't have family out here. But you probably already know that."

Chad chose not to respond to the bitterness in her voice. He *had* known, but he wanted her to confirm it. "You have a protection order against him, issued by the judge this morning, but I have a feeling Derek doesn't really care about a piece of paper."

He could feel her sharp gaze swing to him. "How do I have a P.O. already? I haven't gone in to file it yet."

"My boss spoke to the judge this morning, before Derek went to court."

Lora exhaled softly. "I guess I have to thank you again."

Chad shook his head as he glanced behind him to shift lanes. "We didn't do this for thanks. We realized we were on the wrong side too late, so we're trying to amend the situation. That's why I need to talk to you about a few things."

"What things?" Her voice was wary, and he had to wonder if she was leery of everything anymore.

"Well, if you don't have a place to stay, we're going to assign a couple of people to keep an eye on you for a while."

"The hell you say!"

Chad glanced at her. Her hands were clenched into fists and her expression was livid.

He forced his voice to stay calm. "Let me tell you why."

She eased back in the seat. "I don't want more people watching me."

"I know you don't, but what about your daughter? You can't be with her twenty-four seven. And from what we were told when Derek hired us, he wants the girl back."

Lora barked out a laugh. "No, he doesn't want her. His mother does. She's the one driving him."

Chad thought she was right. Mrs. Malone had come to the original interview and had supplied several of the "facts" about Lora's unsuitability as a parent. "Well, regardless of who wants her, your child is definitely at risk."

She was quiet for a long time. Chad could feel the anger radiating off of her, but it couldn't be helped. The girl had to be protected.

"How long do you think you'll have to watch us?"

Chad sighed, flicking the turn signal to the right. "Honestly, I don't know. He has to go to court for this assault and hopefully he'll get time for it. But his mother may continue to pursue guardianship. I think the best thing you can do is exactly what you've been doing. Keep your nose clean and provide a safe environment for Mercedes. Unless you have a boatload of money hidden away that you can tap to completely disappear, you're kind of stuck where you are, dealing with things as they come."

Lora knew everything he was telling her was correct, but it was a bitter pill to swallow. She literally had to bite her tongue not to argue.

"Do you think he'll get time for this?" She waved a hand at her face and wrapped wrist.

The investigator shrugged, swinging the wheel with one hand. "If we have anything to say about it he will."

He tossed her a roguish grin, startling her, and Lora wished she could be charmed by him. If she'd been any other woman, he would have appealed to her. The only thing she could appreciate was that he was big and made her feel a little more secure in the strange environment. And his eyes seemed kind.

Lora stared out the window. Her face throbbed, but she knew she wasn't going to use the painkillers in her purse. She'd taken the bottle only because it was more expedient than arguing with the doctor. Derek was known to show up at inopportune times, protection order or not, and she couldn't risk Mercy's safety for her comfort.

The thought of having people follow her deliberately, with her knowledge, sickened her. It defeated everything she had worked for to get away from Derek. During their marriage, she had endured bodyguards everywhere, watching them do everything. Derek was used to it; he'd grown up that way. But to Lora it had been humiliating. None of them had ever stepped in when Derek had beaten her, and their sly glances afterwards told her they would do the same if they ever got the chance. She wasn't sure they hadn't.

Her mother had taught her to be independent. And now, the thought of giving up that independence was abhorrent to her. But she would do it. For the sake of her child, she would do it.

"Okay. We'll accept your help. For now."

Chad nodded. He had known what her answer would be. "We'll try to be as unobtrusive as possible, but if anything seems out of the ordinary we will make ourselves known, so you may want to say something to Mercedes. I don't know what you've told her about your situation, but you may want to think about having a little talk with her. She's going to ask questions anyway when she sees you."

"Mercy," she murmured. "Not Mercedes."

Chad gave her a nod. "Mercy."

Lora sighed at the thought of explaining everything to her sharp-eyed little girl. She was already protective of her. Recently, Mercy had started to show signs of anxiety, not eating correctly and coming into her room at night. Lora knew she fed off of her own worries, which made her guilt all the heavier to bear. It was a vicious cycle.

She dropped down the visor mirror in front of her, then flipped it right back up, disgusted. Nothing she could do to change it anyway. When she got to the house, she'd just have to try to smile her way around her daughter's fears.

All of that went out the window when they pulled into her driveway and there was an unfamiliar black Town Car parked there. Before she could get her seat belt off, the front door of her house opened and Derek's mother walked out, carrying her crying daughter. The sitter scurried along behind, cell phone to her ear. She was obviously pleading with the older woman not to leave yet and talking to somebody else on the other line at the same time.

Lora saw red. Before the car had even come to a stop she was out of the vehicle and running across her yard. All of her hurts were shoved to the side as she rushed to her daughter.

Mrs. Malone saw her coming and pasted a smile to her glossy mouth. "Lora, what a nice surprise."

"Get your hands off my daughter."

The smile stayed on the older woman's mouth, but her eyes chilled. "Well, dear, she's my granddaughter too, you know. I was merely helping you out while you were indisposed."

Lora grabbed Mercy and pulled her into her arms. The little girl burrowed into her neck, sobbing.

The sitter, Heather, rushed to them, crying. "She tried to say she had temporary custody, Lora. I was trying to call you, then I was going to call the police."

Mrs. Malone flashed the woman a scorching look. "I'm her grandmother, you twit. I am allowed to see the child whenever I want."

"No," Lora snapped. "You're not. Not unless I say, and I most definitely didn't."

The older woman smoothed a hand down her black dress as if she hadn't a care in the world. The arrogance on her face was enough that Lora almost laid into her. But then she'd be no better than Derek.

"I want to see my granddaughter, Lora."

For a second, there was a flash of honesty in the woman's face, and genuine pleading, but Lora didn't let that sway her. "Mercy will never be allowed into your home, not as long as Derek is a part of your life. Do you see what he did to me?"

She stepped into the other woman's space, making sure Rosalind got a good view of the ten different shades of color around Lora's swollen eye. Rosalind's gaze flickered and she looked away. "I'm sure if you had spoken with him like he requested months ago it wouldn't have come to that."

Lora snorted in disbelief. "It's just so natural for you to come to his rescue. Leave, Rosalind." Cradling her daughter, Lora backed away from the older woman.

Rosalind lifted her hand to stroke down Mercy's back, then folded it away against her stomach. "You need to realize, Lora, that I will be in my granddaughter's life, and so will her father, whether you want us to be or not."

She lifted her chin and walked to the Town Car. The driver didn't have time to get out to open her door before she was inside and waving at him to drive.

Chad stood on the concrete watching the car pull away. He'd been a solid warmth behind her when she confronted Derek's mother and she appreciated the fact that he had let her confront the woman on her own. It wasn't until the black car was out of sight that she let herself sink to the ground.

Mercy's crying started to lessen, until she leaned back and saw her mother's face. Then the sobs started again.

Lora held her daughter as tight as she dared and whispered that she was okay into Mercy's tiny little ear.

Chad called Duncan as soon as the car disappeared and related what had happened.

"So, she planned to sneak out with the girl while Lora was incapacitated. Isn't she sweet?"

Chad snorted. "If you had seen this piece of work, you would have known she wasn't sweet. That woman could make the devil sweat, if you ask me. She was not happy to be thwarted, let me tell you."

Duncan sighed on the other end of the line. "Well, we'll step up with the protection then. Did you clear it all with her?"

"Kind of. She's not happy about it but I think she'll be more accepting of it now." Chad shifted on his feet, feeling like he needed to reach out to the little girl. She was sobbing as if her little heart were broken. Lora rocked her back and forth on the cement sidewalk, talking to her softly. The sitter stood by, wringing her hands.

Lora stood to adjust the little girl to her hip.

"I need to go, Dunc. I'll call you back in a while."

"Okay. Keep your eyes open."

"Always."

Little Mercy had calmed somewhat. She surveyed her mother's injuries with fear in her eyes, though. "Did Derek do that?"

Lora's eyes darkened, but her chin tipped up. "Yes, he did, honey. But I'm okay now. Did your grandmother say where you were going?"

Mercy's little chin quivered as she shook her head back and forth. "No, but she said we were going on a trip. And she wouldn't let me bring 'ansom."

Chad frowned at the word. Ransom?

"Well, I'm sure Handsome would have been very upset if you had gone on a trip without him."

Mercy nodded. "I told her that but she wouldn't listen. She kept saying we need to go, we need to go. And she yelled at Heather."

Lora looked up at the sitter, who still looked upset. "What did she say to you?"

Chad stepped up behind them. "Let's go into the house to talk about this. Get out of the view of the neighbors."

Lora didn't say a word, but she did wrap her girl into her arms and walk into the house. The sitter, Heather, looked at him with fear in her eyes. Chad held out his hand. "Chad Lowell. I'll be watching over Lora and Miss Mercy for a while."

The emotion in the woman's eyes eased but she didn't reach out for his hand. She crossed her arms over her narrow chest and turned to follow Lora inside. Chad frowned at the look she tossed him over her shoulder, as if he were going to attack her from behind.

A chill settled in his gut. He'd seen behavior like that before in his own family, from his sister. She'd married young and had children young, and been a battered wife by her early twenties. Lora and Heather both had that look in their eyes.

Inside the house, the sitter had obviously tried to put the rooms to rights. The potting soil had been swept from the carpet and the blood was gone from the walls. The back patio glass slider was still a gaping, open wound though.

"Do you have any plywood or anything big enough to cover the hole?"

Lora shook her head, settling onto the couch. Mercy was still wrapped around her mother like a little monkey, but Chad got the impression that the little girl was doing it for her mother.

Chad pulled his phone from his pocket, swiping the screen. He thumbed out a text message and sent it. Almost immediately the phone buzzed in his hand with a response from Roger. He would be here within an hour.

Chad motioned for the sitter to have a seat. "Can you tell me what happened, Heather?"

The woman was actually older than Chad first thought. A little more experienced.

"She knocked on the door, and when I answered she just walked in like she owned the place. She said she knew Lora had been hurt and that she had come to get Mercy until Lora was better."

The woman looked at Lora. "I'm truly very sorry. I didn't know who had hurt you and her story sounded so believable. She just acted like she was supposed to be here. It wasn't until Mercy started to put up a fuss that I became concerned."

Lora ran her hand over her daughter's pale blond hair over and over again, obviously reassuring herself that she was fine. "It's okay, Heather. That's just how they are. They roll in as if they own the place and take over."

"I tried to call the hospital but you had already been released. When I couldn't get your cell phone I started to call the police. That's when you pulled in."

Chad felt bad for the woman. She was feeling a lot of guilt right now for being taken in. "I'm glad we got here when we did."

Lora glanced at him, then away without saying anything.

Chad felt like she barely tolerated his presence. Actually, they both made him feel like a disgusting bug they wanted to crush under their shoes, but he couldn't do anything about that. They needed protection. He would be cognizant of their issues to the extent he could. He would eventually give them the space they needed, but not until their safety was assured.

"Heather, I think you can go home now. I appreciate everything you did for us and I'm sorry you had to deal with my crazy in-laws."

The other woman shook her head. "No worries. Believe it or not, I've dealt with worse."

She gathered up her bag and gave Lora a hug. "If you need anything, just give me a call. I'll come over any time."

Lora nodded and walked Heather out, closing and latching the door behind the other woman. She held Mercy the entire time.

When she turned she leaned against the heavy oak door, staring in dismay at the shattered slider.

"I've got a buddy coming over with supplies to fix it."

She nodded, than sank back down into the couch. Mercy sagged into her, drifting off to sleep. Chad wanted to move close enough to run his hand down the little girl's hair, but didn't dare with prickly momma bear watching over her right now.

He was becoming emotionally invested in the pair. Was it because he'd watched over them for so long he felt like he knew them? Or was it because he wanted to be a part of their little unit?

His protective instincts definitely went into overdrive when he was around them. He flexed his jaw where the asshole ex had hit him. Then he looked at Lora's swollen face. If he'd been there just a few seconds sooner, he could have saved her that.

It was uncomfortable in the living room. They didn't have a lot to talk about. At least, not that she was *willing* to talk about.

"I'm sorry I didn't get to you sooner."

She shrugged. "Not your fault. Even if you had been here he still would have come in. That's just the way he is."

Chad hmm'd under his breath. "He would not have come through me."

She glanced at his gnarled hand, then away.

He felt the look like a blow, though he should have been used to it by now. Words crowded into his throat in his defense, but he clamped his jaw shut.

Lora had been through a lot. She didn't have to cater to his sensibilities.

Hell, she probably wouldn't have faith in any man. No matter what shape he was in.

Chad turned to the slider door. It looked like the ass had simply crashed through when she refused to open it for him. "Did you know he was here? Before he crashed through?"

Lora still sat on the couch but could see him. Her eyelids had begun to sag. She shook her head. "I had a suspicion he would be here, but I didn't see him before he broke in. He grabbed me from behind and we crashed into the wall. He knocked my head somewhere and things kind of went dim."

Chad looked around the room. Though Heather had tried to clean the blood from the walls, there was still a stain in the hallway. It would have to be painted over.

"That was pretty ballsy of him to think he could take you like that."

She snorted. "That's Derek, all right. Ballsy to the end. He'll probably blame me for making him crash through the glass to come get me. He never recognized the divorce and only signed the papers because his mother forced him to. He's got a contempt of court somewhere, and I hope that it will have a bearing on this."

Chad frowned. "I'll let Duncan know that he has other charges pending."

Pulling his phone from his pocket, Chad typed off a quick text to Duncan and cc'd John. If anybody could find background dirt, it would be John.

There was a knock on the front door. Chad peeked through the hole first, then unlocked the deadbolts. Roger grinned on the other side of the door, hands full of equipment to repair the mangled slider. Chad ushered him in and introduced him to Lora.

He didn't miss her glance to Roger's prosthetic arm, or the way she tightened her grip around her daughter. She nodded to the other man and turned her bruised face away.

Chad and Roger worked on the door for a solid hour, sweeping up glass and draping plastic to keep out the cool air, but it would need to be replaced. Lora had carried her daughter into the depths of the house and returned to stand nearby, arms crossed protectively over her stomach.

Chad wanted to tell her they were done and it was as tight as Fort Knox, but she could see with her own eyes that it wasn't.

"It's as good as we can get it for now. I know of a contractor that would be willing to come work on it, but it may have to be after his regular work hours."

Lora nodded. "That's fine."

Chad called his buddy Rich and told him about the situation. He promised to be over early the next morning.

Roger eventually left for work, leaving Chad alone in the house with Lora and the girl. The way she paced, he knew she didn't want him there, but he tried to be as unobtrusive as possible. Several times he caught her dozing in the chair, but she refused to actually go to bed. When the exhaustion finally caught up with her, he found her curled up in her daughter's bed. He peeked into the room and little Mercy held a finger to her lips to make sure he stayed quiet, then snuggled back into her mother's arms.

Grinning, Chad left the room, closing the door softly behind him. That little girl was really something.

STILL NOTHING. HE watched the street below and several blocks out, waiting to see the hunched figure come out of the alley.

He'd been waiting for weeks.

Duncan heard the phone ring, but didn't think anything about it until Shannon stepped to the office doorway. Her eyes were wide with alarm. "You need to answer line one. Truman Medical Center Lakewood in Kansas City, Missouri."

Swiveling the chair away from the window, he reached for the phone. "Wilde."

"Hello. This is Dr. Alex Hartfield with Truman Medical Center. We have a patient in our facility we're trying to identify. He had a business card with your name on it in his coat pocket. The male appears to be mid-thirties, brownish hair and beard, a bit over six feet tall. Ring any bells?"

Duncan rocked back in the chair, staggered. "Yes, ma'am. I think it may be Aiden Willingham. He's been missing for several weeks. Is he okay?"

"He is. We didn't get him directly. One of the local urgent care centers did. A trucker found him in the back of his truck, hypothermic and delirious. It's pretty amazing that he recovered as well as he did, because he truly was on death's door. His core body temp had gotten down to eighty-six by the time he came in here. He's underweight, bordering on malnourished, but we've got him hooked up to IVs and we're pumping good stuff into him. We had to sedate him because he became frantic when he roused. Do you know anything about his medical history?"

Duncan sighed. "I believe he's former military, just from the interaction I've had with him. I filed a missing person's report with the PD here in Denver and they were unable to find any kind of service record on him for any of the branches. From my experience though, he appears to be suffering from PTSD."

The doctor hummed on the other end of the line. "I agree. He is sedated right now because he knocked one of my nurses to the floor. I have a psych consult scheduled for this afternoon."

Duncan cringed at the thought of what the guy would have to go through. "Do you have a VA he can transfer to? They might be better equipped to deal with the PTSD."

"Well," the woman murmured, "we do, but unless we can confirm his service record I can't just drop him off on their doorstep."

He rocked back in the chair, shifting his hips to ease the ache. Thoughts chased through his head. No, he didn't know Aiden very well, but if he could ease the vet's suffering in any way he would.

"Tell me where you are, Dr. Hartfield, and I'll hop on a plane."

Duncan started planning even as he wrote directions from the doctor. John could take over while he ran to KC. Shannon knew most of what he had his fingers in anyway, so between the two of them the business would be fine. Hell, he didn't even really need to tell anyone what he was doing.

After he hung up from the doctor, he shoved a few things in his desk and got ready to leave. Shannon peeked in as he was getting ready to go.

"Was that good news or bad?"

Duncan grimaced. "Well, good overall but troubling. I have to go to Kansas City."

She nodded as if she already knew. "Want me to make you a flight?"

He nodded and limped past her. "John in his office?"

"Yep."

Palmer was hunched over his keyboard when Duncan walked in, but he glanced up. "Hey. I have a lead on why Malone is being such an asshole. I'm gonna dig a little deeper then I'll send you a report."

Duncan nodded. "Good. I have to run to KC for a bit. They found Willingham."

John sat back in his chair in surprise. "No fuckin' way..."

"I don't know what's going on, but I need to get to the bottom of this guy."

John wheeled away from the desk. "Absolutely. Go dig. And let us know what's going on. There's nothing here we can't manage while you're gone."

Shannon walked into the office and handed Duncan a slip of paper. "Your flight is booked. I only made it one way because I didn't know what kind of time frame you were looking at. You have two hours to get to the airport."

He took the paper and folded it away into his wallet. "I don't know either, but I'll keep you posted on what's going on."

Duncan walked out of the office building knowing he had a team at his back that would take care of everything.

CHAD'S NIGHT RELIEF came in the smiling form of Zeke Foster tapping lightly at the front door. Chad let him in, giving him space to get through the entry. The big man reached out for a manly shoulder bump and Chad was surprised. Zeke was one of the more standoffish guys in the office.

"Hey, big man."

Zeke grinned down at him and Chad had to take a second to remind himself what the guy had looked like before. Just a couple months ago Zeke had gone in and had another reconstructive surgery, smoothing out some of the scar tissue on his face. Ember, his kind-of girlfriend at the time, had gone ballistic because Zeke hadn't told her he was going in. "Ember still as awesome as ever?"

Zeke shook his head in wonder. "More so every day. I don't know what she sees in me, but I'm never letting her go."

Chad grinned, truly glad that his buddy had had such a change in his life. Not too long ago they'd been hanging in the bar window-shopping. None of them actually had the balls to do anything about the women they saw. They'd been publicly shot down too many times.

Ember had been different though. She'd never looked at any one of them like they were to be pitied, though the group had been pretty rough. Something about her and Zeke together totally worked. She saw the good guy he was at heart.

Chad sighed at the contentment he could see in his buddy's face, but he couldn't be petty about it. Zeke Foster truly deserved that happiness.

The big man rested a hand on his shoulder. "You okay, boss man?"

Chad nodded, forcing a grin. "Heck yeah, I'm just wondering where I can get a wingman now. You've changed your hours to be with Ember and her son more, and Ortiz left for the rich and famous with Grif."

Zeke snorted. "Sorry, dude."

Chad could tell he wasn't, though. And if he had the kind of home life Zeke was now getting used to, he wouldn't either.

"Ms. Malone has gone to bed, and I think I may just sack out on the couch for tonight. If she wakes up and finds you in her house, she'll freak. I didn't have a chance to tell her you were coming."

Zeke grimaced and his massive shoulders shifted. "I'd have t-t-tried to get here earlier if you'd let me kn-know sooner."

Chad waved his words away. "Don't worry about it. If you hear her getting up, wake me to run interference."

Zeke nodded and turned for the back of the house. “Can do, boss man. Get s-some sh-shut-eye.”

Chad laid on the couch that night prepared to jump up at the slightest noise, but all was quiet. He debated taking his leg off to let it breathe, then decided against it. Toward dawn, he finally let himself slip away.

CHAPTER THREE

LORA GRIMACED AT the sun beaming in the window behind them, then immediately wished she hadn't. Her face throbbed, and as she shifted she realized her hip did too. She hadn't moved all night; that was why. She'd slept like the dead. Mercy sprawled like an angel beside her, sheets pushed away. Her long, blond eyelashes left little crescent moon shadows on her round cheeks, and her soft little mouth hung open as she breathed.

Moving slowly, she brushed a finger down her daughter's ivory cheek. The long restless day and semi-sleepless night had given her some perspective over the situation. Derek wasn't going to stop trying to get Mercy. Neither was his mother. Unless something truly drastic happened, her ex was going to be an albatross around her neck for a long time to come.

The thought made her want to cry.

She forced herself out of bed, groaning. Every damn muscle in her body ached. Her head throbbed and her sprained arm pulsed with pain. Advil and coffee were at the top of her to-do list. Pausing at the bedroom door, she leaned her ear close but couldn't hear anything.

Was the investigator still here?

His misguided guilt seemed genuine, so he probably was.

She tiptoed out into the hallway, her heart pounding, straining to listen. She thought she might have heard cloth rustle in the living room, but she wasn't sure. Padding down the hallway, sticking to the wall, she peered into the room.

Morning sunlight shafted into the room, trying to chase away the darkness. The tall, brown haired investigator had sprawled on her couch, making it look tiny. His cowboy boots were still on, legs hanging over the arm, and he had a frown on his face, so he didn't seem comfortable. She tamped down her concern. A few years ago, she'd have gone out of her way to make sure a guest in her home had everything they needed, but the fact that he was even in her house right now was as far as she was willing to go. Yes, he'd been hired to do a job. That didn't mean it didn't chafe.

As she turned for the kitchen, she held her breath to move quietly.

"Ma'am?"

Lora screamed and jumped back from the monstrous form in the kitchen doorway, tripping over a pair of shoes as she backed away. Her feet tangled and she smacked against the wall, but miraculously kept her feet. She held up her injured hand as her left scrabbled for a weapon, knowing he was too close to her to get away.

But the monster didn't move.

"Lora, hey, it's okay."

Chad had lurched to his feet and now approached her slowly, hands held out, blinking sleep from his eyes. "This is Zeke Foster. He's one of our investigators. My night relief."

Lora panted as her eyes flicked in the semi-darkness of the room. The shape in the doorway hadn't moved. As she watched, his hands raised as well.

Gulping air, she tried to ease her racing heart, but she'd been on a hair-trigger for too long. She leaned against the wall, quivering, and fought angry, frantic tears.

"He got here after you fell asleep. I stayed last night to try to talk to you first, but I didn't hear you come down the hallway. I'm sorry."

She shook her head. "It's okay," she whispered. "I just overreacted."

The investigator stepped closer and she fought not to tense.

"I can't be here twenty-four hours a day. Zeke will probably be my relief on most days."

The man in the kitchen doorway took one small step forward into the light and Lora had her second shock. His face was a map of scars and at first she had to wonder if it was a trick of the fickle light. But the longer she looked, the more clear he became, and the bigger he seemed. He loomed in her doorway, almost brushing the top jamb with his blond hair. Stacked with muscle, he still seemed intimidating to her, even with his hands up.

She looked at the other investigator, Chad, and caught his gaze. Kindness gleamed from his blue eyes. "I know, he's a big SOB, but he's a good man, I promise you."

In a little over a day she'd begun to trust his words, because the sick knot of tension in her stomach began to ease. Her eyes returned to the giant's shattered face.

He rubbed his hand over the marks, almost self-consciously. "I kn-know it's shocking. S-sorry."

Her heart clutched at the stutter.

"I w-was trying to find your coffee."

Lora blinked and stood away from the wall, straightening her t-shirt. "It's in the cupboard below the coffee maker," she whispered.

The big man gave her a thumbs up and a grin, then returned to the kitchen. She heard a cupboard door open and close. Within a few seconds, she heard the gurgle from the machine.

Chad stood watching her. "Are you okay? Can I get you one of your painkillers? Or an icepack for your face?"

Shame overtook her. She hadn't even stopped in the bathroom before coming downstairs. The damage from yesterday had to be even prettier today. "No, thank you. I'll get some Advil and coffee and I'll be fine."

Chad seemed to take her at her word. He gave her a small smile before he turned for the kitchen.

Lora escaped to her room and bathroom. The bed was still in disarray from Derek attacking her. She hadn't wanted to deal with it last night, but she would today. Everything would be set back to rights today. The alarm clock on the floor blinked twelve o'clock, and she wondered what time it actually was. She would have to call off work. Mercy would not be going to school either. If Derek tried to get her, it could be disastrous.

When she flicked on the bathroom light, tears came to her eyes. It physically hurt, but she also couldn't believe how far she'd fallen that she was so unconcerned with her looks. Her looks were what had grabbed Derek's attention to begin with. She huffed in exasperation. It was too early in the morning to think about right now.

She used the bathroom and washed her face, looking at the shower longingly. Maybe later. After she'd gotten used to having weird people in her house.

Gritting her teeth, she ran a brush through her long hair, trying to drag out the snarls. She peeked under her bangs at the stitches at her hairline. Once they came out, the scar wouldn't even be noticeable. Though her face was a mass of bruises right now, they would fade over time. And as long as the swelling went down, she could cover most of it with makeup. She'd gotten very good at that over the years.

Feeling better, she grabbed clothes from her closet and changed, finding more bruises. Her stomach ached and she thought she remembered him punching her at some point.

Standard MO.

When she entered the kitchen, Chad sat at the table, but the big man had left.

"I told Zeke to go home for now. He'll be back tonight."

She nodded and poured herself a cup of coffee, inhaling deeply. In spite of the burning heat, she took a sip. Not bad.

Lora moved to the opposite side of the table from Chad. He didn't move or even look at her as she settled into the chair, just sipped at his mug of coffee and looked out the window to the backyard.

She cleared her throat. "I'm sorry I reacted the way I did earlier. I didn't know anybody else had come inside the house."

He glanced at her and grinned. "No biggie. Zeke's had people react to him like that before, so he probably didn't think anything of it."

Lora frowned, feeling even guiltier at the misassumption. "It wasn't because of his scars. I didn't even see them at first. He was just this big shape backlit by the sun. I though…well, I thought it was one of Derek's goons or something."

Chad looked at her for a second, then away. "Okay. I'll let him know."

She looked at the arm curled on the table in front of him, curiosity eating at her. All three of the men she had seen had some kind of … deformity. Injury. She wondered what the heck had happened to them.

His eyes caught hers. "How are you feeling otherwise?"

Her cheeks heated, even through the bruise, making it ache. "Sore. Like an elephant tap-danced on my face."

Nodding, he quirked a brow. "No offense, but you look like an elephant tap-danced on your face."

She snorted in surprise, gasping as the split in her lip tugged in a smile.

Anger flashed in his eyes and she jerked back, startled at the change.

The investigator noticed her reaction and shook his head. "I'm sorry. It just pisses me off to no end that a guy would do this to a woman. I'm a Texas boy. Our women are treated with the respect they deserve. I want to take your ex out and beat the shit out of him, then hang him by his balls for the vultures to eat."

Her throat tightened with emotion and she had to look away. Very few people had ever stood up for her and it was shocking to hear those words uttered out loud. She dragged in a deep breath. "Well," she whispered, "if you ever do let me know so I can be there to help."

The man across from her laughed out loud, nodding. "Agreed."

A curl of amusement swirled through her, taking her by surprise. It had been so very long since she'd felt any kind of light-heartedness. Even when she played with Mercy, she had to stay on guard. Because she was the only one *to* stay on guard.

Maybe having the guys around would let her relax just a bit.

"So, how will this work when I have to go back to work? I called off today, by the way. Obviously."

She made a motion with her hand then turned her face away from his scrutiny.

"Well," he drawled, "we'll have to stay somewhere in the vicinity of both of you, so another guard will have to be brought in. If we're moving a lot, I may just make it an even four, what we call a fire-team."

Lora cringed at the thought of other men being around. "Mercy is the priority. I want her to be protected at all costs."

Chad blinked at her. "And you don't need protection?"

She shook her head. "I would take this and more every day as long as she's safe. I don't want the family anywhere near her."

He tilted his head, as if trying to figure her out. Lora let him see the determination in her face.

"Well, if we have anything to do about it they won't touch either one of you. How 'bout that?"

He grinned at her and Lora felt her own tight mouth ease. The man had serious charm.

The humor in her died away and she shoved away from the table. "I'm going to go take a shower before Mercy wakes up."

Without giving him a chance to respond, she left the kitchen. It wouldn't do for her to be friendly with them.

Chad watched Lora leave the kitchen, her narrow back straight as an arrow. He thought they'd kind of been connecting, but apparently not. It was always best to have some cooperation from the party you were protecting. Having a group of men basically overrun your life probably didn't make a person particularly friendly, though.

Something occurred to him and he pulled his phone from his pocket, swiping the code in then pressing a speed dial button.

Palmer answered on the second ring.

"This better be a fucking emergency," he growled.

Chad glanced at the digital readout at the corner of the screen and cringed, but it was too late to hang up. "Morning, Gunny. I didn't wake you, did I? It's after six thirty."

"I'm awake now. What do you want, Lowell?"

Chad choked on a laugh as he heard Shannon grumble in the background.

"I was wondering how far along you were in the hiring process for the woman pilot. Did she pass her background?"

Palmer sighed on the other end of the line. "With flying colors."

Chad laughed at the pun. "You're awful sharp for this early in the morning."

"Why do you need to know?"

"Because I think it would be a good idea to have a female involved with this case. I haven't sat in on any of her interviews. How does she strike you?"

"No nonsense, sharp, built like a brick shithouse. Probably won't take any of your crap. Diagnosed PTSD years ago, but she got counseling early and has done well, according to her files. Her bird was shot down in oh-seven in Anbar Province. Busted her up pretty good. She's got rods in her back but it doesn't seem to be slowing her down."

"Huh. And…"

"And her file is on Duncan's desk, waiting for approval."

"So she's ready to go, then? Okay, I'll call Duncan."

"Hold on, Lowell. He's not around right now and it's not a good time to bother him."

"Why?"

"Somebody in Kansas City found that homeless dude he's been looking for. I thought for sure he'd done himself in, but apparently not."

Chad sat back in his chair, shocked. "Damn, I didn't think he'd still be kickin' either. How the hell did he get to KC?"

Palmer snorted. "A trucker found him in the back of his rig about froze. Dropped him off at an urgent care."

Shit. He hoped the guy was okay. Damn. Duncan had final approval on all hires. "I'll at least send him a text message to let him know what's going on and see if we can bring her in temporarily."

"She's not a usual MP, Chad. She'll have to be given a crash course in everything."

"So what's with the puns today? Seriously?"

Palmer barked out a rough laugh. "Didn't mean to that time."

"If she's half as good as you say, I need her here. Lora cringes every time we're around her. She freaked when she saw Zeke in the kitchen. I think having a woman here with her will make things easier."

Palmer hmm'd on the other end of the line. "If you say so. Contact Duncan. If he says she's a go we'll get her moving."

"Okay, Gunny. Thank you. Tell Shannon I'm sorry I woke you up."

His partner snorted and hung up on him without another word.

Chad typed off a text to Duncan and shoved his phone in his pocket. When he looked up, Lora's little girl stood at the kitchen doorjamb. She was about the cutest thing he'd ever seen with her messy blond hair and rumpled PJs.

He grinned at her, trying to remember if he'd cussed while talking to Palmer. "Good morning, sunshine. Your mom's in the shower."

She blinked at him, clutching that multi-colored stuffed animal to her chest. "I know. I heard her." Watching him from the corner of her eye, the girl padded to the opposite side of the table where Lora had just left and climbed onto the chair. "We're late for school."

Glancing at the clock on the wall, he realized they probably were. "I think your mom decided to stay home today. Is that okay? An extra day to watch cartoons?"

She glanced at the living room, then back and shrugged.

"Are you hungry? Maybe I can make you something to eat."

Her lips moved back and forth. Maybe she was hungry and just didn't want to say.

"If I scramble some eggs will you eat them?"

She nodded.

Chad prayed there were eggs in the fridge to cook.

As he stood from the chair he did a visual down the long hallway to the door and out the back window to the yard. Everything seemed in order. A typical cold, frosty Colorado morning.

Digging a pan from the lower cupboard, he set it on the smooth-top stove and turned for the fridge. Eggs were front and center, along with some ham and cheese. He held the items up for the girl's inspection and she nodded, looking more excited.

Chad wondered if Lora would eat a couple of eggs. He hadn't seen her eat anything yesterday. When he asked Mercy, she nodded her head. Cracking a couple more into the bowl to beat, he hoped she would at least eat a bit.

"So, what do you like to be called, little miss? Mercy or Mercedes?"

"Mercy."

He nodded to the crumpled animal clutched in her arms. "And his name?"

"'Ansom."

"Handsome. That's right. For some reason I thought it was Bill."

The little girl's eyes went wide and she shook her head. Chad turned back to stir the eggs, wondering if a six year old was too young to charm. Opening cupboard doors, he drew two small plates from the shelf and piled some eggs onto one. He crossed the kitchen and placed it in front of the child. "Miss Mercy, your eggs, madam." He bowed from the waist, and when he looked up, her little pink lips were fighting a smile.

When he set the plate in front of her, she poked at the eggs experimentally before taking a bite. Once she knew they were good she started eating. Chad set a glass of juice in front of her and was just dishing out the second plate of eggs when Lora walked into the kitchen. Her pretty green eyes flashed with anger as she took in her daughter eating and him standing at the stove, spatula in hand.

"Just make yourself at home," she snapped. "I'll feed my daughter, thank you very much."

Tipping his head, Chad handed her the plate of eggs. He brushed his hands on his jeans and turned the heat off, moving the pan away from the burner. "No problem. I apologize."

Giving Mercy a wink, he walked out of the kitchen.

Mercy blinked up at her.

"He made you breakfast and it's good."

Lora looked down at the plate in her hand with a sinking stomach. "He made it for me?"

She nodded her head. "And he didn't put nonions in it."

Lora smiled at the common complaint. "No onions, huh?"

She looked down at the plate of food and her stomach rumbled. It had been a while since she'd eaten. And he knew that. She forked a pile of eggs into her mouth. They were as good as they looked, and within just a couple of minutes, they were completely gone. Then the guilt really moved in.

It had been petty of her to yell at him; he'd only been kind to the two of them, in spite of her prickliness. Common decency forced her to leave the kitchen to find Chad and make it right.

Lora searched the front of the house but didn't find him. She peeked out the windows out of habit as she walked deeper into the house. In Mercy's room, she finally found him. He was pressing on the frame of the window above her bed. He glanced at her from the corner of his eye, but didn't say anything.

"I'm sorry I snapped at you. Thank you for making her breakfast. You didn't have to do that."

He shrugged his shoulders. "Had to do something. She was wasting away in front of me. I thought she was gonna eat that nasty dog she carries around."

Lora snorted, amused in spite of herself. "That nasty dog is actually a nasty bear."

He turned and gave her a weird cringe. "Really?"

She nodded.

Chad shook his head sadly.

"And thank you for my breakfast, too. It was very good."

He widened his eyes at her. "You ate my eggs? I just wanted you to hold the plate for me."

Lora's mouth dropped open in disbelief, and she started to sputter out an apology, until he held up a hand, grinning. "I'm kidding. I made those eggs for you." His eyes drifted down her body. "You need some meat on your bones."

Lora flushed as his eyes traveled over every inch of her in a too-thorough scan, sending goose bumps racing across her shoulders and down her chest. She shuddered at the feel of her body responding with awareness.

Chad was watching her closely. "Are you okay?"

She nodded her head automatically and backed out of the room. "Thank you for the breakfast. I'm going to…go straighten the…the mess in my room."

Trying not to run, she escaped, retreating to her bedroom. She circled to the opposite side of the rumpled bed and sank down onto the mattress, breathing heavily. She looked down at the front of her t-shirt and the unmistakable evidence that her body had recognized his interest. Her nipples pressed against the soft fabric.

It scared her to death.

Why had she reacted like that? It had been years since she'd wanted any kind of physical relationship with anybody. Derek had ruined that for her.

At first, their relationship had been sublime. They'd met at a party almost seven years ago. She'd been going to college for an English degree, working her way through school on her own dime. It had been an unexpected free weekend not waiting tables when she'd accepted the invitation to a party.

As soon as she'd walked into the crowded room, Derek's gaze had connected with hers. Within just a few minutes he'd approached her, charming her with sweet compliments. Lora had relished the attention from such a handsome guy. Derek had been a total gentleman, getting her drinks and dancing with her. Against her better judgment, she'd let him drive her back to the dorm that night, but he'd left her at the front door with a chaste kiss on the cheek.

The next morning he'd call to invite her on a date and she'd accepted. The attention he'd lavished on her had been like rain falling in Death Valley. Lora's mother had died the year before and the loneliness and depression had almost swallowed her under.

Hindsight was twenty-twenty though. With her emotions out of balance she'd been easy pickings for his manipulative nature. He'd walked in and made her life better, made her swallow the dream.

Derek's mother had been just as devious and it was obvious where he'd learned the skill. She'd been the motherly figure Lora had craved. When the subject of marriage had been brought up, she fallen for it completely, and them. She and Derek had married in a quiet ceremony on the family's estate in New York.

It wasn't until she discovered she was pregnant two weeks after they married that things started to turn sour.

Lora returned home early from the doctor's office, ecstatic about her news, and headed upstairs. She wanted to be ready when Derek came home. But Derek was already home. She found him in a clinch with one of the house maids. In their bed, no less. The young girl had run from the room crying. Lora had laid into Derek, calling him names. When she told him only small men cheated, he went off on her. He dazed her with a punch to the jaw and immediately slammed her to the bed facedown. He'd bound her hands with his silk tie and looped it around the bedpost. That had been the first time he'd raped her.

When she'd reported the incident to the police, she'd been given the brush off. Only years later did she realize how deep the corruption went around her. The Malone family owned their quiet New York town, and they used the influence any way they wanted.

Lora looked down at her lap, her surroundings fading away. The past rushed up to snatch her into its depths.

Her heart was trying to race out of her chest. The throbbing in her head twisted her stomach with nausea. Holy hell, what happened last night? She raised her hand to her face, and the swelling under her fingers told her exactly what had happened. He'd laid into her again.

She sighed into the darkness, then caught her breath, rolling her head to the right. Good, he was gone. She didn't have to worry about waking him when she moaned as she rolled out of bed.

As her feet dropped to the cold marble floor of their bedroom, she paused, caught by how many times she'd done this before. When had it become an accepted routine that he would beat the shit out of her, fuck her till he fell asleep, then go drink himself into oblivion, leaving her to clean up?

She couldn't even remember. Too long.

She looked down at the t-shirt she'd worn to bed. Blood from her bloody nose had dripped down onto her breast, then dried brown. Gross. There were other things on her she didn't even want to look at. She thought one of the guards had been in the room as well. Had he taken part in decorating her? She couldn't remember. If he had it had been when she'd been unconscious.

She eased forward onto her feet, moaning as her internals settled low. Fluid flowed down her thighs. Somebody had penetrated her.

Disgust coated her tongue as she caught sight of herself in the mirrored closet doors.

Lora realized she was standing at the used dresser in her new house, looking into the glass, fists clenched at her sides. She exhaled the stale air in her lungs and wondered how long she'd been out of it. She hated the dream but didn't know how to change it. The same scene had played over and over again in real life until it was ingrained in her gut.

Derek had kept her under his thumb for three years. That first rape had caused her to miscarry the baby she'd been so excited to tell him about. He'd blamed her, of course, because she hadn't told him about it right away. Depression had been her constant companion then, eating at her will to live.

Six months later she'd gotten pregnant again, in spite of the furtive precautions she'd taken. One of the hardest decisions of her life was to decide whether or not to tell him about the pregnancy. Eventually she did and, to her complete shock, the abuse stopped completely. Rosalind treated her with a tiny bit of respect and things felt like they were looking up.

Derek wanted to name the baby Mercedes after his favorite brand of car. When she'd looked at him as if he were out of his mind, the flash of rage in his eyes made her fear for her safety. And that of the child's. So she'd bitten her tongue and gone along with what he wanted. Again.

When the baby was born, they'd gone through an almost honeymoon-like phase. They nurtured the child and spent some good, quality time together. But it hadn't lasted. Within a few months, they'd gone back to the way things were before.

Lora shook off the melancholy. She had things to do and wallowing in the past wasn't getting her anywhere.

SIX HOURS AFTER he left Denver, Duncan walked into Truman Medical Center. Dr. Hartfield had left permission for him to see Willingham, though he wasn't technically family. The volunteer gave him directions and pointed out the elevator.

As Duncan limped off onto the seventh floor, it was hard not to be sucked under by his own memories as the smell seeped into his lungs. After so many years, he thought it would be easier, but no. Every time one of his guys got hurt, or somebody needed something for a vet, he was there to lend a hand or a shoulder.

Blue signs counted down the room numbers, odd numbers on one side, even on the other. Seven twenty-eight was directly across from the nurse's station and had a glass window. Had Willingham really been causing them so many problems they needed to watch him twenty-four seven?

Apparently. Duncan cringed when he realized the man's arms and feet were buckled to the bed with leather straps. "Fuck."

Aiden appeared to be deeply asleep. It gave Duncan a chance to look him over and he was dismayed at the change in the man. He'd lost a lot of weight, and even beneath the beard his skin looked sallow, as if his body were fighting off a deadly disease.

A nurse stepped into the room. "Are you Mr. Wilde? The doctor told me to page her when you got in."

"I am."

She tossed him a smile and left to page the doctor.

Duncan circled the bed and reached out to rest his hand on Aiden's bony shoulder. "Hey, buddy. Looks like you've had a heck of a time recently. We'll get you fixed up."

There was no reaction physically, but Duncan thought perhaps he breathed a little bit easier. He sat in the plastic chair beside the bed to wait for the doctor.

Duncan had answered all the emails and messages he could on his phone and was debating going to find coffee when a woman entered the room. Tall and lean, her dark auburn hair was pulled back into a low ponytail. Heavy, black-framed glasses covered her eyes and she seemed very young. But she approached him like she owned the place.

"Mr. Wilde? Dr. Alex Hartfield. Nice to meet you."

She shook his hand and turned to the figure on the bed. "I assume this is your Mr. Willingham?"

Duncan nodded. "It is. Definitely leaner and a little more cleaned up. He was homeless when I met him."

The doctor cringed. "Well, that would explain his leanness. I have a feeling this guy's been in a lot of other crap, though, because he has serious scars all over his body. Knife wounds, bullet wounds. It looks like his ankle has been rebuilt at some point. Knee's been ripped up. He has surgery scars on his right shoulder. Marks on his wrists as if he were bound for a long time."

Duncan cringed, wishing he knew the man's history. If he had to guess, it sounded like Aiden had been Navy SEAL. Or black ops. He'd have to call in some serious favors to find out. Palmer wasn't going to find anything.

A nurse brought in a syringe and handed it to the doctor. Two burly orderlies stood at the door. Duncan eyed them. "Are those necessary?"

The doctor turned and blinked at him. "They are if he freaks out when I give him this shot and he doesn't recognize you. I'm hoping for hunky-dory, but expecting a fight."

Duncan sighed and stepped to the opposite side of the bed, leaving his cane hanging on the bedrail. He rested his hand on Aiden's shoulder as the doctor injected the IV with part of the shot. "We'll start with a small dose and see if he rouses."

A subtle quivering started in his arms.

"You need to step back, doctor."

The words had no sooner left his mouth than Aiden Willingham was wide awake and fighting the restraints. Duncan pressed against his shoulder but even malnourished the other man had a lot of fight in him. "Willingham! Aiden! Stop. You need to settle down."

The orderlies started to move in but Duncan waved a hand for them to stay where they were. "Aiden. Look at me." He pitched his voice low and calm, in spite of the situation. "Aiden, you need to calm down before they knock you out again."

The leather restraints creaked and snapped as the younger man fought, but something must have filtered in, because his eyes snapped to Duncan's.

He grinned at him. "You need to settle down, soldier. You're makin' these civvies a little jumpy."

Aiden blinked heavily, then looked at the people grouped around the bed. His head swung back to Duncan. "You need to let me go," he rasped. His whole body quivered with tension, though he'd stopped thrashing. Muscles bulged in his arms as he pulled against the restraints. "I can't be tied down. I can't be tied down."

Duncan couldn't help but feel for the guy, and wondered if they weren't doing him more emotional harm by keeping him restrained. "You need to be calm then. They need to know you're not going to hurt them or yourself if they let you go."

Desperation lit Aiden's brown eyes. "I won't hurt these people. I swear."

Duncan believed him, in spite of the evidence to the contrary.

The doctor didn't look as convinced. "I don't know. He already hurt one nurse."

Aiden jerked his gaze to her. "What?"

The doctor nodded. "One of the nurses was knocked down when you were first brought in. She's fine. Just bruised."

Closing his eyes for a moment, he grimaced. "I'm sorry I knocked her down. I can't be restrained. It will truly drive me insane."

Duncan didn't envy her position. If she let him go and he did hurt somebody, it was her responsibility. She pursed her lips for several long seconds before finally nodding. "You better be a man of your word, Mr. Willingham, because if you hurt one of my people I'll make sure you're locked up for a very long time."

Aiden nodded and some of the tension eased from his body as they leaned in to unfasten him. Everyone in the room held their collective breath when he was finally free, waiting to see what would happen. Grimacing, Aiden sat up in the bed, rubbing his wrists, but he didn't make any other moves to cause alarm.

The doctor pulled the stethoscope from around her neck and held it up. "Mind if I examine you?"

Aiden stared at her for a long moment before shaking his head.

The examination was quick and perfunctory, but Aiden's body quaked with tension by the time she was finished and moved away. Duncan eased away just a bit to reach his cane to lean on, his hips aching from holding Aiden to the bed.

Aiden looked up as Duncan moved away and fear flashed through his eyes.

"I'm not going anywhere. Just adjusting."

"Where am I?"

"Kansas City, Missouri."

If he hadn't been watching, he'd have missed the tightening around the other man's eyes.

"You apparently climbed in the back of a tractor-trailer to get here."

Aiden blinked at him but didn't say anything. He looked over Duncan's shoulder to the window outside, as if the bleary sky would be able to tell him where he was. "How long have I been here?"

Duncan shrugged. "You've been gone from Colorado for several weeks."

Aiden dropped back against the bed. Though there was no other outward reaction, Duncan thought he was shocked at the amount of time that had passed. "You don't remember?"

He shook his head.

Duncan could ask him what happened in the alley later, when the people were gone.

The doctor shooed everybody out. "I'm sorry we had to take the steps we did, Mr. Willingham, but I wasn't going to let anyone else get hurt."

He avoided her gaze but nodded his head. With a final glance she left the room.

Duncan turned and eased down into the chair, legs stretched out in front of him. His hip was aching like a sonofabitch. "So how much of your trip do you remember?"

Shaking his head, Aiden scrubbed his hands over his face. "Not much. Cold. I remember the cold."

Duncan snorted. "Well, you were damn near a popsicle when you got out here. You're lucky the driver found you when he did."

Aiden cringed. "Am I?"

He didn't like the tone of the other man's voice. "Yes, you are," he told him firmly. "Do you have family or someone I need to contact?"

Blankness settled over Aiden's features. "Nope."

Though his gaze was steady, Duncan felt like he was being lied to. "Well, if you think of somebody, let me know and I'll get a hold of them."

"I won't."

He'd gone blank-face and Duncan had a feeling he wouldn't be forthcoming with anything else about his family situation.

"Were you coming this direction for a reason?"

Aiden stared at him. "Nope."

Again, deception. But it wasn't like he had any hold over him. He could lie all he wanted to. "I'm trying to help you out, Aiden."

"I'm pretty tired. I'd like to sleep for a while."

Duncan thought about leaning back in the chair and telling him to go ahead, but he didn't want things to get antagonistic. Instead, he pushed to his feet, fighting to keep the grimace from his face. "Okay, Aiden, I'll let you rest. As soon as I get settled into the hotel I'll call the nurse's station and leave them my information."

"Don't worry about it."

Frowning, he looked at the man on the bed. "I want you to have it."

"I don't need it."

Without saying anything more, Duncan left the room, disappointed at Aiden's reluctance to accept anything.

CHAPTER FOUR

THEY SPENT A quiet day in the house.

Chad paced the living room, restless. It had been quiet outside and inside for too long. Lora had been cleaning the bedroom where she'd been attacked. She'd made several trips with soiled sheets and bags of trash. At one point he'd offered to help. She'd stared at him for several long seconds before shaking her head. "No, thank you."

The little girl played in her room for a while then wandered into the living room to watch TV. As she clicked through the channels, Chad felt her eyes watching him. He lifted an eyebrow at her in question.

She glanced back at the TV, but her little mouth was working, as if she were trying to keep in the words. "Mommy gets mad sometimes."

Chad grinned. "Yes, she does, darlin'. But most mamas do sometimes. It didn't bother me. I'm used to getting yelled at."

Her pretty green eyes, so like her mother's, widened. "Why do you get in trouble?"

Sighing, he sat on the couch beside her. "Well, many reasons. I usually try to do good, but sometimes I get in trouble whether I want to or not."

Nodding, she folded her legs Indian style. "Me too. Sometimes Mommy yells and I don't know why." Her voice lowered to a whisper. "I think it's because Derek keeps bugging her."

Chad nodded. "Probably," he agreed just as softly. "Maybe sometime soon we can do something about that. Don't worry about him."

Her little head dropped down. "He keeps coming after me, but I don't think he likes me."

Cringing at the hurt he heard in her voice, Chad reached into his pocket, trying to lighten the mood. Unable to help himself, he pressed a quick kiss to the top of her head and handed her the candy. "I'll let you have this if you don't tell your momma I spoiled your lunch."

Her tiny little fingers plucked the Smarties from his hand and curled them away. She looked up at him with a grin, bouncing on the cushion. "I won't," she whispered.

Chad left her sneaking little candies and watching cartoons. When he stood up from the couch, movement in his peripheral caught his attention. Lora was trying to fade away down the hallway. He followed after her as she retreated into the bedroom. "Did you hear?"

Her gaze darted from his, but she nodded. "Thank you for trying to ease her mind. I think sometimes I don't realize how intense I get trying to be everything for her."

"Well, you've done a good job up till now. And this is just a minor setback. We'll try to get this mess untangled and then we'll get you back on track."

She folded her arms across her chest and he noticed she'd taken a shower. Her blond hair was pulled back in a ponytail, but she had bangs over her forehead, covering the gash and bandage. What concerned him, though, was her wrist was not bandaged. He noticed the ace wrap on top of her dresser and started to straighten it. "You should wear this. It'll help your arm heal faster."

Pink tinged her pale cheeks. "I tried to wrap it but couldn't get it to stay."

He tossed the bandage out, letting it untwist. She tensed up but didn't move away as he stopped in front of her. "Hold your arm out."

She held it out thumb up, with her other hand cupped beneath it for support. Chad's jaw clenched when he saw the bruising running up her pale arm. Fingerprints from her husband and from the strain itself. Dragging oxygen into his lungs, he fought for something to say. "Your daughter is a sweetheart."

Some of the tension eased from her frame. "Yes, she is. She is my reason for life."

"I can see that. And I think it's mutual. She worries about you a lot."

"I know," she whispered. Her throat sounded tight.

Chad wrapped her arm as carefully as he could, uncomfortable that he was giving her a close-up look at his own damage. *Only fair, I guess, considering.*

She cleared her throat as he wound the bandage around and around her arm, and he knew what was coming. "What happened?"

He shrugged. "Iraq happened. I got burned in an explosion. Landmine."

She cringed. "I'm sorry."

"Why?" He forced a grin. "You didn't do it."

She blinked as if she were caught off guard by the way he reacted to it but didn't say anything more.

Just as he fastened the Velcro to the ace wrap, the doorbell rang. Chad made sure he got to the door first, peering through the peephole. Frank Norcross stood outside, tool belt slung low around his hips. Chad grinned as he tugged open the door and greeted the man.

Frank cringed when he saw the damage to the back door but thought he could get it fixed fairly quickly, with some modification. Lora stood, arms crossed, as he explained that a French door, with one side fixed permanent, would offer more security. She nodded in agreement and told him to do what he needed to do to seal off the hole. Chad helped him measure it before Frank left for the hardware superstore.

The door was framed and installed, though it took him until late into the evening to get it finished. Zeke arrived for his rotation, and for a while they all sat and watched Frank do his magic. A line of tension immediately went out of Lora's shoulders when he told her it was done and showed her the completed product. She seemed especially appreciative of the deadbolt, extending it and retracting it several times to get used to the feel.

Frank wrote up the invoice and handed it off to Chad. Lora watched the exchange and anger tightened her features. As soon as Frank left, she held her hand out. "I'll take the receipt, please."

Chad smiled and shook his head. "Nah. We'll take this one." Actually, it would be coming out of his own personal account.

She took a step forward, brows furrowing over her eyes. "No, it's my door."

"No, it used to be your door before I forgot my head up my ass and you had to deal with a dickwad invading your home." He winked at her. "Take it with good grace. Say thank you."

Growling beneath her breath, she shook her head. "Thank you. You didn't have to do that."

Chad dug some Smarties from his shirt pocket. He offered her a roll, but she wrinkled her nose in distaste. The expression was unbelievably cute on her stern face and he couldn't help but grin at her.

Lora blinked at him and turned away without responding.

Sighing, he left Zeke in charge of their care and headed home. He'd been wearing the same clothes for entirely too long.

Walking into his apartment, the silence was striking. At Lora's house, either Lora or Mercy were always making some kind of noise. Cleaning, cartoons, giggling, whispering. His apartment was bland in the extreme. Yeah, he had his electronics, but they didn't have life. Even in the deep of night, Lora's house pulsed with life.

Shoving his depressing thoughts aside, he dug in his refrigerator for something to munch on. Nothing. He ordered takeout and headed to the bathroom to clean up while he waited.

The heat of the shower relaxed his body, but his mind continued to work, trying to figure out how to get rid of the puke trying to run Lora's life. High-powered people always had skeletons in their closets. The way Derek treated Lora hinted at something he was used to doing, so maybe there were other women he'd been involved with that hadn't had a great experience. Maybe he could mention it to John.

Plus, the guy came from an investment family. They'd made money off of other people. They always had secrets.

He washed the sleeve for his prosthetic, then sprayed antibacterial in the prosthetic itself and left it in the bathroom. Hopping to the kitchen on his right leg he grabbed a bottle of water from the fridge, snatched his tablet from the charger on the counter and headed to the living room. He'd just sat down when the doorbell rang. Mmm,

General Tso's chicken. The dinner of champions.

Tiredness dragged at him, but the thought of seeing Dodd in his dreams again didn't hold any appeal. Maybe if he surfed himself into tiredness, he'd leave him alone for the night.

LORA KNEW THE big guy with the scarred face was down the hallway, and there was another guard outside, Killian or something, but she still found herself pacing away the night, worrying.

Derek had been pissed when she'd denied him access to Mercy a couple of months ago. Tired of arguing, she'd finally agreed to take the multi-colored bear he'd brought for her, hoping that if she gave in on that aspect he'd leave her alone. Surprisingly, he did.

Derek's visits and calls had become more frequent recently. Trying to reconnect on their anniversary was a total crock, but he'd had to try to exert his dominance over her again. When the judge had granted her divorce, she'd chosen not to pursue child support, just so that she would have no strings tying her to the bastard.

Too bad he didn't recognize anything from the courts.

Lora heard a thump from the front of the house and her stomach clenched. Creeping down the hallway, she leaned her head into the living room to see if she could identify what had made the noise.

The front door was standing wide open and she heard feet running outside. Plastering herself to the wall, she eased toward the door to see what she could. The front porch light was on, but it only reached about ten feet out. Vaguely, she could see two figures wrestling in the grass.

Sliding back into the hallway she rushed to Mercy's room. When she heard another thud, she sped up and swung the door open to her daughter's room. From the light of the security pole outside, she could see the hunched figure of a man trying to force open the window.

Icy fear shot through her but she lunged for the bed, ripping back the covers. Mercy wasn't there. "Mercy," she hissed.

"Here, Mommy."

Lora looked to the left and found her daughter coming out of the closet, bear clutched by one ear. Her eyes were wide with fright but she was calm as she came to her. Lora looked at the man at the window. He had stopped trying to pry into the room and just stood watching her, black mask over his face. Suddenly, he raised his gloved fist and shattered the glass with the big flashlight he had in his hand.

Lora jerked Mercy by the hand and slammed the door as they ran out of the room. Once out though, she wasn't sure she wanted to go toward the front of the house. At least, not until she heard from the big guard.

As if she'd conjured him from her thoughts, the man came running around the corner from the living room. His rough face was flushed with exertion. Blood ran down his chin from a busted lip and he was panting heavily. "Are you okay?"

Lora nodded, holding Mercy against her legs. "Another was trying to get into Mercy's room. He broke the glass."

"Is he still there?"

"I don't know."

Zeke slid past her and into Mercy's bedroom, but returned seconds later shaking his head. Reaching into his hip pocket, he pulled out his cell phone, thumbing in a number. With the other hand he guided them into her bedroom. Lora could hear the phone ringing on the other end of the line, then Chad's drawl pick up.

"We've got visitors. You better g-get over here."

Short and sweet. Zeke was a man of few words. He shoved the phone back in his pocket.

Guiding them around the bed, he nudged them toward the closet. "Wait 'til I come back."

And he disappeared.

Lora huddled into the corner of the closet, her arms wrapped around Mercy, and counted off the minutes. Fumbling on the floor, she found a tall heel and held it like a hammer, ready for anything that came through the door. Her heart thudded heavily and she wondered what was going on. She didn't want Zeke to be hurt. Or the other guard. Or anybody for that matter. But she refused to let them have

Mercy.

Though they hadn't announced their names, she had no doubt who the men worked for. She was only a little surprised Derek hadn't shown up to supervise the attack himself. Seemed like the narcissistic thing to do.

Within a surprisingly short amount of time, Zeke was knocking on the closet door. "You c-can come out now."

Lora walked out, keeping Mercy behind her. For some reason, she'd expected there to be another mess for her to clean up, but everything was as she'd left it. When they went down the hall to the living room, Chad was at the front door. "Are you okay? Both of you?"

He stepped close enough that she could have walked into his arms if she'd wanted to. Lora frowned and shook her head, unable to believe she'd contemplate doing something so crazy.

Mercy had no problems flinging her arms around his neck though, then pulling back to tell him about the experience. Chad nodded at everything the girl said, but Lora could tell he was thinking internally. He caught her eyes. "I need you to pack a bag."

Shit. Blinking, she turned without argument and headed toward her room. She threw essentials into a small suitcase, then turned to the heater vent in the floor, debating. For several long seconds, she wavered in indecision before going to her hands and knees and pulling the grate from the floor. Reaching inside, she dragged the plastic wrapped package from its hiding place and stored it in her bag along with everything else. Then she went to Mercy's room to pack. Within just a few minutes she was back at the kitchen. Mercy was watching TV quietly while Zeke and Chad watched the windows.

Lora was having second thoughts about leaving. "Are you sure this is necessary?"

Chad held an arm out to guide her into the kitchen. "Your home was just broken into. Again."

Lora understood what the investigator said, but it didn't mean she had to like it. This was her home. And Mercy's home. Her daughter would be devastated if they had to uproot everything while they waited this thing out.

"I need time to think."

Chad nodded once. "That's fine. But we don't have a lot of time. If they try to break in again, it will be with more men. You don't want to be here when they do. If we leave, he won't be able to serve you with any documents, either. I can guarantee your safety and Mercy's, but you have to trust me."

Unable to help herself, she snorted. "I've heard that before."

"But not from me."

As she looked into his vivid blue eyes, she could see his determination to do what was right.

"How long would we have to be gone?"

He shrugged. "I'm not sure. It depends upon how quickly Duncan can get his contacts moving. It may be a week or it may be three months. Derek is after you and Mercy. You, for throwing him over. But I feel like he wants Mercy for some other reason."

Lora blinked as a domino suddenly fell into place in her mind.

"She's a partial stock holder. I thought it was strange when I signed the papers with him, but if the business is having problems, maybe he needs her leverage."

Chad pursed his lips and nodded. "If he gains custody, he gains her shares, basically."

Lora looked at her young daughter watching TV. "Why would he try to take her then? I would have to sign over guardianship and he knows I won't do that willingly."

He tilted his head. "So maybe he's aware of that and he feels the only way to manipulate you is by force."

Lora sank down to the kitchen chair behind her, her knees suddenly weak.

"Regardless," he continued, "I think we need to get you out of Dodge. Make you disappear. Things are escalating. If Zeke and Killian hadn't been here, she would probably have been taken."

A shudder rippled through her. She couldn't imagine losing her daughter to that man. The thought was enough to make her sick.

The solid weight of a hand settled on her shoulder and she tensed.

But as soon as the weight was there it was gone again. "We'll take care of both of you."

She looked up at him and knew he believed he could keep her safe. Years of frustrated struggling came back to her, and for the first time in longer than she could remember she wanted to let somebody help take care of Mercy. The two of them had been constant companions for her entire life. It would be hard to relinquish some of that control, but she had a feeling she was over her head with Derek. If he wanted to take their daughter, she had no doubt he would try. And his mother would be right there trying with him.

"Okay."

A bubble of tension eased in her spine. Chad smiled at her, bright teeth flashing, and she felt heat bloom in her cheeks. She clamped her jaw in desperation, sending pain shooting through the side of her head. Yes, he was cute, but men only brought pain.

CHAD CALLED DUNCAN, in spite of the crazy hour. "Dude, don't you ever sleep?"

The older man chuckled on the other end of the line. "I could ask you the same thing, smartass. What's going on?"

Chad filled him in on the details, ending with tonight's altercation. "I need to get them out of town. And we need to make this bastard squirm."

"Agreed on both counts. Has she given us any usable information about his business?"

"Well," Chad sighed, "the daughter is a partial stockholder. I think that's the only reason why he wants her."

"Hell." The silence stretched on the other end of the line. "Okay, how many people do you need?"

Chad thought for several long seconds. "At least two. Maybe three."

"We'll make it an even four-man squad, that way you'll have better coverage. I'd rather you have too many than not enough, and this is our fuck-up, so we'll clean it up. I got your text about the female, and as long as you're comfortable with Rachel as one of your four, you have my blessing to take her with you. And Zeke."

Chad frowned. "I hate to take Zeke away right now. Preston?"

Duncan paused on the other end of the line. "Preston's not on anything major. I'll let him know. Who do you want for your fourth?"

"Flynn."

"Really? Are you sure?"

"Yes."

The former SEAL was a bit of a wild card, but was a truly impressive fighter. He wouldn't like it where they were going, but he would deal.

"Done, then. I'll let them know they're on. I'll also start digging a little harder. I've got a buddy at the Federal Reserve Board that might be able to look into things."

Snorting, Chad shook his head. "Why am I not surprised you have a buddy there? Seems like you have buddies everywhere."

Duncan laughed. "Well, yeah. I served for a long time. You know that. Had a lot of men under my command. A lot of them have gone on to other careers. Hell, I'm meeting some of their sons now."

Was that a note of sadness he heard in Duncan's voice? Nah…

"So, how's your bum?"

Duncan snorted. "Well, he's got issues, but I think he's reachable. I may have to be out here for a few days."

"Okay, we'll be gone by the time you get back. Do you want to know where?"

"Nope. The less I know the less I have to testify about. Just stay safe and keep our people safe. Keep your phone on you."

"You know I'll do all of that. Thanks, Dunc. You be safe too."

"Will do."

Chad hung up his phone slowly, details swimming through his head. The logistics of making six people disappear for an unknown amount of time would not be easy, but he knew he could do it. More importantly, he knew where he could do it.

Damn, he had a lot of phone calls to make. And very little time to do it.

WHEN DUNCAN RETURNED a few hours later, he half expected Aiden to be gone. He pushed the door in and peered around the little corner to the bed. Aiden lay in the exact position he had been in before. It was as if he'd been so wiped out he didn't have the energy to even shift.

Duncan could sympathize. It seemed like he never felt rested anymore.

Turning, he looked down the hallway to the waiting room. He could park in there for a little while, catch up on some emails. Planting his cane, he started for the room.

Aiden's auburn-haired doctor walked out of one of the rooms a little ways down the hallway and turned to the right, her head tilted down to the clipboard in her hand. Since she was going the same direction he was, she hadn't seen him, which was fine. It gave him a chance to check her out. Although with that long white doctor's coat on, it was kind of a non-issue. The color of her hair stood out like a neon light though, curling down her back to below her shoulder blades.

Duncan was actually surprised he was even vaguely interested. It had been so long since he'd had even the faintest hint of curiosity. Had to be the red hair.

The doctor paused and knocked gently on the door to her left. As she stepped into the room, she glanced up, her gaze catching on his for the barest second before she disappeared from view.

Duncan paused. Had he actually seen the flash of awareness in her eyes? Or had he imagined it? She knew he was walking behind her—the sound of his cane on the floor had a distinctive sound from his feet.

Shoving into motion again, he shook his head. There was no damn way she'd looked at him like that. And even if she had, she was a damn baby. There was no way he'd consider touching that.

CHAPTER FIVE

THEY ALL MET at the office. Though it was four a.m. in the morning, Mercy was bright-eyed with excitement as she looked around curiously. Lora, on the other hand, had gone into mother-tiger mode. She surveyed everyone with suspicion, if not outright alarm. When she caught sight of a stone-faced Harper lounging in the meeting room, trimming his nails with his knife, she paled and shifted to the opposite side of the table, tugging Mercy along behind her. She settled into a spare chair in the corner with Mercy on her lap.

Rachel, the new hire, thrummed with excitement though she never moved. Chad held his hand out to her as she stood. "I've not had the chance to meet you yet. Chad Lowell."

She grinned at him, shaking strongly. "Rachel Searles. It's a pleasure to meet you. Thank you for the chance to do this."

At first glance, Rachel seemed pretty and open. Her honey blond colored hair was pulled back in a tight ponytail and she was dressed in fatigues and a T-shirt. Then he realized how strong she was. The woman was stacked with muscle. Not so much to lose her femininity but definitely enough to intimidate most men. If she hadn't been standing in a group that was all over six feet and moderately to heavily built, in Harper's case, she would have dwarfed most average men.

Chad motioned to the others in the room. "Have you met the other yahoos?"

She nodded, her golden eyes darkening just a bit. "I have."

Flynn cleared his throat. "Can we get some details now or what?"

Glancing at the belligerent former SEAL K9 handler, Chad fought a grimace. He had hoped some of the attitude would wane if Flynn were given something more challenging than the computer work he'd been doing. He'd been hired a few months ago, with conditions. Flynn struggled with PTSD like they all did, from losing his K9 in the war, but his felt different for some reason. Chad couldn't pinpoint what it was exactly, but it was unsettling. The counselor swore his treatment had progressed.

The darkly-bearded man stared at him hard, as if daring him to say something about his attitude.

Chad motioned to Lora and Mercy sitting behind him. "We're on a security detail until further notice. We're bugging out because the perp, a former client, has tried to acquire the target, his daughter, twice now." He smiled at Mercy, determined to keep her calm and protected. "Duncan needs time to manage the sitch on this end."

"Where are we going?"

Glancing at Rachel, he hesitated. "I'll tell you when we get there. The less people that know where we are the better. You were aware of that when you signed on for this operation, right?"

She nodded. "Yes, sir. Sorry."

Flynn snorted. Rachel turned to look at him, but didn't say anything.

Chad wondered what kind of an idiot he was throwing this crew together.

"Cash transactions only. No cards. This guy has ties to the financial world, so we're not going to make it easy for him to track us. We'll take two vehicles. Harper, are you up to driving?"

The other man nodded, expressionless as always.

"And I'll take my truck. It's a long drive, boys and girls, so be prepared."

Lora looked shell-shocked. He wanted to reach out and reassure her, but they needed to get going. "Are you okay?"

She blinked at him. "What about my job and my house? My car?"

Chad had left directions with Shannon on what to do, but he hadn't told Lora. "We'll inform your job what's going on, to a certain extent. If they hold your job until this thing is over–great. If not, we'll set you up in another position. Mercy's school will also receive a note about the situation, with directions to contact us should somebody inquire about you or her. The house will be locked up and we'll make sure your vehicle will be stored in your garage. We'll take care of your bills right now. If you want to jot down a note to our receptionist with your account numbers and the names of the companies for your utilities, it would make our job that much easier."

Lora's mouth had dropped open. "You can't do all this. Nobody can. These are my responsibilities."

He nodded. "I know. But we don't have time to hang out waiting for you to tie up loose ends. He's tried to…" he paused, looking pointedly at Mercy, "twice now. And I'm not so sure that your 'anniversary visit' wasn't the first attempt."

She sank back in the chair and tears came to her eyes. The thought had obviously not occurred to her.

Chad gave her a minute to gather herself, aware of the others in the room. He turned to look at them. "Get your gear together."

They moved at once, though Flynn tossed him an aggravated look as they left the room.

Chad knelt down beside her chair on his good leg and dared to reach out to touch her elbow. "I'm sorry I can't give you more time to adjust to this, but we need to go. The sooner we go the safer you'll both be. Let me worry about the details. You take care of her."

He ran his finger down Mercy's nose, tapping on the end, and she grinned at him. "We have to go on a trip. Are you ready? And Handsome?"

She nodded and slid from her mother's lap to step closer to him. "That man was kind of scary."

"Which one?"

"The one with the dark hair."

Chad nodded and reached out to rest a hand on her shoulder. "Flynn's just kind of grumpy. He won't hurt you."

It actually surprised him that Harper wasn't the one who had scared her.

Mercy clutched her dog, bear, whatever it was, and sighed. "Okay."

Lora looked resigned to what was going on, and he had the striking thought that maybe he was running her life like the bastard ex was trying to. "If you really don't want to leave, we can try to tough it out here."

She shook her head, giving him a tight smile. "No, I know leaving is best. It's just hard. I've fought for everything we have and to walk away from it is harder than I expected." She swallowed. "You know, I actually had a plan to leave if things got desperate. I don't understand why I'm dragging my feet now."

She shook her arms out and stood, heading toward the table. "Give me a minute to write a few things down and I'll be ready."

Chad pushed to his feet, anxious to get going. While Lora worked on her list, he walked down the hallway to the employee lounge. There was a group of lockers on the back wall. Inside his, he pulled out one of his alternate legs, the blade prosthetic. He hoped he didn't need it, but he'd rather take it than not have a backup. He stuffed his spare clothes in the bag as well. They'd probably have to stop on the way to buy a few more things to add to their wardrobes, but this would do for a few days.

When he returned to the boardroom, Lora clutched her list.

"I couldn't remember everything, but I think I got most of it. Some of the account numbers I couldn't remember."

Chad smiled at her. "No biggie. Shannon is a whiz with this kind of thing. She'll figure it out. You'll have to leave you cell phone too."

She didn't seem too upset as she handed it over.

"Okay. Let's go."

Chad walked her out of the room, down the hallway and dropped the list and phone on Shannon's desk. Then he guided them to the elevator where their bags waited. "We're bugging out! Are you ready?"

Mercy giggled and nodded, dancing beside them. "Bugging out!"

Lora smiled as she watched her daughter, and Chad thought that maybe everything would be okay.

WHEN DR. HARTFIELD walked into the waiting room where he'd set up his impromptu office and sat down in the chair across from him, folding her legs elegantly, he expected an update on Aiden.

"Would you like to go down and get a cup of coffee in the cafeteria? I'm dragging, and if you're going to be here as late as you were last night, you probably need food too."

Duncan sat back in the chair, surprised at her boldness. But he shouldn't have been. She seemed confident in her skin and her abilities as a doctor. She couldn't have gotten where she was today if she hadn't had balls.

As he looked into her dark kelly green eyes, unhidden by her chunky black glasses, he wondered where all the arguments went he'd been giving himself a couple hours ago. "I can take a coffee. And a sandwich."

Gathering his cane, he pushed to his feet. Pride made him try to minimize his limp, but he gave up on that pretty quickly. If she was interested in him anyway, the quickest way to turn her off was to show her everything.

As she led him from the room and down the hallway, she made sure to walk beside him slow enough that he didn't struggle. Years ago it would have frustrated Duncan to make people curb their speed for him, but he'd come to the realization that they could walk away from him and he would be fine with it. He would get there eventually.

She pressed the elevator button when they drew close enough, then leaned against the wall. "Looks like you can set up your operation wherever you happen to be. What branch of military were you in?"

"Marines."

The woman got a funny look on her face and nodded her head. "Should have known."

The elevator doors hissed open and he made a motion for her to get on first, then he followed. "If I'm not mistaken, you have the look of a brat."

Laughter pealed out of her, stunning him with its clear beauty. As she looked at him, mouth spread in a smile, eyes creased with laughter, he knew he was in deep shit.

Duncan felt more alive than he had in a long time. Alex Hartfield was an interesting woman. What the hell she wanted with him, he didn't know. At first he thought she was looking for a father figure to take care of her, but she quickly dispelled that notion. She and her Marine father were on excellent terms, and as they spoke Duncan realized he had known a Hartfield in Iraq. When they connected the dots, he felt like an old man. Yes, that was her father. They'd not been in the same unit, but they'd pounded the same dirt. The difference being her father had never been seriously wounded.

Duncan would still be over there if that helicopter hadn't come down on him and his guys.

When Dr. Hartfield asked about his injuries, he gave her the list. Clinical, details only. But when she rested her hand on his and he looked into her eyes, he lost his distance. "The biggest injury was to my soul, though. I lost a lot of good men over there."

She tightened her hand on his, her eyes going moist with tears. "But there's nothing you could have done," she whispered.

He shrugged.

Pulling his hand away, he began to gather up his trash. They were in territory he had no interest in rehashing. "When will Aiden be able to be released?"

Her eyes cooled as she watched him but she accepted that he needed distance. "As long as he starts to eat correctly over the next day, I should be able to let him go in a few days. He has to eat first."

Duncan nodded and waited while she got to her feet. He took her plastic tray from her and dumped the trash, then held out a hand for her to proceed back the way they came. This had been a nice break, he told himself, but it was time to get back to real life.

LORA WATCHED THE miles fly by. They headed east for a while, but she realized they were kind of making a loop. At one point they backtracked completely and took a different exchange on the freeway. Chad talked to the big, black, military-looking vehicle behind them a couple of times, but they didn't think they were followed.

After a few hours she started to see signs for Texas. "Are we going to Texas?"

He nodded, glancing away from the road to see her reaction.

Lora didn't know how she felt. It was as good of a place to hide as any, she supposed. "Are we going somewhere in particular?"

His eyes shifted away, and for a moment, he looked a little uncomfortable. "We are. A little place about an hour south of Amarillo called Honeywell, Texas."

She had never heard of it. "What's in Honeywell, Texas?"

He grinned at her. "Not much of anything really. Couple restaurants, couple gas stations, a grocery, a feed store. There's a little movie theater that plays matinees on the weekends."

She narrowed her eyes at him. "You've been there before?"

Winking at her, he passed a vehicle. "I might have grown up there."

Lora didn't know what to think. Why on Earth would he take her to his home? "Mind explaining that to me?"

Chad sighed. "Well, we're not connected in any way, so I thought it would be a good place to hide you out. My family has a ranch down here, several thousand acres, and it's easy to lose yourself on the land. My dad gave me a chunk of the ranch to try to get me to come home a few years ago, but I wasn't interested in moving back. It's nice to visit once in a while, but I doubt I'll ever live there again."

"And your parents are okay with you bringing a strange woman and child home with you?" She thought his cheeks might have flushed just a bit.

"Well, they'll probably get the wrong idea, but that may actually work in our favor. I, um," he coughed into his hand, "well, anytime I come home I have visitors. Of the female persuasion. Maybe if they think I'm off the market they'll leave us alone."

Lora shrank back in the seat, cringing. She didn't want to belong to any man. Did he actually think she would go for that idea? Her gaze furious, she opened her mouth to respond, but he held up a hand.

"I'm sorry, Lora. We'll come up with another story. No big deal."

She looked at his clamped jaw and realized he was offended. Why the hell would he…her eyes fell to his left hand, hidden at his side. Ah. He had scars on that side of his neck, too, and she wondered for the first time how far down they reached. It had to have been incredibly painful, what he'd gone through.

Chad had put himself out there to help her, help them both actually, and she'd cut him off at the knees. Shame fought with her instinct to protect herself at all cost. "I can't…I don't know that I would be able to fake being with you. Physically, I mean."

If anything, his jaw hardened even more. "No problem," he snapped.

She clenched her fists and gave a sharp cry, frustrated that she'd hurt him even more. "I can't do physical. Me. I can't do that."

Some of the tension went out of the fist clutching the steering wheel and he glanced at her. "Okay. I can understand that. We'll come up with something else then."

Lora wanted to cry, and scream, and most of all she wanted to punch Derek Malone. The man had ruined her life and Mercy's life, and she didn't know if they would ever be the same. She missed being a woman, letting a man touch her without shrinking in fear. Dinner out, dessert in. Sharing every day with someone important. For a few precious months, she'd had that.

Chad turned on the radio and concentrated on the road, letting her off the conversational hook. Mercy slept quietly in the back seat, worn out from all that had happened in the night and morning.

Looking out the window, she tried to imagine the life she had before, but it was so shrouded in all the crap that came after. A tear slipped down her cheek and she was glad she had her head turned away.

THEY ARRIVED IN Honeywell, Texas a little before noon that day. As Chad idled through town, he looked for changes. There was a new green awning on the restaurant. One of the gas stations had closed down, but there were two new ones on the other end. One of those pharmacies that landed on every corner of the big cities had popped up and he wondered how it had enough business to warrant its existence. Other than that, everything looked the same. The sun shone down harshly, glaring off the hood of the truck and into his eyes. As he drove out the other end of town, he started to accelerate.

"Just a little bit more."

Mercy was chomping at the bit to be out of the truck. She'd done really well for the most part, but for the past two hours she'd been wide awake and ready to get out. On their last gas break he'd found her a coloring book and crayons. That had kept her occupied for about thirty minutes. I Spy had only lasted ten minutes with the boring landscape. Knock-knock jokes had lasted a few minutes before his repertoire was exhausted. When he started making them up, she knew, and gave him such a disgusted look. Finally he told her to count cows.

When she complained that there were more cows than stars in the sky, Lora had grinned for the first time since they'd started out. Chad hoped that the mess he'd created hours before could be forgotten. How humiliating.

But it only got better when he rolled onto the Blue Star Ranch. His mother came down the porch steps and embraced him the way she always did, then turned to Lora, huddled in her sweater. "Oh, honey, Chad told me you had issues with your ex, but I guarantee you he will treat you so much better."

"Mama," he growled. "We're not together like that. We came down to get away from a situation for a while."

But she wrapped Lora in her arms and completely ignored his words, treating her like a long-lost daughter.

Dad gave him a look as he stepped forward, pulling him into a hug. "You know how she is, son. You should have known she'd react like this."

Chad shook his head. "I know, but damn. It's good to see you, Dad."

His father looked trim and healthy, buff colored cowboy hat cocked at an angle to shield his face. Garrett Lowell wore a hat like he'd been born in one. Hell, maybe he had.

Car doors slammed behind him and Chad turned to introduce the group. "Dad, this is Harper, Flynn, and Rachel. They'll be staying with us for a while."

Dad's face creased as he smiled and bright blue eyes, so like his own, twinkled with welcome. "Glad to have you here, all of you. Please, consider this your home for as long as you need."

Harper turned to survey the area, wraparound sunglasses completely concealing his eyes. Flynn walked to the corner of one of the outbuildings and stared out. Only Rachel stepped forward to shake Dad's hand. Chad appreciated that at least one of them could be fairly normal.

"Well, grab your bags and come on in."

"Dad, I think we're going to stay on that piece you gave me. In the old foreman's house. Sorry, I should have told you when I called last night, but I didn't think of it."

His face fell and Chad hated to disappoint him, but his father rallied. "That's perfectly fine. At least you're here. We'll still get time to visit."

Chad nodded, determined that they would. Once they got settled and onto a routine, they would talk.

Mercy and Lora had disappeared into the house with his mother. He heard Mercy's little giggle and turned for the kitchen. Of course that's where they'd be.

His mother had already poured glasses of milk and unwrapped a plate of cookies. Mercy chewed like she hadn't eaten in forever, though they'd stopped for breakfast not long ago. She seemed fascinated by his mother.

Francine Lowell was known far and wide for her cooking, and wasn't ashamed of her enjoyment. Nicely rounded, she was the perfect stereotypical rancher's wife. She could get up at five to feed twenty men, then ride the range looking for cattle, her perfectly done up gray-streaked brown hair never moving. Chad considered her one of the most competent women he knew and he loved her to pieces.

Though she did tend to steamroll. Even now she was asking Lora about her history. Lora, wide-eyed and cornered against the counter, looked overwhelmed.

"Mama, really? Let the poor woman chill out a bit before you interrogate her. She came here to relax, not be attacked by a nosy busybody."

Francine's mouth dropped open and she swatted Chad with a towel. "You haven't had anyone around to remind you of your manners, Chadwick. How dare you talk to your mama like that?"

She grinned then, taking the sting from her scolding. "Oh, I've missed you, son. I'm so glad you came down."

He pressed a kiss to his mother's hair. "Me too, Mama. Just be nice to Lora, okay? Try to rein in your natural steam-roller personality."

"I will, dear." She turned to Lora. "I'm sorry if I overwhelmed you. That wasn't my intention. You're welcome in my home no matter what. If Chad says you need to relax, this is a good place to do it. There's not a thing you need to do here."

She turned to the refrigerator and started to pull platters from the shelves. "Chad, I thought you all might like some lunch. Go get your friends and bring them in."

Chad didn't know whether to be humiliated by his mother's antics or laugh his ass off at the interaction between her and the guards. Rachel was easy. She seemed to fit into any situation. As soon as she entered the kitchen she started to help with the meal. Harper moved to the bay window in the dining room and stayed there, a hulking, intimidating figure watching the landscape. Flynn gave the most curious reaction. Considering the attitude he'd shown Chad for the past eight hours, he'd expected the same when confronted with his mother. But he dipped his head and started 'yes, ma'am'-ing everything. Okay, seriously? The Atlanta boy had manners? So not right.

Mama parked Lora in a chair in the corner and clucked over her, making sure she was comfortable and had a glass of iced tea at hand. Then continued to fill the table with what he realized were all of his favorites. Fried chicken, homemade noodles, cinnamon apples, green beans. He grinned as Dad sat at the head of the table, his normal seat.

It was one of the strangest meals he'd ever participated in. Mama wanted to put everyone at ease, but to people like them who didn't talk nearly as much as she did, it merely made things awkward. Mercy chatted with her best, going on and on about the cattle she'd seen.

They made it through lunch quickly. When he told her they wouldn't actually be staying in the house, her crestfallen expression made him feel bad. The relief on Lora's face, though, was unmistakable. A bit faster than was polite, he hustled them all out of the house to the vehicles. Flynn hoisted bags of leftovers into Harper's Hummer and waved goodbye to her. Chad pressed a kiss to his mother's forehead, promising to be back the next day to talk for a while. Shaking Dad's hand, he hopped into the truck and took off down the driveway.

"Are we leaving, Chad?"

He looked into the rearview mirror at Mercy's disappointed face. "No, darlin', we're just going to a different part of the ranch. We'll still be able to see the main house, but it will be a little more private for us."

She frowned, looking out the window.

Chad turned down the lane near the front gate, a little overgrown now that it wasn't used as much. They drove for the better part of a mile, the incline steadily climbing until they reached a rocky slope. A long, low ranch house was nestled into the mountain, the stone front partially camouflaging it. A good-sized barn, big enough for a few horses if they wanted, sat back in the pine woods off to the right, as well as a good-sized paddock for grazing.

The foreman that used to live here had had several kids. There was a wood-framed swing set in the dry front yard, surrounded by mulch. Mercy leaned up to get a closer look as he parked the truck.

"Mommy, can I go swing?"

Lora glanced at him to see what he thought and he nodded to her. "I think she'll be fine up here. We can see people coming from miles away, literally. The back of the mountain is pretty much impassible. Let her run."

"Okay, Mercy. But just stay on the swing set, okay?"

Her little blond head bobbed. "I will Mommy, promise."

Chad let himself into the house. It didn't look like anyone had been here since he last had, more than a year ago. Dust coated the surfaces of the furniture. Heading to the back of the house, he flipped the master switch on the power box and turned the water valve to 'open'. The hot water heater started to hum.

Moving from room to room, he made sure no critters had gotten in. Lora explored as well, removing dust covers here and there. There were three bedrooms. Lora and Mercy could share one, and the four guards could share the other two. They would be working alternate shifts, so it would work out.

When he left the bedroom, Harper had just ducked through the front door. Chad motioned to the bedroom behind him and told him the schedule. The big man nodded and moved to drop his bag inside the bedroom door, then moved through the rest of the house, obviously memorizing the layout.

"I'm going to hike out back," Harper told him.

Chad nodded, understanding that he would be a while. The former SEAL sniper preferred the outdoors and it suited him. He would only come indoors when he absolutely had to. Harper's first priority on any new op was to find the most advantageous, defensible position.

Flynn sat in a chair on the front porch. "Just what exactly are we supposed to do out here?" he grumbled.

"Protect Lora and her daughter at all costs until we find a way to get the ex off her tail."

Flynn scowled at him. "I know that. I mean out here." He motioned to the broad expanse of open land surrounding them.

To Chad, the open land around the house presented all kinds of opportunities. "Sorry, Frogman. I'll find work for you to do, if that's what you're worried about. You won't be bored. Sorry there's no water around."

Flynn snorted, pulling his cell phone from his pocket. "I'll be damned. At least there's service."

Chad left him scrolling through the screens of his phone.

Their biggest priority was to give Duncan time to dig into Derek's business to look for dirt. He needed to talk to Lora and see if she had any further insights. Any information they could gather would be better than what they had now, which was very little.

Chad found Lora hanging clothes in the closet of her bedroom, next to a few of Mercy's little things. She was staring off into space, holding a hanger when he stepped into the room, so he made a little extra noise so that she wouldn't be startled. She looked up with a faint smile tugging the corners of her lips and Chad ground to a halt. The old yellow light above her head softened the bruises on her face and he could see the attractiveness she tried to hide with her bulky sweaters and crossed arms. That one small smile gave him an insight into her personality he didn't think she would want him to know.

That she played her looks down deliberately.

It didn't hit him until just that moment, but he had never seen her dress to be seen. Every item of clothing she wore tended to be tan, pale green or cream. No glaring colors or fabrics. Nothing to draw the eye. She wanted to fly under the radar of attention and she made choices to do that.

She looked up when he stepped into the room, her green eyes soft. Within a split second, they had chilled to a frosty green.

He hated to see that look settle into her eyes. For the first time in a long time, he wished a woman would look at him and smile, just because he belonged to her. Chad swallowed, his throat working, as the realization took root in his gut.

No, he didn't want 'a woman' to look at him that way; he wanted Lora to look at him that way.

She tilted her head at him, fine brows raised in question. "Are you okay?"

Blinking, he gave a sharp nod. "Just…thinking about something. Sorry."

She shrugged. "I was hanging clothes. And wondering how long we'll be here."

Chad sighed and moved in a bit closer. "I'm not sure. Flynn just asked the same thing and I guess it depends upon how quickly Duncan can investigate your ex. People with money have things to hide. We just have to find his dirty secrets. I came in to ask if there's anything else you could think of that would help us do that. I need to call Duncan to check in."

Lora blinked and shifted around him to stand at the window. Outside, pine trees swayed in the breeze. The wind gusted a little, sending dust skittering across the yard. She seemed fascinated, eyes darting back and forth. "I don't know what would help. He's an egomaniac. I think you've realized that. Thinks he's better than everyone else. Believes he's God's gift to womankind, whether they want him or not. Derek Malone grew up privileged. And he had no problem taking what was denied him."

Anger built in his gut. It was obvious to him that Lora had fought against Derek for a long time.

"Do you know if he was involved with anyone else?"

She shook her head. "I was the only one he married; I know that. I'm sure he had affairs, though. There was a long stretch during my pregnancy, most of it actually, when he wouldn't touch me. I'm sure he had something on the side. Maybe a couple of somethings."

Chad smiled at the tone of her voice. "I don't think you cared, though, did you?"

She graced him with a small smile. "No, I didn't. Derek Malone lost his appeal within a few weeks of marrying him."

That one sentence reassured Chad as nothing else had. If she had lingering feelings for the scum, it would be difficult to pursue charges against him.

"And tell me about the business. Were you involved with it at all? What was his regular schedule like? Did he go to work every day nine to five?"

She snorted. "Never. He had an office at the company but he only went in sporadically. Rosalind wanted him to take a larger, more active part in the company at first, but I think even she has begun to realize what a fuck-up he is. As far as I know, he still goes into work but he doesn't get the same projects he used to."

Chad laughed out loud at her words. She'd cussed. He raised his brows at her in surprise and she turned a little pink. Then she managed to laugh a little as well.

The change in her face was truly something to behold. The plain clothes and the bruises on her face faded away, and the beauty beneath peeked out, dazing him for a long moment.

"Rosalind is the driving force behind all of this. As crazy as it seems I think she may actually care about Mercy. I know Derek has a vague need to be with his daughter, but he doesn't realize the kind of engagement and support a child needs. He's too much of a child himself."

Chad knew men like that. Several of them, in fact.

"I'll pass this info on to Duncan and see if there's anything he can use."

She nodded, turning back to the window.

Chad hated to interrupt her again, because she seemed content just looking out the window. "I'm going to run down to the house for an hour or so and talk to my parents. I'll be back as soon as I can. I, uh," he cleared his throat as she turned to look at him again. "Do you mind if I bring a pony back for Mercy? We have an old guy by the name of Taco that lives for little kids. I thought it might be fun for her."

Lora blinked, obviously startled. "I think she would absolutely love that. Thank you so much."

Chad nodded once and headed toward the kitchen, glad that she'd gone along with the fun surprise. Flynn sat at the kitchen table, dismantling his sidearm. There were pieces scattered everywhere and music played softly from his phone, but he looked up when Chad entered the room.

"I'm going to run down to the house and talk to my dad. Do you need anything?"

The SEAL shook his head. "Nah. I'm good here. Rachel's on the girl. I think Harper went walkabout."

"He did. I suggest you do the same when you're exterior."

Flynn gave him a lazy salute and focused back onto his scattered pieces.

As Chad headed toward the truck, he spied Mercy on the swing set with Rachel watching over her. They both waved as he pulled away. When he glanced into the rear view mirror, Lora had stepped out onto the front porch to watch her daughter. The late April sun was shining on them, highlighting their golden heads.

CHAPTER SIX

HIS MOTHER WAS ecstatic to see him again, though she was disappointed he was the only visitor. He stayed long enough to catch up with family gossip and to try to impress upon her that he didn't want anyone to know he was at the ranch, but he didn't think she got the message.

"But surely you wanna see Tara Johnson? She married that Clapper boy for a while but it didn't work out."

Chad cringed at the thought of the heavy cloud of perfume that followed Tara wherever she went. She'd been one of the worst when he'd come home to recover after he'd gotten out of the hospital. And while she seemed to have a heart of gold, she'd been so pitying toward him that it had turned his stomach.

"Mama, I appreciate that you want me to reconnect with people around here, but I'm down here for work. I'm protecting a woman from her abusive ex, and that ex can't have any whiff that she's here, or he'll come down after her."

His mother frowned. "Tara Johnson does not know this woman's husband, so how would he know?"

Chad could only shake his head at his mother's stubborn streak.

"Don't call her, Mama."

He allowed a little of his sergeant's voice to come out and she seemed a little startled. Before she could recover, he stood up from the table. "I'm going out to the barn to see Dad. Hey, do any of the grandbabies have any spare clothes around? Lora and Mercy only brought a few changes of things. And maybe some boots?"

Mama stood up, a smile creasing her face. "I have just the thing. I always keep clothes here."

Chad knew she did. The Lowell homestead was the hub of the

family. He'd be surprised if he didn't see one of his brothers or sisters today. And it seemed like there were always kids around.

"I'll be back in after I talk to Dad."

But his mother had already disappeared down the long hallway of the house.

His father was in the main barn, as Chad had expected. His older brother Brock was there as well, bent over the rear hock of a sorrel gelding tied in crossties. The horse had cut his hoof just above the coronary band and Brock was bandaging the wound. He glanced up when Chad walked in, but didn't stop what he was doing.

"Hey, Dad. Brock."

"Chad."

He stood quietly beside his dad, absorbing the relaxed atmosphere inside the barn. Horses chewed hay in their stalls, or hung their heads lazily over the stall doors. He could fee the tension easing out of his body.

They watched Brock finish wrapping the foot, then stand up. Chad felt the drag of Brock's eyes as he surveyed him up and down, lingering on his legs.

"Pretty boots. How you doin', little brother?"

Chad cringed at the derision he heard in Brock's voice. "Fine, Broccoli. How are you doing?"

Red flushed the big man's face and he took a step toward him, tipping his cream-colored hat back with one finger, but Garrett held his hand up. "Don't start bickering already. You're grown men. You need to act like it."

Brock gathered up the materials he'd used on the horse and turned away.

Chad followed his dad as he walked beyond the horse to the other end of the barn.

"Why do you antagonize him?"

"Me?" Chad stared at his father incredulously. "Are you serious?"

Garrett shook his head. "I don't know why the two of you can't get along anymore."

With a sigh, Chad leaned against the side of the barn. "If you ever figure it out let me know, would you? I've been wondering for years."

And he had been. When they'd been kids, he and Brock had hung out a lot. Chad had had a serious case of hero worship for his big brother, and Brock had seemed to enjoy the attention. Chad had known early on that it would be Brock taking over the ranch one day, so he'd looked for other options. He'd joined the Marines and the family had been overjoyed. Brock had been too. After he'd been injured, something had changed. Brock had closed off, becoming surly and difficult. He'd been the most irritating part about visiting home.

Well, the women had been the worst part. But Brock had been the second worst.

"So, how's the business been? Guard anybody interesting lately?"

Chad grinned at his father's question. He always asked the same thing. "Nah. Nobody you'd know. People like Lora and Mercy."

Grinning, his father removed his hat long enough to swipe a hand over his head, smoothing the still thick gray hair. "That little one is going to be a handful. I think she could talk the horns off a bull, if you know what I mean." He plopped his hat back on his head.

Laughing, he agreed with his father's assessment of Mercy. "She is a sweetie. I don't think her mother realizes how sharp she is."

Garrett laughed. "She will!"

They laughed together like Chad had never left and it made him happy. The guys at LNF were great friends, but there was no replacing actual family. It had been months since he'd seen his mom and dad and he'd missed them.

"I thought I'd take a few horses up to the house, if you didn't mind. It's a little easier to get around that hill on horseback than foot."

"It is. I've got some I can send you. That little one might want to try out old Taco, too."

He and Dad were too much alike. "I thought so, too. I was going to ask if I could take him along."

Garrett nodded. "The old boy needs the exercise."

Within a half hour, he'd loaded two horses and a scruffy pony, as well as their tack and a couple bags of feed. Chad shifted the truck into gear and listened to the pull on the motor as he left the barn lot. He slowed down on the rutted path up to the house, and when he pulled in front of the house, Mercy stopped swinging long enough to come over and see what he was doing. Chad crooked a finger at her as he unlocked the rear gate of the trailer.

Taco was the last to be loaded, so he was at the rear. Chad untied the lead line and tugged the old guy down to the ground. Mercy gasped at the sight of the little reddish-brown horse with the white blaze and crept forward cautiously, but stopped several feet away. Taco reached his muzzle out to her, asking for attention, but Mercy curled her hands away carefully. Going down to one knee, Chad held his hand out to her.

"This is Taco. He's been on the ranch for many years. I rode him when I was little."

Mercy's green eyes, so brilliant in the clear day, widened dramatically. "Really?"

Chad nodded. "A couple of my sisters did too. All the little kids that come to the ranch have been Taco's buddy. He loves little kids. I thought he would be a good friend for you while we're here."

Mercy stepped forward but leaned in toward him for protection. Chad wrapped his arm around her.

"Let me see your hand."

She held it out and he spread her fingers, placing a peppermint from his pocket on her flat palm.

"Hold your fingers completely flat like that, then hold the candy out."

She did as he told her and the pony stole the treat. Mercy giggled and held her hand out to Chad for another, but he shook his head. "No, he just gets one treat at a time. Look how round his belly is."

Mercy laughed and burrowed into his hold as Taco took a step toward her. The old pony reached out his muzzle and Chad showed the little girl how to stroke his nose and the side of his neck. Once she realized the animal wasn't going to hurt her, Mercy stepped out of the circle of his arms and moved around. Chad gave her a quick course on animal safety.

"If you're good maybe your mom will let you ride him. I brought his saddle."

Mercy stopped and looked at him, her big eyes filling with tears before she bolted up the porch to her mother. Lora knelt down beside her and wrapped the sobbing girl in her arms before carrying her inside.

Chad was shocked at the sudden turnaround and didn't understand what he'd said that had upset the little one. He'd have to talk to Lora after Mercy had calmed down.

Had the thought of riding Taco scared her? That had not been his intention at all.

He unloaded the horses and settled them into the barn. Hefting a fifty-pound bag of sweet feed over his shoulder, he made sure to plant his feet securely as he carried the bag into the tack room. When he turned for the second bag, Harper stood behind him, bag draped over his shoulder as though it were a towel. He handed the bag to Chad with one hand, his right hand never leaving the menacing sniper rifle he carried.

Chad grinned at him. "Find anything interesting?"

Harper scowled. "Cows and brush, interspersed with big boulders good for cover. And the occasional pine tree."

Sounded about right.

"I found a good spotting location up on top. I'm going to hang out up there for a while. Just came down for a radio."

Chad nodded. "Take one from the kitchen. Flynn set them up."

With a single nod, the former sniper headed for the house, weapon at his side.

Chad unloaded the rest of the tack from the truck to the tack room. By the time he was done, his leg was aching from carrying the unfamiliar weight. He'd also strained his hand when one of the saddles slipped from his grip. He should have just let the thing fall to the ground, but he made a grab with his bad hand. The fragile skin at the bend of his wrist had torn and now dripped blood to the ground.

As he walked into the house, he caught Rachel's eye as she came around from the back of the house. "I'm going to go crash for a couple hours. Flynn is supposed to be sleeping now, but he's up if you need anything."

"Roger," she said with a nod.

Her gaze caught the blood dripping from his hand but she didn't say anything.

Smart woman.

Flynn sat at the table, pretending to be absorbed in the movie on the screen of his tablet. The reassembled sidearm was now on his hip. Chad had seen his eyes dart to the door, then back. The man was aware of everything that went on around him.

Chad repeated the same message he had to Rachel and headed down the hallway. Lora and Mercy had the master bedroom with the attached bathroom, so he stepped into the one in the hallway. He washed his hands and blotted at the seeping skin on his wrist. Rummaging beneath the sink, he found an assortment of first aid products.

Running cold water over the skin break, he let it soak for several long moments before turning off the tap and blotting it dry. He hadn't been moisturizing it the way he should have been. The stretches were easy, he could do them anywhere anytime. It had become habit to just prop his arm against a doorjamb or wall and lean. But getting a bottle of lotion out just wasn't convenient. Even when he had the time he didn't always think about it.

The bleeding had stopped by the time he quit blotting it, but he kept the cloth against his wrist. He needed a shower before he bandaged it.

As he shifted his weight, his lower leg pinched. If felt like he had a raw spot in there. Leaving the bathroom long enough to grab a pair of sweat pants, he headed back into the bathroom.

This bathroom wasn't set up for 'combat modified', but he could make it work. Twisting the knobs on the shower, he warmed the water. Stripping off his clothes, he closed the lid on the commode and sat. When he tugged the prosthetic from the stump of his lower leg, it seemed to take a heavy breath. He rolled the fabric sleeve down and off and surveyed the blotchy red skin. Damn. He'd definitely left it on too long. Swinging his legs into the shower, he stood carefully, conscious that if he fell, he'd have people banging at his door in no time. He snapped the shower curtain shut and leaned into the heat of the water. Man, that felt good. Bracing against the shower wall, he soaped his body, paying particular attention to the end of his leg. It needed moisturizer as well, and the leg and sleeve needed to air out.

While he'd become accustomed to dealing with his missing leg, it was still a disadvantage when on assignment. Just taking the time to care for the damn thing was an inconvenience. If he didn't take care of it now though, the irritation would get worse.

He finished up his shower and reversed the process to get out of the tub. Toweling dry, he looked for moisturizer under the sink, but there wasn't any. Damn. He'd have to get the bottle from his room.

Rinsing the sleeve in the sink, he laid it on the edge while he pulled the sweats on, then he readied a bandage. Ah, Neosporin. The cool salve felt really good as he applied a dressing and wrapped gauze around the skin break on his wrist. Though he'd gotten after Lora for not wearing her bandage on her wrist, he had to admit it wasn't easy to wrap yourself, but he'd had many, many years of practice. Within seconds his burnt hand was hidden beneath layers of gauze.

His room was across the hall and down a few feet from the bathroom. Bouncing on his right foot, he made his way to the room and inside. He propped his leg beside the bed and draped the sleeve over the short foot post of the queen-sized frame. Not exactly what it was meant for, but it would do.

Digging in his duffel, he found the bottle of non-perfumed anti-itch moisturizer and started rubbing it onto his leg. Damn, that felt good.

There was a knock on his door before Flynn stuck his head in. His gaze didn't even flicker to his leg, because he'd seen it all before.

"What's up, Flynn?"

"The woman is out here fussing. She won't say anything outright, but I think she's looking for you. The little girl is in bed."

Chad sighed and glanced at the alarm clock on the bedside table. Going on eight in the evening. He needed to get some sleep. "You can tell her I'm awake. If she comes back, great, if not, I'll sleep for a while. My sleeve is wet. I can't put it on yet."

Just the thought of putting his leg into a squishy, cold sleeve made him shudder.

The thought of Lora seeing him like this made him shudder in a different way. But maybe it was time. Needing to minimize the impact, he rolled the leg of the sweats back down over the leg.

Flynn ducked out of the room and moved down the hallway. Chad listened to him go, and realized his breathing had changed. The thought of Lora coming in now put him on edge, for several different reasons. One, he didn't think she realized he was missing a leg. He adjusted the prosthetic beside him, placing it at the exact corner of the bed. There was no doubting now. Two, he hadn't let a woman see him without his leg for years. Granted, with the sweats on, she wouldn't see anything that might gross her out, but this was damn near naked for him. Fuck, he'd rather be naked than show off his stump. Not having his leg on put him at a severe disadvantage, and he was curious what she would do with that power. Plus, he hadn't put a T-shirt on yet either. The rough skin down his left side was on display.

This was kind of the big test, whether she realized it or not. As he sat there, heart thudding and palms sweating, wondering if he had time to cover up, there was a knock at the door.

"Come in."

Lora ducked her head in the door, similar to how Flynn had. She smiled slightly when she saw him sitting on the bed, but her green eyes were serious. "I'm not bothering you, am I?"

He shook his head. "Not at all. Come on in."

She stepped a little further inside the doorway but didn't let go of the door itself.

Chad knew the exact moment when she spotted the leg. She opened her mouth to say something, but nothing came out. Her gaze rested on the prosthetic at the corner of the bed, then flicked to his sweats. The left leg was obviously gone; there was no hiding that.

She blinked and finally lifted her troubled eyes to his. "I didn't realize. You never said anything."

He shrugged, struggling not to hide as her eyes ran up his chest.

She had to be getting a hell of an eyeful. "It's not something you can just throw out there in the middle of conversation. And it hasn't been convenient to talk about much of anything. We've been busy."

Lora nodded, her eyes drifting back down his chest. "Yes, we have."

Chad shifted, his body heating under the weight of her eyes.

She closed them with a wince and shook her head, and he felt lacking. "I wanted to tell you I was sorry for the way Mercy reacted." She took a heavy, shuddering breath, and looked at him again. "I think you kind of brought up some memories. One of the only things Derek ever promised her was a pony of her own. It was just a message on the answering machine, but she took it to heart."

Chad winced. "I wondered if it wasn't something like that. I'm sorry. I didn't know."

Lora moved a little further into the room, letting go of the door. "It wasn't your fault at all. You were trying to make her happy. And I truly appreciate that."

"Should I take Taco back down to the main house?"

She shook her head, blond hair swinging around her battered face. "No. Can we keep him up here for a while? I think she'll figure things out in her own time and she'll want to see him again."

Chad gave her a single nod. "We can. The old guy doesn't take a lot of care."

She smiled slightly. "Is he really as old as you are?"

With a chuckle, he shifted on the bed. "Older, actually. One of my sisters got him for her birthday and he was several years old then. Ponies aren't like normal horses. They're tough little bastards."

Lora grinned and even laughed a little.

Chad watched her expression lighten and felt like the sun had come up. He was an easy-going guy, fairly funny, or so he thought, but Lora was a tough nut to crack. And after what she'd been through, how could he blame her? That little laugh gave him hope for more.

And the fact that she hadn't freaked about his leg was encouraging.

When he focused on her again, she was looking at him, considering.

"What?" he asked.

Frowning, she motioned to the prosthetic. "I didn't even realize. You move so normally."

Chad tried not to wince at the inference that he was abnormal.

"I've had many years to practice. I lost it in '07, same time as this." He lifted his bandaged hand.

"Why is it bandaged?"

He snorted. "Because I'm stupid and haven't been taking care of it. I need to moisturize it every day and things have been a little busy recently."

It was her turn to wince then. "I'm sorry we've messed up your schedule."

Chad shook his head. "No biggie. Really." He motioned to the duffel. "I pack with the expectation of everything. It'll be fine in a day."

Lora shifted on her feet as if she still had something to say. "I wanted to let you know that I appreciate everything you've done to welcome us here. I mean, this is your family home," she sighed. "I would never wish trouble to follow us here, but I can't help but worry."

He had his own worries about that, not that she needed to know. "My parents are very understanding. There's such a small chance of Derek finding us. I do believe you're safe for however long we need to be here."

Almost immediately, her shoulders relaxed and he could almost see some of the worry ease away. Chad wanted to go to her and wrap her in his arms, but he didn't think she would be good with that. Instead he offered her a grin. "Enjoy your time on the ranch as much as you can."

She nodded and he thought he saw the glisten of tears in her eyes. "It is beautiful here. I meant to tell you that earlier. I'm a city girl, so all this quiet is kind of…odd." She motioned to the darkening evening outside the window. "Are there predators up here?"

He glanced out the window. "Occasionally we might see a mountain lion, but most often you'll hear the coyotes howling. If you hear it, don't be alarmed. They very rarely come near people."

Lora folded her arms and he could see the doubt in her expression.

"Maybe I could get you on a horse. That would probably ease Mercy's mind about Taco."

Big green eyes widened, then winced in pain. She pressed a hand to the bruised side of her face. "I don't know if I can take that much excitement."

He forced a grin. "You may like it. Controlling an animal like that."

An odd expression crossed her face before she nodded. "I may, actually." She glanced out the window. "I'll let you get some rest."

With a final glance at him she slipped out the door.

Chad slumped on the side of the mattress, wrung out. It was always disconcerting taking off his Superman costume, but "Lois Lane" had seemed cool with everything.

Stretching out on the bed, he stared up at the ceiling, going over their interaction. The final few seconds played through in his mind. She'd looked at him, over his chest, but her gaze hadn't drifted any further. She hadn't even glanced at his leg before she'd walked out the door.

CHAPTER SEVEN

LORA WRAPPED HER arms around herself and walked down the hallway to the bedroom she shared with Mercy. The poor little thing was tuckered out after traveling all day and playing, and she'd fallen into a sorrowful heap on the bed. Handsome was now clutched in her arms.

As a mother, she wanted her daughter to be cautious, but she didn't want her to hide away because of her past. Yes, Lora had tried to keep her sheltered from her father as much as she could, but there would come a time when the little girl would either fade away or use this experience as a jumping off point for a truly momentous life. Obviously, she hoped the latter.

Every few months, Derek would come up with some scheme to insert himself into their lives. Showing up with tickets to the circus or the zoo, then leaving it to Lora to explain why they couldn't go with him. It had become such a fight.

And she always felt like the bad guy.

Whenever Derek would do something like that, she made sure to try to follow through with Mercy herself. Some of the stunts he tried to pull were completely out of her budget, but for the most part she felt like she made sure Mercy had experiences.

When Chad had offered to bring the pony up, she didn't think it would cause such a meltdown with her daughter. Several months ago, Derek had tried to surprise her with a pony at the house, but Lora had taken Mercy out of town for the weekend, not believing he'd actually follow through with the message he'd left. By the time they'd returned, the pony had been gone, but the mess remained. She'd had to explain to Mercy what had happened.

Heartbroken, the little girl had refused to talk to her for several hours.

Lora had thought that Chad's pony would bring her some happiness. She'd have to talk to Mercy in the morning.

Crossing the room, she sank down into the chair beside the window, dragging a discarded sweater across her lap. The sun had gone down and evening was deepening. She should have been thinking about going to bed, but her mind refused to settle.

It didn't help that they were in such unfamiliar surroundings. This was nothing like her little suburban house in Denver. Literally she could see for miles here. Mostly cattle and long sweeps of brown land, but it was still picturesque. A little strange not seeing jagged peaks outside her window, but she could deal with it.

Chad fit here. Laid back and calm, he seemed comfortable. Those cowboy boots made sense. Outside, especially. He'd said his dad had given him this acreage to try to get him to come home more often and she could see the appeal. Though the buildings in the suburbs made her feel secure, the expanse of land here thrilled her heart with its wildness.

She could make a life with her daughter out here and not give Denver a second thought.

She flashed back to Chad driving the truck into the yard. He'd seemed very natural introducing Taco to Mercy. Her throat tightened as she remembered how Mercy had burrowed into his arms when she'd gotten frightened.

Lora wished she could do that as well.

On nights like these, she ached with loneliness. Chad sitting bare-chested on his bed had seemed so appealing, even though she'd been shocked at his appearance. She'd had no idea he was missing a leg. That was kind of a huge thing to overlook, but she'd been lost in her own issues for too long. Heck, she couldn't even remember him limping or anything, other than when he wheeled her out of the hospital. But she'd thought that had been acting.

She'd been taken off guard, too, when she'd seen the defensive insecurity in his eyes. It was obvious he hadn't wanted to tell her but he felt he had to.

The thought of him experiencing something so traumatic that he'd lost a limb made her gut clench. The war overseas was a distant thing, easily put out of mind when daily life intruded. Mercy had asked about a couple of news segments she'd seen, but Lora remembered now that she'd reassured her and changed the subject. She had effectively buried her daughter's head in the sand along with her own.

As traumatic as the sight of his prosthetic leg had been, her reaction to his bare chest had rocked her more. Chad was muscled but lean. Actually, he could stand to put on a few pounds. But her gaze had been drawn to his chest and abs over and over again. Skin wrinkled over his muscles and his pectorals had rippled when he'd made a motion. There was also a tattoo on his left shoulder. All she could see from where she was standing was a dark blob. Without conscious thought, she'd crept a bit closer to him.

Maybe she felt safer with him *because* he wasn't perfect. She could see imperfections down the left side of his chest and neck, and there were freckles sprinkled across his upper shoulders. And when he grinned, she could see he had a crooked tooth at the bottom front. He didn't seem to care though. Maybe part of his appeal was that he didn't care what he looked like. He seemed okay with the scars and superficial marks, but the amputation made him insecure.

Derek had been the extreme opposite, always going to the gym and working out with his guards. There had been a private gym in the bowels of the family home. She'd never gone down there though Derek had urged her to all the time. She remembered a scene just a couple weeks after she'd had Mercy. His voice rang so clearly in her head.

"You need to tighten up those arms. And your belly is disgusting. I don't care if you did just have a baby."

She snorted. Even though she'd been disgusting, she'd apparently been okay enough to fuck.

Lora shook away the thought. It had happened years ago.

Chad was the first man to appeal to her physically. Too bad she'd never do anything about it.

LORA WOKE UP the next morning strangely energized. Mercy was chattering at her like a magpie, and she'd apparently forgotten about her breakdown from the night before. Lora found ingredients for pancakes in the cupboards and heated a griddle on the countertop. It was a little difficult juggling things with her good hand, but she managed.

The huge, shaved-headed guy came in from outside and glanced at her in the kitchen.

Lora took a deep breath. "If you'd like pancakes, there are plenty."

He tipped his head to her. "Thank you."

He disappeared down the hallway, carrying the big rifle like it didn't weigh anything. Mercy's eyes widened when she saw it but she didn't say anything.

Chad came in next. His eyes widened when he saw her cooking and he grinned. "Pancakes are the way to a man's heart."

Lora flushed and turned back to the griddle, unwilling to engage in that conversation. "Maybe we can get in some groceries?"

He leaned against the counter beside her and crossed his arms. He'd found an old ball cap somewhere and it sat cocked over his eyes. "We can. Why don't you make a list and we'll send somebody down."

She nodded, wondering who they would send. Hopefully Rachel. She'd professed not to be a cook, but maybe she could at least maneuver a grocery store.

Mercy bounced up and down in her seat, excited to be out of school. She stuffed huge chunks of pancake into her mouth, dripping syrup down her chin and shirt. Lora swiped at her with a napkin, but it did no good. "You're going to need another bath if you don't close your mouth on that syrup, girl."

Mercy giggled and chewed away.

Chad had left for a moment, heading down the hallway, but he returned within just a few seconds. Lora felt him enter the room behind her and didn't need to turn her head. She gathered a fresh plate and a stack of pancakes and handed it to him.

He stood in front of her, but he didn't take the plate until her eyes connected with his. "You don't have to cook for this group. We're used to takeout and gas station food. We can make do anywhere they put us." His eyes squinted as he smiled. "But the occasional home-cooked meal won't go uneaten."

A smile tugged at the corners of her mouth as he finally accepted the plate. "You need to eat better. You're too skinny."

Something dark flittered through his expression before he turned toward the table.

She snapped her mouth shut and turned back to the griddle, shocked that she'd made such a personal observation. What business was it of hers that he didn't eat right?

Flynn was on watch, but as soon as Chad finished his breakfast he went outside to relieve him so that he could eat. Lora thought she had made enough, but by the time Flynn was done, she had to wonder. Rachel was sleeping and Harper was the last to grab a plate. He drowned his cakes in syrup and went to stand by the window to eat.

Lora grabbed the last few and wrapped them up for Rachel to have later.

Flynn went back outside and within a few minutes, Chad was back.

"Can I go see Taco again?"

Lora looked at her daughter in surprise, then Chad. He nodded. "Of course you can, sweet cheeks. Clean up and I'll take you out."

Mercy jumped up from the table so fast she was a blur. Lora swiped the last of her mess away.

"Are you sure you have time to do this?"

His brows shot up. "Of course. The other three are on surveillance rotating through. I'll be with the two of you for the most part. Doesn't matter what we do as long as I stick with you."

Lora's heartbeat accelerated as she realized he would be with them exclusively. Brushing her hands down her jeans, she gave him a tight smile. "Okay then."

Mercy bolted out from the hallway and they trooped outside. The morning was cool, but not uncomfortable, and when they entered the barn the horses nickered.

"What are they doing?" Mercy asked, giggling.

"They're talking to each other," Chad told her. "And telling us hello."

He crossed to the stall at the very end, where a nose peeked over the weathered barn door. Taco shook his head and squealed when Chad stepped in, and seemed very happy to see people. Chad fastened a green halter on him and led him out, tying him to a ring set into the wall. The pony looked at Lora and Mercy from under a shaggy mane as if waiting.

Chad handed Mercy a Smarties from his pocket. "Think you can share those with Taco?"

Mercy nodded and bent her blond head to unwrap the cellophane. She popped one in her mouth, then held a second out to the pony. Taco lipped the sweet carefully from her hand making Mercy giggle again.

Chad held a bristle brush out to her. "You need to take care of any horse you have and I know for a fact Taco loves to be brushed. You'll put him to sleep."

Lora's throat tightened with emotion as she watched Chad instruct her daughter in the proper care for a horse. And he was true to his word. Within just a few minutes, the pony's head had drooped and his eyelids were flickering.

Chad suddenly looked up at Lora and motioned to her to step inside one of the empty stalls. "Do you mind if she rides?" he whispered.

Lora lost her thoughts as the scent of his sweet breath hit her. "N-no. As long as you're with her."

The man in front of her gave her a serious look, as if he knew his nearness affected her. "I'll take care of her, I promise."

And she knew he would.

Turning, he stepped out of the stall. "Would you like to try to ride him?"

Mercy looked up at him thoughtfully, her brow furrowed. "Yes, I think I would." She didn't mention yesterday.

Tears came to Lora's eyes at how grown up her daughter sounded. As Chad brought a small saddle from the tack room and showed her how to put it on, she realized how much her daughter had grown in the past year. Picking her up had become a chore–not that she'd change anything about her at all. But it was becoming more difficult. It seemed like every time she turned around they were having to shop for new, better fitting clothes.

As Chad showed Mercy how to tighten buckles and straps while moving carefully around the horse, Lora thought about how fast the time had flown. It seemed like just yesterday she'd been cradling her belly, counting down the days before her child came into the world. Then, once she had, she'd been counting the days till she could get out of the house.

It seemed like she went from one calamity to another, doggy paddling to keep her head above water and the sharks away.

Shoving all that aside, she watched her daughter be lifted to the saddle of the old pony. She now wore a little red helmet with Velcro straps beneath her chin. Mercy's eyes gleamed with excitement, but she stayed quiet as Chad told her to do. Lora wished she had a camera to capture the delighted look in her daughter's eyes, but Chad had made her leave her phone at the LNF office.

Chad untied the lead rope from the ring and walked the pony out of the barn. Lora walked beside Mercy to make sure she stayed steady, but her daughter didn't seem to need her. Walking her in a circle in the sprouting grass, Chad watched her constantly to make sure she was secure.

After they'd done half a dozen circles, Lora stepped out of the way and let them continue alone. Mercy held her back straight but flexible, as she'd been told, and clutched the saddle horn in her little hands.

Lora's attention shifted to Chad as he walked backwards to watch Mercy. Didn't he worry about tripping over something doing that? In all fairness, she'd never seen him trip, but it could happen.

Chad pulled the pony to a stop as Flynn jogged around the side of the house. "We've got a truck coming up the road."

The easy atmosphere immediately charged. Chad turned for the barn, lifting Mercy down as he did. Lora reached for her daughter as he tugged the pony inside the barn.

"Why don't you just stay here for a minute," he told her. "I'm sure it's a friendly, but we'll just make sure."

She nodded quickly and guided her daughter into the empty stall, watching his back as he left the dimness of the barn. Straight and tall, he walked toward the possible threat with no hesitation.

Lora ducked inside the stall and waited. Once the truck pulled into the turn-around and quieted, she heard the rumble of voices, but she controlled her curiosity. Only when Chad called out her name did she walk out with her daughter.

Chad's father was in the truck and he tipped his hat to her when she drew near. "Ma'am."

"Mr. Lowell."

He shook his head, his face creasing in an easy smile. "Garrett is fine. No fuss here."

Lora smiled as much as she could and nodded. Mercy clutched her hand and kind of hid behind her. "I think we're going to go get cleaned up a little bit, Chad."

He gave her a wave and watched as she walked away.

"She's got some cute under those bruises," his father murmured.

Lifting his brows, he turned back to his father. "Yes, she does."

Garrett rubbed a hand over his lean jaw. "Could be there's a little more to this job, huh?"

Chad shook his head and leaned against the side of the truck. "Nah. She's not interested in anything like that and I don't know if I am either."

"Boy, it'd be a hard man that could deny that baby, though."

Grinning, Chad looked after the retreating pair. His father had always loved the little ones. "I know. We just put Taco away. She wasn't wild about him at first, but this morning she hopped on him and rode like she's been doing it for years."

Garrett grinned. "No kid I know has been able to deny Taco's charm."

He reached for the two bags sitting beside him. "Your mama was a little put out you didn't come back for these yesterday. There's kids clothes and some she found of your sister's for Lora. She said she didn't expect them back. And here's a couple pairs of boots."

Chad took the plastic shopping bags and boots in one hand. "Okay. Tell her I'm sorry and thank you. I did forget to go back to the house." He shrugged.

"Well, now that you're feeling guilty, I'm supposed to invite you to dinner. Tomorrow night. Cheyenne's coming with her crew."

Wincing at the thought of the noise level in the house, he pursed his lips. "I'll see what Lora says but don't be surprised if it's a no."

Garrett nodded. "I told her the same thing but I can only get so much through to your mama, you know that. Think about it and let me know."

Turning the ignition, his dad shifted the truck into gear and rattled down the drive.

Chad stared after the retreating vehicle until Flynn stepped beside him. "You look just like your dad."

"Yeah, I get that a lot. If you get a chance to meet my brother, we look even more alike."

Flynn snorted and walked away. Chad stared after him for a minute, wondering what Flynn's point had been.

He walked the bags into the house. Lora stood at the sink, washing dishes. The ace bandage that had been wrapped around her arm was in a pile on the table.

"I don't know if you should be using that arm yet. We can do the dishes."

She glanced at him over her shoulder. "The hot water actually feels good on it."

"Are you a steaming hot bath kind of person?"

Chad could have happily bitten his tongue off right then, but the words were out. Lora narrowed her eyes at him before giving a single nod. "I am. I love to soak in a hot bath after Mercy goes to sleep. It's my treat after a long day."

Chad filed that away. She would love the bathhouse then. He held the bags up. "My mom gathered some clothes up for Mercy. Just jeans and stuff that she can play and get dirty in. I think there might be some stuff in there for you, too. And boots."

She dried her hands on a dishtowel hanging from the cupboard and turned for the bags. "She didn't have to do that. I'll give them back when we leave."

"I don't think she's worried about it. My nieces and nephews are mostly bigger than Mercy so they're not really needed."

She struggled with the knot at the top of the bags and he could tell her sprain was bothering her. "Why don't you let me rewrap that wrist? It's only been a couple days since you hurt it."

"Since Derek hurt it, you mean."

He frowned at the bitterness he heard in her voice. "Yes."

She settled into the chair, sighing. "Sorry I growled."

He grabbed the pile of bandage and located the end, letting the rest hang and unravel. "You're fine. I'd growl too if I were in your position. I'm glad you realize it's not your fault. A lot of women that go through the abuse you did would believe it was their responsibility."

She shook her head, sending her blond hair swaying. "No, I knew it wasn't my fault pretty early. Although Rosalind has done her best to bury me under guilt. None of this was Derek's fault, she said. It all came down on my head."

Chad positioned another chair in front of her and motioned for her hand. "Well, I understand a mother supporting her child but that goes beyond normal. I wonder if she was brought up in the same kind of environment, or if Derek's father did the same thing to her."

Lora sighed. "I think she was. Just by some of the things they've said, I don't think Derek's father was much of a peach either. He died years ago, before I came on the scene. And that makes me feel sorry for her. But as soon as I hint at understanding, she swoops in for the kill."

"That's how predators are."

Chad wrapped her wrist and fastened it with the Velcro end. He wanted to hold her soft hand for a few more seconds, but that would probably make her uncomfortable.

"Thanks, Chad."

He forced a grin. "No problem." He held out a piece of candy.

"For being such a good patient."

She looked at him askance, as if she didn't know what to think. But she eventually smiled and took the piece. "Only because it's a Starlight spearmint."

Chuckling, he unwrapped his own piece.

"Is that a bottomless pocket or what?"

He wiggled his brows at her and leaned forward. "Maybe. Would you like to feel?"

She cocked her head as if considering. "I better not. My daughter is pretty quiet. I should see what she's into."

Gathering up the bags, she started down the hallway.

"Hey."

She turned back to him.

"My mother wants us to come down for dinner tomorrow night. No answer right now, but maybe you can think about it? My sister Cheyenne will be there and her critters. Might be fun for Mercy."

She nodded and slipped away.

Chad dried the dishes and put them back in the cupboards.

Rachel came into the kitchen, hair pulled back into her usual ponytail. "Did I hear a truck?"

"My dad stopped in for a minute. Hey, you up for a trek into town?"

Rachel nodded. "Of course."

"Cool." He grabbed the list Lora had made from the counter. "I need you to go to the grocery store."

Her golden brown eyes widened and she looked a little worried. "Uh, okay. I can do that. Yes, sir."

Chad almost grinned at her bewildered expression. He pulled a credit card from his wallet and handed it to her. "If you have problems using it have them call me."

She nodded and folded the card and list, slipping it into her jeans pocket. "Can do."

"Also, check out that drug store. Maybe you can pick up a few things Mercy can play with."

Rachel nodded. "Of course. Anything else?"

Chad thought for a moment, but nothing occurred to him just then. "Keep your phone handy and try not to talk to a lot of people." He crossed the room to the hook beside the front door and retrieved his keys. "No craziness."

Grinning, Rachel took the keys. "I'll be good, boss. No worries."

And she was. Within a few hours she had returned, laden with groceries to fill the cupboards and fridge and enough toys that three six-year-olds would have a tough time playing with them all.

But the happiness on Mercy's face was worth it. There was TV, if you could get the antennae zeroed in on something. It was kind of a waste of time to mess with, so she had to keep herself occupied. Rachel had also gotten a couple of board games, so they were all eventually roped into playing.

Chad wished he could take a group picture without their knowledge, because nobody at the office would ever believe that Harper had agreed to play a kid's game. Or even Flynn, for that matter. They were both good men, but unapproachable and brusque at the best of times. When Mercy approached them with her eyes so big and hopeful, her sweet little voice pleading, they hadn't been able to tell her no. Now they all sat around the kitchen table, taking direction from the girl as they worked around the Candyland board. She seemed to prefer to lean against Harper for some reason though. Maybe it was his gruff voice when he answered her or even just the fact that he was so much bigger than she was that she felt protected. For whatever reason, if there was a spare moment, she stayed with him.

It was the most relaxed he'd ever seen Lora. She was still leery of the men, but maybe the more she was around them, the more at ease she would be. When Mercy swept the board with a play, she even laughed with her, tugging on a hank of her hair.

It was one of the most enjoyable nights he could remember having himself.

When Mercy's bedtime rolled around, they all seemed reluctant to go to their duties. Her bright little disposition was a bit contagious. Hell, he'd even seen Harper's lips tip up in a slight smile. Flynn hadn't seemed so remote either.

That night he dreamt of ponies and little girls shaking him so that he could hop in and play a game. Death didn't visit him until almost dawn, but when it did it arrived with a vengeance.

Dodd had just handed him his rifle again. Chad checked it over and went through the motions he knew he had to before the dream would end. They had the same conversation they'd had for years, and when the other man took off at a jog, Chad knew that nothing he said would change what was about to happen.

"Dodd, follow..."

...the footprints.

For seven years he'd never been able to finish that sentence. The pain that roared over him was the same every single time. It obliterated his sight and hearing. Knocked him unconscious for several long minutes.

Vaguely, Chad knew tears were leaking from the corners of his eyes, but the dream would not release him from its grip. He saw Dodd lying on the ground, his clear blue eyes staring at him in surprise. But he never blinked.

Chad fought to rouse, but he'd gone without sleep for too long. Even with the trauma the dreams brought, his body needed the relaxation.

The dream suddenly morphed into the blazing, screaming agony of singed nerve-endings reporting to his brain. Then the amputated foot tried to report in, and it slammed into a severed wall. He'd never felt such ungodly pain. Blinking in the glaring light, he realized he'd been moved to the hospital room and he was coming out of his morphine fog. Blindly, he groped for the pain pump beside him, but he couldn't find it. When he cried out for help, nobody answered his call. He was left writhing with no relief from the agony.

A cool hand pressed to his brow, surprising him into stillness. Chad was afraid to move because he didn't want the pain to come back. The hand brushed his short hair up away from his forehead, then settled back, the thumb stroking his eyebrows.

When he blinked his eyes open, he found Lora leaned over him, her hand the cool relief he felt on his head. As soon as he blinked up at her, she pulled away, folding her arms across her chest. There was just enough light in the room from the coming dawn that he could see the fear in her eyes.

"I called out your name, but you didn't answer. I thought there was something wrong."

Chad scrubbed his hands over his face, hoping she hadn't seen the tears at his temples. It was embarrassing enough crying out in his sleep loud enough to rouse her. "I'm sorry I woke you." He cleared his tight throat.

She shrugged her hunched shoulders. "I wasn't actually asleep. Are you okay?"

He nodded his head and sat up, only then realizing the sheet was torqued around his hips. His legs were covered, though, which was an incredible relief. As off-balance as he was right then, he didn't think he could take the horror he would see in her eyes if his legs were exposed. "I have…dreams."

Dreams. Such a weak word for the terrors that haunted him.

He kicked his legs over the side and grabbed his discarded t-shirt, stretching it over his head. When he looked at Lora again, she was just dragging her eyes away from his chest.

Chad paused, shocked that she would even be interested after the show he'd just put on. He tugged the shirt smooth.

When he looked up again, she had disappeared.

CHAPTER EIGHT

LORA HURRIED NEXT door to the room she and Mercy shared, more shook than she wanted to be. When she'd heard the sound next door, she hadn't known what it was, but she'd known she had to investigate. Nobody had answered her knock and the rustling inside had continued. When Chad had cried out, she'd pushed the door open and peeked inside.

The tall man thrashed on the bed as if demons were after him. Then he'd writhed as if in incredible pain, reaching out for help. She'd been in that kind of pain before, and nobody had helped her, but she was helpless to deny him comfort. Stepping forward, she'd rested her hand on his brow and crooned to him that everything would be okay. He'd kicked the sheets aside and his amputated left leg had caught her gaze, making her pause. He reached toward it as if it had just been injured. It didn't look painful now, but the pain that had to have accompanied the injury was surely horrendous. It was no wonder he had dreams like this.

She'd tossed the sheet over his legs just as he stilled beneath her hand. She allowed her thumb to stroke his brow, fascinated at the smoothness of his skin. Her gaze had drifted down to rest on his pectorals. There was a smattering of dark hair across his chest, sweat soaked from the dreams, that led south beneath the rumpled sheet. But there was also a layer of scars down his side, older and not nearly as bad as his hand. She dragged her eyes back to his face. His lids were just fluttering open. She pulled her hand away and folded her arms. But when he sat up, abdominals flexing, she'd been unable to drag her gaze away before she'd been caught staring. Even now, it made her cheeks heat with embarrassment.

Lora rubbed the fingers of her right hand, remembering the feel of his soft skin. The thrill that had shot through her as she'd calmed him had been unlike anything she'd ever felt before.

When she'd been a girl, even into college, she'd dreamt hazy dreams of a man taking care of her simply because he loved her. Derek had nurtured that dream, then squashed it. But there was still the faintest hope that she could have a normal life. Even after the crap that had gone on, Chad made her yearn for things out of her reach.

Shaking her head at her ridiculous fancies, she crossed to her bag and dug out the romance novel she'd thrown in at the last minute. Another ridiculous waste of time, according to Derek, but once he'd been gone, she'd relished buying them.

Besides, they helped while away the hours she couldn't sleep.

When Mercy woke an hour later, she made her breakfast. Chad came in from the front as she was spooning sausage gravy over bread and his eyes lit with happiness. Lora was struck by the change in him from just a few hours before.

There was a guarded look in his eyes, as if he felt he had exposed too much of himself to her. Lora found she didn't like him feeling uncomfortable because of her, so she made an effort to be more pleasant than she had been.

"Can I ride Taco again?"

Chad's gaze flashed up to hers in question and she nodded. "If you promise not to complain when we do some work tonight."

Mercy scrunched up her little face. "Work?"

"You're missing school right now. But I brought your reading book."

Mercy looked a little put out until Chad pushed away from the table and said he was ready to go. Mercy raced to her room for her borrowed jeans and boots and was back within just a few minutes. She grabbed Chad's damaged hand as they walked out of the house, and didn't even seem to notice his hesitation.

Lora turned off the burner and covered the gravy so that the other guards could have some breakfast when they came around. Then, slipping on the borrowed boots, she followed after her daughter.

She was brushing Taco as if she were trying to get every speck of dust off his hide. Chad settled the saddle over the old guy and tightened the band around his belly, then put a bit and bridle on.

"I'm going to help you out for a little bit, but I think you'll be able to control him today."

Mercy's movements paused and she looked up at Chad wide-eyed. "Really?"

He nodded and took the brush from her hand, then lifted her to the back of the pony. He strapped the little helmet onto her head. "Hang on now and we're going to walk to the paddock in the back, okay?"

Mercy nodded and clutched the horn in front of her. Lora followed along behind, as excited as her daughter.

Chad let all three of them into the wood plank paddock in the back. The other horses were still in the stalls so it was empty. The paddock itself only stretched about fifty feet long and about twenty-five feet wide, not very big, but definitely big enough for a little girl and a pony.

Lora fastened the chain on the gate behind them and leaned against the rails, but Chad waved her over. "If you're going to be riding, it won't hurt you to know this either."

He went over the steps for making the horse go and stop, and how to turn him left and right. It seemed fairly simple to Lora and Mercy seemed ready as well. Finally, they were ready to go. Chad walked along beside Mercy as he gave her instructions, but he eventually just stood in the middle of the space while they circled him.

Lora couldn't believe how confident her child looked. The pony wasn't very big, but he definitely made her feel taller.

They rode for about ten minutes before Chad walked over to lean against the fence with her. "I think we may have created a monster."

Lora's heart stalled in her chest at the affectionate possessiveness as he referred to her daughter and she could only nod.

"As long as you don't mind, I'll let her ride every day. It'll give her a distraction for the time we're here."

She nodded again and pulled her sweater tighter around herself. "I would appreciate that. It's obvious she loves it."

Mercy completed another circle of the ring and turned the pony to go in the other direction.

"Mercy," Chad called out. "If you click your tongue and kick him a little with your feet, he'll move into a trot. Just hang onto the horn and if you feel like you're sliding, pull back on the reins and tell him whoa!"

She grinned at them as she passed and did exactly as he told her. And almost immediately bounced out of the saddle to the ground.

Chad raced across the ring to help her up, but Mercy only giggled as he brushed her off. Lora knelt beside her, but Mercy didn't want her attention. "Can I get back on? I'll hold on better, I promise."

Chad straightened her helmet, lifted her up onto Taco's back again and she took off. This time she held on.

They watched Mercy ride for the better part of a half hour before Lora finally suggested they give the old pony a break. "You don't want to wear him out," she told her daughter.

Mercy's eyes widened with alarm. "Oh no, I don't want to do that."

Before Chad could reach for her, she slid off the saddle to the ground.

"My legs feel funny."

She danced around until she got her land legs again and raced into the barn to grab the brush to use on the pony.

After they settled Taco, they headed to the swing set.

"Have you thought any more about dinner?"

Lora frowned. "I don't know if it's a good idea." She made a vague motion toward her face.

Chad surveyed her face. "I don't think it's as bad as you think. The swelling is completely gone and the purple around your eye is fading." Before she could pull away, he brushed a fingertip over her lower lip. "And the split is gone."

She frowned. It had only been a few days. She doubted she looked as good as he said. Maybe makeup could cover some of it.

Sighing, she squinted into the late morning sun, knowing that she was about to cave. "What time do we need to go down?"

"Mama always serves dinner at six."

Lora glanced at him, reluctant. "I guess we can go."

Chad grinned and she forced her eyes away from the sight. He was too tempting as it was without him gushing over her.

But she had to remember that this was his family as well, and if he hadn't seen his parents for months, he probably hadn't seen his sister and her kids either.

"I'll be ready then," she sighed. "And Mercy will, too."

CHAD LEFT BEFORE he did something else to spook her. She hadn't recoiled when he'd stroked her lip, but he wasn't going to push his luck. He wanted to take her in his arms and try to ease the tension he could literally see in every line of her body. Even without the bruises, her face tended to be tense. Nobody should live like that. It wasn't healthy.

Heading back into the barn, he grabbed a bridle for one of the geldings and saddled him up. The horse seemed eager to go so he turned him up the hill at a good canter. Within just a few minutes though, he had to slow him down. Rocks on the trail were treacherous, and he'd never hear the end of it if he damaged one of his dad's prized Quarter horses. Toward the top of the hill, he slowed even further. Harper was camped out up here somewhere.

The other man found him, stepping out onto the trail in front of him. Chad gathered the reins as the horse reared, almost unseating him. He shook his head at the big guard.

"You bastard," he laughed. "You almost put me on my ass on the ground!"

Harper smiled slightly. "You make too much noise."

Chad slid to his feet, shaking his head. Looping the reins over the horse's head, he tied them to the branch of a tree before following the other man onto the overgrown path. Harper had managed to find a slight game trail, just barely big enough for his huge body to squeeze through the brush. Chad angled his body and followed.

When they reached the plateau where Harper had set up his look-out, Chad was impressed. "I didn't realize you had this kind of range up here."

As he stood at the top of the hill, he was overcome by a sense of history, in the land and his family. Hell, even in Texas. Though he'd gotten used to being stationed in many different places for the Marines, this would always be his touchstone.

LNF was his career now, but he wished he had the freedom to come home more often.

Harper had created a hollow to lay in at the top of the knoll, well shaded but far enough out on a promontory that he could see for miles in several different directions. To the south were more long sloping sweeps up to jagged hills. To the east, the main road onto the ranch. There was a long-range spotting scope pointed in that direction and Chad knew for a fact Harper already recognized every truck on the place. It's what he did. Settled in, took stock and picked off the bad guys.

"Been quiet?"

Harper nodded, eyes hidden behind the wraparound sunglasses. "Your brother does a lot of running."

"Yeah." Chad dug the toe of his boot into the rock. "Used to be Dad running everywhere all day, but Brock's starting to take on more responsibility. He's built for being in charge."

They didn't say anything for a few minutes. Chad tipped his face up to the breeze blowing up the incline. "I love this place."

Harper sighed beside him. "It does have its appeal. Reminds me of Iraq."

Chad looked at him, surprised. "No way."

The big man nodded once. "Inhospitable. Unforgiving. The heat hasn't kicked in yet, but I think it'll boil your brain in the summer."

Chad laughed out right. "Oh, you are so right. I grew up here though. I guess it kind of resembles Iraq, but I can see the differences." He pointed into the distance. "You've never seen meat on the hoof that good looking anywhere but Texas."

Harper gave him a wide grin and tipped his head in agreement. "I will agree with you there."

"We're heading down to the house for dinner. You up for a visit?"

Harper turned to him, but Chad still couldn't see his eyes through the shades. "I think I'll hang up here."

"Okay. Maybe we'll bring you some leftovers."

Harper gave him a lazy nod and Chad headed back down the slope. The horse waited patiently and when mounted took off at a steady clip toward the barn.

CHAPTER NINE

LORA WATCHED THE clock tick over another minute and her anxiety mounted. A few more minutes and they would have to leave for dinner. She tucked her hair behind her ears, then moved it forward again. She'd left it down in the hopes that it would hide some of the bruising she'd been unable to cover with makeup. Even with that, it was obvious she'd been beaten.

Disgust coated her tongue. She'd left that life behind. Derek didn't have any right to mess with her anymore.

She walked out to the kitchen with her chin up. Chad looked up from his phone and frowned, then his lips spread in a broad smile. "You look like you're ready to kick ass."

Lora tilted her head. "I kind of feel like that," she admitted.

"My family isn't going to attack you."

She shook her head, stepping closer. "It's not your family. I'm just…tired of worrying. Tired of Derek monopolizing my life, even when he's not around."

Chad pushed to his feet and Lora realized he had cleaned up as well. He wore a fresh t-shirt and jeans and the ball cap was missing. He'd spiked his short hair with gel and shaved his lean jaw. The scent of a tangy body wash reached her and she wanted to inhale more.

Maybe if she walked toward him he would just open his arms…

Lora cringed and Chad immediately stopped moving. She huffed out a breath and waved her hand. "It wasn't you. I just…had a thought that I shouldn't have."

He raised a dark brow at her but she refused to elaborate.

"Do I look okay?"

She ran her hands over the pale blue blouse and jeans she wore, worried that it was too informal. When she'd shoved things in her bag, she hadn't thought about dinner like this.

Chad's bright blue eyes drifted over her slowly and Lora forced herself to stand still, though his appreciative survey was making her prickle. His gaze slowed at her hands on her hips, drifted down to her socked feet, then back up to meet her eyes. "I think you look perfect."

Lora had to look away then because the sincerity in his expression was enough to make her tear up. She grabbed her jacket from the back of the chair where she'd draped it and slipped her shoes on at the door. Stepping outside, she called for Mercy.

The little girl leapt off the swing several feet in the air and raced to her, followed closely by Rachel. "You better be careful doing that, you little imp," the guard called to her.

Mercy giggled and climbed into the open truck door Lora held open, then Lora slid in beside her daughter.

They rattled down the hill in silence. Flynn had agreed to go for exterior coverage and Rachel would stay inside, though Chad had told her he doubted there was need inside the house.

When they arrived, Flynn headed toward the barn, probably to secure an outlook from the second floor. He made an odd motion with his hand at his side before he disappeared inside.

Before she could wonder further, Chad slid out of the truck and moved to open their rear door. He held out his broad hand and she stared at it for several long seconds, before sliding her own inside and allowing him to help her down. As soon as was polite, she released him, though her body resonated with the touch. Mercy parked herself on the step and fell into his arms with a giggle.

Growling at the little girl and tickling her, he set her on the ground, then turned to grin at Lora. "I think you raised a daredevil."

The daredevil clammed up and hid at Lora's side when they entered the house. It seemed like there were kids everywhere, but Lora realized it was just three moving very fast.

A little girl with some of the brightest red hair Lora had ever seen skidded to a stop and held her hand out to Mercy. "Wanna go see the big cow in Grampa's office?"

With a glance up at her mother, Mercy took the little girl's hand

and they raced off.

"Hello, Grace," Chad called down the hallway. "It was nice seeing you Grace."

A faint voice called back "Hello, Uncle Chad".

Chad looked at her with an odd expression on his face. "You may want to check on her soon. It's hard to tell what Grace will get her into."

Two taller girls, their hair almost matching strawberry blond, slammed into him with yells of "Uncle Chad". Lora moved out of the way of the melee until their greetings were done. Chad stood up and made a motion to Lora. "Girls, this is Lora O'Neil. Say hello. Lora, this is Carolyn." He held his hand over the taller girl. "She's ten and thinks she knows everything. And this is Savannah." He brushed his hand over the other girl's head. "She's eight and she does know everything."

Savannah nodded her head, arms crossed over her narrow chest and grinned. A tall woman stepped up behind them. "Girls, go help Grandma with dinner."

They did as they were told, though not without putting up a fuss.

The woman that had sent them on their way held out her hand. "Cheyenne. Very nice to meet you, Lora."

Lora shook her hand reluctantly. If there was ever a woman to make her feel inadequate, it was this one. As good-looking as Chad was, this woman had him beat by a mile. Striking bone structure, piercing blue eyes with deep auburn hair. But she had a smile as fun and good-natured as Chad's, and when she wrapped her arms around her little brother, she could see the love between them.

Lora stepped back and turned as Francine came through the room to meet them. She allowed the older woman to wrap her in an easy hug, and for the briefest second allowed her body to relax. Then she forced herself to pull away. It wouldn't do to get attached to this family.

She tried to remind herself of that several times over the course of the night, but it got harder and harder as the night went along. Chad was a real stand-up guy and his family loved him desperately. Well, everybody except the brother. Brock was another beautiful Lowell sibling, but his personality definitely veered to the more serious. While the rest of the family joked and played around and the kids ran around being kids, he sat in one of the chairs in front of the fire and dozed, a glass of whiskey balanced precariously on his knee.

"Don't worry about him," Cheyenne told her as she plopped down onto the couch beside her.

In spite of herself, Lora truly enjoyed the woman. She was strong and opinionated and had made a life for herself and her girls when she'd walked out on her cheating, abusive husband.

"Is he the oldest?"

Cheyenne cocked a brow at her. "He is, but he never used to be this serious. It was only after Chad got injured in Iraq when he turned downright sour. Then it was like everything suddenly got real for him. I don't know." She shook her head slowly. "He used to be this great guy, willing to do anything for you. He still is, but now he's going to bitch at you while he helps you."

Lora grinned with her. "You guys have another sister too, right?"

"Mm, Emily. She's down around Houston settin' the business world on fire. I'm not even sure what exactly she does. She makes a lot of money, I know that."

"And you're a teacher, right?"

Cheyenne grinned. "Third grade. Old enough I don't have to wipe their noses but not old enough to be snots yet."

Lora laughed out right, because it was so true. She worked in the high school at home and the kids had so much attitude about everything.

"Chad said you were getting away from your ex. What is it about small-minded men that make them feel like they need to be brutal?"

"I don't know," Lora sighed.

"Your face doesn't look bad. My ex broke my jaw once. Had to be wired shut for two months. Not a very fashionable look but man, what a great diet plan." She glanced at Lora out of the corner of her eyes. "We came here to stay for several months while I took his ass to the cleaners. This is a good place to be."

"I hate to put your family in this position. If he does find us I would feel terrible."

Cheyenne shrugged. "I don't think little brother is concerned. And we've got good men working at the ranch, so if anything looks out of the ordinary they'll let him know."

"Are you here in town?"

The other woman nodded. "You know you always end up back home. Makes it easy for the grands to see the animals, and vice versa. My parents still believe they're getting the better end of the deal."

Lora laughed out loud and then caught herself, tamping down the laughter, fear suddenly clutching at her throat.

Cheyenne turned toward her and grabbed her clenched hands. "Don't you dare curb your enjoyment of anything. Don't let him ruin you like that."

Tears flooded Lora's eyes at the other woman's understanding, and when she wrapped her in a massive hug Lora let her. For several long seconds she let Cheyenne comfort her, unbelievably touched that this stranger could relate to her on such a basic level.

She pulled away and wiped her face. Cheyenne wiped her own eyes with the backs of her hands. "I know where you're coming from," she whispered, "but you have to be strong enough for that little girl to come out strong on the other side. You use any resource you can to achieve that end. Do you hear me?"

Lora nodded, knowing every word Cheyenne spoke was the truth.

"I will. It hit me this morning that I was tired of hiding from life," Lora admitted softly. "I was so scared to come down here and meet all of you and it was because he taught me to be that way. If I didn't perform the way I was supposed to, I would know it later that night. I'm tired of living in fear of every situation."

Cheyenne nodded. "Yep. You reach the point that you just say fuck it. And what better time than right now, supported by more people than you ever have been before?"

She was completely right.

"Where were you years ago when I met Derek? I really could have used your input then."

Laughing, the other woman gave her a one-armed hug before pushing up from the couch. "I was probably dealing with my own Derek. I'm gonna go see what the girls are into."

Lora watched her go and sagged into the couch.

That's where Chad found her a few minutes later. He was carrying two bowls of ice cream. "May I join you? I bring treats," he sing-songed in his deep voice.

Lora scooted over but she needn't have worried. Chad sat on the other side of the couch with a couple feet of space between then. He handed her one of the bowls. Their fingers brushed for the barest second before he pulled away. Lora looked down at the bowl and the triangular piece sticking out of it. "What is this?"

"Taste it," he told her, shoving a huge spoonful into his own mouth.

Lora took a small bite of the cream, delighted when she realized it was cinnamon. "Oh, this is good."

"Mama made the sopapillas. They're just tortillas baked with cinnamon and sugar, but she's made them all my life."

"I'm beginning to see where you get your sweet tooth."

He grinned at her. "A meal is not complete without some kind of dessert."

Before long he was scraping his bowl clean and setting it aside. "I hope Cheyenne didn't make a nuisance of herself."

Lora shook her head. "No, she didn't. Actually, she told me some really insightful things. Things that I knew, but needed reaffirmed, you know?"

Chad turned on the cushion a bit, resting his left arm along the back. "She's not always had an easy time of it. We didn't like her ex when we met him. Brock and I had known him years ago and he was an ass back then. But we couldn't tell Cheyenne. She thought she was in love and that she could change him. It didn't work that way. By the time I came back from overseas, she was dealing with some serious shit. I wasn't much help to her back then."

Lora gave him a look. "I think you had your own issues to deal with then."

He nodded, his eyes glazing over as he stared off into the distance. Lora's hand twitched and she wanted to offer him comfort. Twisting in the seat, she reached her left hand out to rest on top of his.

Chad jerked in surprise at her touch on his scarred skin, then stilled. His eyes met hers and if Lora had been any other woman, she would have leaned forward to press a kiss to his lips. They were close enough and the gently shaded room encouraged the intimacy. But she wasn't that woman, no matter how much she told herself she wanted to be. Stroking him softly, she pulled away.

The sudden, sharp clink of glass rang through the room. They both turned to look at Brock. He'd moved to the small liquor table a few feet away and was pouring himself another drink, sloshing it over the edge. He must have felt their scrutiny because he looked up. "Oh, sorry, did I interrupt you? I was refilling so that I could watch the rest of the show. Have to say, bro, Cheyenne's first half was more exciting."

Chad cocked his head at his brother's words and Lora thought she saw a hint of anger in the tightening of his expression. She was embarrassed. Brock had been sitting several yards away on the far end of the room, head tipped back on the chair. She'd thought he'd been asleep.

Damn. They'd said some not so nice things about him.

"Why are you so bitter, Brock? You get worse every time I see you."

The older brother snorted. "Maybe it's *because* I see you, little brother."

Lora sucked in a breath at the hurtful words and turned to look at Chad. His expression didn't change, but she could imagine the hurt he had to be feeling.

"What the hell is your issue with me? We used to be better than this. We used to hang out together and be friends. What changed?"

Brock shook his head.

"Was it because I came back broken? Less of a man than I used to be?"

Brock blinked and seemed a little shocked that Chad believed that.

He looked down at the glass in his hand and shook his head again, harder. "You're not broken," he said softly.

"Then I wish my brother was around. I'd have liked to have seen him this week."

Chad pushed to his feet and held his right hand out to Lora. Without a word, she let him help her up out of the deep couch. They walked out of the room without a backward glance, but Chad paused in the hallway.

"I'm sorry about that. I don't know what's gotten into him. He's usually not so rude."

"It's okay. Maybe he has stuff going on in his life too."

"Hm. Maybe."

Chad guided her into the kitchen. All four little girls had their heads bent over glittery craft projects and barely looked up to acknowledge them. Mercy did finally, and her eyes drifted over Chad's lower legs, making Lora wonder if the other girls had been talking.

"Little Mercy has fit into the group like she's always been here," Francine gushed, running a hand over her daughter's mussed hair. "You've done a wonderful job raising your little girl, Lora. She's so polite."

"Thank you. I appreciate hearing that."

Cheyenne held a bundle of cloth out to Chad and he folded it under his arm, then caught Lora's eye. "Would you step out here, please? I have something to show you."

Lora lifted her brows in surprise, but followed after a last glance at the kitchen. Cheyenne caught her eye and gave her a big wink and a smile. Chad guided her down a hallway and into a mud-slash-laundry room, then out the back door.

Glancing back to make sure she followed, he led her across a wide deck and down a few steps to a flagstone path. Though the surrounding area was rocky and didn't have a lot of vegetation, Francine had managed to make her backyard into a nice retreat. There were flower beds everywhere just beginning to bud, and bushes lined the smooth path. There was a building a little ways away and that was where Chad led her. As he opened the front doors, Lora realized it was a gazebo housing a huge hot tub. She looked at him in surprise. "I never expected to find this hidden out here."

"Yeah, it's camouflaged pretty well." He handed her the bundle of cloth. "Cheyenne is about your size and she said you could borrow this."

Lora let the bundle fall open and realized it was a bathing suit. Anxiety clutched her stomach and she automatically shook her head.

Chad took a step closer to her and leaned down, just a bit. "Before you say no, I want you to take a deep breath and know that I would never let anyone hurt you. I promise you I won't turn around. I give you my word. Harper is on the hill watching the entire area, Flynn is in the barn and Mercy is in the house with Rachel and the family. Everybody is taken care of. You need to take a few minutes for yourself."

He turned away from her then and gave her his back, standing at the front of the building.

Lora looked at the temptation. The water was steaming. She wondered if it was as hot as it looked. Reaching out, she ran her fingers through the water. Oh, it felt so good. She glanced at Chad's broad back. She knew for a fact she could strip naked and dance the tango and he would not turn around. He'd given his word. The gazebo was enclosed, the shutters drawn. Tiny little LEDs cast enough light to see by, but that was all. Nobody would see her.

Screw it.

Before she could talk herself out of it, she stripped out of her clothes, dropping them onto a low bench along the wall. Cheyenne's one piece slid up over her hips easily and fit her surprisingly well. A little gappy in the boob area, but there was nothing to be done for it. She then unwound the ace bandage from her wrist, dropping it on top of the clothes. Crossing to the stairs she slid a foot into the water, moaning at the warmth that welcomed her. Stepping all the way into the tub, she lowered herself into the water and pushed to the side. Shuddering with the sharp temperature but relishing it, she settled into the corner of the tub, her head resting on the back edge.

The heat sank into her bones, chasing away the chill of the past few months. It was the warmest she'd been in as long as she could remember. "This is heavenly, Chad."

He chuckled quietly but didn't turn around. "I thought you'd like it. My mother is a soaker too, bubble bath, the whole bit, so my dad built her this a few years ago. She likes to take midnight breaks, when the ranch is completely quiet."

"Does your dad join her?"

"Mm, sometimes. When she can talk him into it."

Lora swirled her hand through the water, restless.

"Chad," she hesitated.

"Yes?"

He turned his head enough that she could see his face in profile, lit from behind by the house lights, but he kept his eyes down on the ground. As he'd promised he would.

"Are we safe here?" she whispered.

"Yes," he answered firmly. "I wouldn't have brought you out here if I thought otherwise."

He faced the house, feet planted. Looking at him from behind, his back seemed so broad, his legs so long. She wanted to explore him, to take her time and touch every square inch of his body.

Lora knew though, that he would never make the first move. It would be up to her to do that.

And she didn't know if she had the courage.

Cheyenne's challenging words came back to her, and her resolve solidified.

"Chad?"

"Yes?"

"Can you turn around please?"

He'd been still before, but now it was if he were frozen in time. For several long seconds she didn't even hear him breathe. But then he swiveled on one boot heel to face her.

Lora sank down into the water until only her shoulders were exposed. His gaze traveled over her as if he could see more, though.

"Would you join me?"

Lora actually heard him swallow from several feet away and it gave her courage that he was nervous.

"I don't know if that's such a great idea."

"Please?"

He took a step forward across the deck, then a few more, until he stood at the side of the tub. "I'll have to take the prosthetic off," he admitted.

Lora hadn't even thought about that. "Okay." She was struck with something and she grinned. "Want me to turn around?"

She thought she'd been funny but he gave her the strangest look.

"If you keep giving me smiles like that, you can look at anything you want."

Her laughter faded at the sincerity she saw in his shadowed face and her heart started to thud as his fingers reached for the snaps on his shirt. She was suddenly more fearful than when he'd expected her to get into the tub, but this was an edge-of-your-seat kind of fear. Thrilling. Exciting.

As he shrugged the shirt off his shoulders and dropped it to the bench, he paused for several long seconds. "I don't want to scare you or rush you into any kind of situation you're not comfortable with."

She smiled, appreciating the consideration. "I'm good right now. I'm trying to be more willing to engage and enjoy life."

He seemed to search her face in the subtle light before reaching for the snap of his jeans. Lora pushed herself back to the opposite side of the tub and rested her head against the cushion, letting her eyes drift closed. Every little sound he made encouraged her to open her eyes, but she didn't.

"I'm in."

For a few more seconds she kept her eyes closed just to prove she could before rolling her head up to look at him.

The steaming water hit Chad right at the nipple line. His chest hair had darkened with water. Both of his long arms were stretched along the sides of the tub, much like he'd been sitting on the couch.

"Does the heat of the water bother your burns?" she asked.

He watched her as though he was waiting for an insult or something, a heavy frown on his face. "It does a bit. Not too bad. Bothers my leg more."

She cocked her head. "Why does it bother your leg more?"

Chad scowled as if he regretted admitting the weakness. "Because I wear the prosthetic all the time, for the most part. The skin of the amputation itself is very sensitive."

"Is the amputation painful?"

"Not really. Just feels like my leg now."

Lora wanted to look beneath the surface of the water to try to see the amputation, but that would be rude. Besides, he seemed self-conscious about it or something. It had been seven years since he'd been injured. She would have thought he'd be more comfortable with it by now. But who was she to determine that?

Chad watched the emotions play across Lora's face. Curiosity was there, but it didn't seem to be malicious. Just inquisitive. All women were curious before they saw it, but in his experience, the disgust rolled in soon after.

He snorted. They were both hiding. It was ridiculous.

"I, uh, don't have a very good history showing women my amputation. If I remember right, the last one walked out the door in tears of disgust."

Lora narrowed her eyes. "Tears of disgust? Really?"

Chad shrugged. "That was how I took it. Things were moving along good until I stripped down and pulled my leg off. She saw it and burst into tears, scrambled out of bed and disappeared."

Her mouth dropped open and anger sparked in her eyes. "That's terrible."

He gave her a self-deprecating smile. "It was her loss. She hadn't gotten to the good part yet."

Lora giggled in delight, her cheeks flushing, and it was the most enjoyment he'd ever seen her experience. He chuckled with her. Years later the scene was still vivid in his mind, but over time he'd forced himself to look at the humor in it.

He'd had to.

He took a deep breath. "I'll show you if you're interested."

The enjoyment in her eyes dimmed, but it was replaced by resolve.

She nodded.

Before he could change his mind he lifted his hips and raised his left knee out of the water.

Lora moved closer. One long fingered hand lifted, dripping warm water to cup what was left of his calf. She squeezed the tense muscle, then drifted her hand up to his knee and back down. Shaking her head, she tossed him a quizzical look. "I don't understand why she would react that way. This is not disgusting. It's not even stomach turning. It's just skin and muscle and bone."

Chad could have wept tears of gratitude at her no-nonsense words. Instead he clenched his jaw and looked away as he fought to control the wild emotion slamming through him. The touch of her fingers on the most sensitive part of him sent goose bumps racing across his body.

"Can you tell me about the mechanics of the amputation? Is this just one bone or…"

Clearing his throat, he turned back to her. "I didn't directly step on the mine. Another Marine did. But I was part of the blast. The docs on the ground where I was had gotten really good at wound care. I was shipped to Landstuhl within hours, then to Walter Reed. I had a lot of burn issues, too. The leg was easy compared to the burns."

Chad knew he was rambling, but he felt like he needed to give her as much info as he could while she was interested.

"Basically, they clean up the mess and cut above the injury site. The ends of the bones are trimmed and in my case, they grafted a small piece of bone between the ends of the tibia and fibia to stabilize them. Then they reattach the muscles to the end of the bone and wrap the skin around everything."

Her fingers traced the scar of the reattachment and he paused. She looked up at him and he had to clear his throat. "After several weeks of healing they start to fit you for a prosthetic. I've got half a dozen legs at home, but I prefer the one I wear now."

Lora released his leg and he let it withdraw beneath the water, but she didn't retreat across the tub like he expected her to. She pushed to the shaped bench to his left, just a couple of feet away. The deep green of her eyes seemed languid here beneath the subtle lighting, but he didn't see anything unsettled in her expression. She didn't seem to be disturbed by his body.

Gratitude filled him.

"You are one of three women who have ever seen my leg and not been offended or repulsed," he told her softly. "The other two are in that house."

Her eyes flicked to the ranch house then back to him. "I appreciate you telling me. And showing me. That had to be hard."

Chad tried to be unconcerned but he didn't think he pulled it off.

"Now are you going to show me the good part?"

His gaze snapped to her face as his heart leapt in his chest, but before he could say anything she burst into tears. "I'm sorry, I shouldn't have said that," she gasped. She buried her face in her hands and wept.

Chad didn't know what to do. He wanted to draw her into his arms and hold her tight to let her know that they were okay, but he didn't know how she'd react. Instead, he reached out his bad hand and rested it on her shoulder. Lora wept all the harder and seemed to crumple in on herself, but then she turned and seemed to want him to hold her. Chad opened his arms, but stayed where he was. If she wanted comfort he would give it to her, but he wouldn't force it on her.

Lora seemed to need it badly, because she kind of fell against him, burrowing her face into his neck. Chad cupped her shoulders as gently as he could, scared that she would feel trapped and pull away. But she stayed where she was, sobbing her heart out.

"Hey, you're okay," he murmured. "It's okay, Lora."

She shook her head against him. "I'm not okay. I want so much but I'm terrified. Of you and my need. I'm scared of men in general. But I want to be strong like Cheyenne. I want to live the life I've dreamed of for my daughter, but I can't just shove everything aside."

He leaned his head to the side to try to catch her eyes, but she avoided looking at him. "Hey, nobody's asking you to shove everything aside. Certainly not in a night. You just met Cheyenne and let me tell you, she's been working on this version of herself for several years. I think you've done excellent for tonight. I'll hold you as long as you want me to, but that's all. I got excited when you wanted to see my good part–" She snorted and clutched him tighter around the neck. "But I knew you weren't ready. You've already given me so much tonight."

Tightening his hands on her shoulders for the briefest second, he relaxed back against the edge of the tub, still cradling her carefully. They stayed like that for a good while. Lora relaxed into his arms to the point that he thought she'd fallen asleep, but eventually she moved.

"I'm turning into a prune."

She pulled back enough to look into his eyes, then very deliberately moved forward enough to brush her lips against the corner of his mouth.

Chad forced himself to hold as still as possible. But one of the hardest things he'd ever had to do was not turn his head that fraction of an inch to meet her lips. Body straining, he breathed through the need as she pushed to the other side of the tub.

Chad knew he had to get out first, but he was so hard it was uncomfortable to move. When he pushed out of the water, her eyes followed him, as if she were fascinated in spite of herself. He caught the widening of her eyes when she caught sight of his erection behind the soaked cotton of his briefs, but there was nothing he could do about it.

Swinging his legs out, he lowered himself to the bench, draping himself with a towel. "Can you give me just a minute?"

Lora nodded her head, submerged up to her chin in the water, her eyes wide. The tears were gone, but she still seemed fragile.

Chad patted himself dry, talking his body into calming down. He'd had Lora in his arms for the first time and it had been incredible, but torturous. Slamming the door on those thoughts, he shimmied out of his cold underwear. He'd have to go without until they got back to the house. Standing on his right leg he patted himself with the towel again and dragged his jeans up over his damp hips. Glancing over his shoulder, he caught Lora staring at his ass. He took a single hop to sit on the bench while he put his prosthetic on and grinned at her, letting her know he'd caught her looking. Seating his leg into the cup, he rolled his pant leg down and stood to put on his shirt. "You can look all you want."

Even beneath the dim lights he could see the blush that stained her cheeks. And that was enough. Walking out to the opening of the gazebo, he gave her his back, arms crossed over his chest.

It took Lora a few minutes to get out and dried off, but he never moved from his position. He breathed in the still night and allowed his body to calm down.

"I'm ready to go back."

They left their wet things in the laundry room. Lora had rolled the ace bandage to take with her. Before they entered the hallway to the kitchen, she touched his elbow. "I want to thank you for taking me out there. I needed it."

Smiling, he reached out enough to stroke a finger down her cheek. "I needed it just as much," he admitted. And it was true. He had.

Mercy was practically asleep on her feet. They'd been at his parent's house for several hours now and Chad thought it prudent to head back up the mountain. Mama gave Lora a hug and pressed a kiss to Mercy's head. Cheyenne wrapped her arms around Lora and held her for a minute, whispering something in her ear. When they parted, they both had wide smiles on their faces. Flynn and Rachel met them at the truck.

Mercy fell asleep on the short, rough ride up to the foreman's house. After he parked the truck, Chad gathered her in his arms to carry into the house. Lora hurried ahead to open doors and pull down the blankets on the bed. Chad settled the little girl onto the mattress and positioned Handsome next to her, but he moved back for Lora to cover her daughter.

She motioned for him to step out of the room and he waited just in the hallway.

"I wanted to thank you again for tonight," she whispered. "I didn't really want to go down but I'm so glad I did. Your family is amazing."

Chad smiled at her. "They love Mercy. She fit right in with the other kids."

"And she hasn't had very much of that. I mean, she goes to school, but she has no other family to speak of. I was an only child and Derek was as well. I worry what would happen to her if something happened to me." Her eyes filled with tears. "It would kill me if they got their hands on her. She's so good and sweet."

Moving slowly, Chad swiped her tears away. "They won't get her. We'll make sure of that."

She looked at him, weighing his words before she let out a sigh. "I know," she whispered. "I'm going to try to sleep too. Thank you, Chad, for everything."

He watched her reenter the room and close the door softly behind her. Massaging her tears into his fingers, he wished he knew how to proceed. On the one hand he wanted everything resolved, with Lora and Mercy safe. But on the other hand, he wanted the current set-up to continue. Being this close to Lora and her daughter was teaching him how alone he'd been for a long time. He would love to bring them into the family permanently.

Turning down the hallway, he marveled at his own calmness. Given his track record, the thought of being with a woman permanently should have scared the shit out of him.

It didn't.

CHAPTER TEN

AIDEN STARTED TO eat actual food. And talk to a counselor. When he realized that was the only way he was going to make it out of the hospital, he demanded solid food. Dr. Hartfield cautioned him to proceed slowly but with his typical bull-headedness, the man stretched the limits. He started walking, which was drama by itself. He was shaky on his feet but refused to be touched by the nurses and orderlies. They finally resorted to getting him a walker to use. Then they had to take the damn thing away because he was up all the time.

The counselor seemed confused as to what to do with him. "He admits to having issues with flashbacks, but refuses to admit his medical or military history." She shook her gray head. "I've prescribed him a low-dose antidepressant, but I can't do more than that unless he talks to me."

But he never did. The antidepressant seemed to help his mood, but he refused to talk to the counselor any more.

Duncan could only shake his head. He remembered doing the same things when he was in the hospital, stretching every limit he could. How could he blame Aiden for doing the same?

Several times he felt Dr. Hartfield's scrutiny on him, but he refused to acknowledge it. They'd had a nice meal together. That was enough.

Aiden seemed curious about why Duncan stayed around, but after the first day he never said anything out right. Duncan encouraged him as much as he could, but made sure to keep his distance. Aiden wasn't ready to be dug into.

After the third day of steady eating and gaining strength, Aiden got rid of the walker. Duncan knew it was time to talk to him, before he walked out of the hospital without saying a word.

"I want to take you back to Denver," Duncan told him after lunch.

Aiden gave him a narrow eyed look. "Why?"

Duncan kept his body relaxed. "Because it's where you were living."

"Do you actually think I want to go back to that?"

Duncan shook his head. "No, but I can help you get on your feet. You can't have been content living on the streets like that. The company I own is full of crazy idiots like you."

Aiden's eyes flared with heat, then he barked out a laugh. "Is this how you recruit all your people?"

Duncan shook his head. "Actually, I have a file with over a thousand resumes in it of people, former military, that want to be part of my company."

Aiden's hard jaw slackened. "Seriously?"

He nodded. "So, what I'm offering you doesn't happen very often. I suggest you think about it before you refuse it outright." Pushing to his feet, he nodded to Aiden. "I'll be back in the morning."

DUNCAN DID NOT have a good feeling as he walked into Aiden's hospital room the next morning. Kansas City was dreary today, as if warning of impending disaster.

The younger man sat on the edge of the bed as if he were getting ready to take a walk. Some of the flesh had filled in around his eyes and he didn't look so gaunt anymore. Duncan had seen the doctor down the hallway and knew she would be along as soon as she could break away from her other patients.

"Good morning, Aiden."

No response.

Dr. Hartfield came through the door grinning. "Good morning, gentlemen. Aiden, how do you feel today?"

"Like I want to leave."

The doctor grinned at Duncan, obviously under the assumption that Aiden would be leaving with him. "Well, I think we may be able to let you do that. Mind if I listen?"

The stethoscope was tugged from her neck and the ends were plugged into her ears. Aiden tugged his hospital johnny flat and sat up straight. The doctor listened to his breathing front and back, then moved the device lower to listen to his gut sounds. "I think you're well on your way to good health." She turned to Duncan. "Be sure he eats at least five times a day until he gets back up to weight."

Duncan shook his head. "I can't guarantee he'll do that. Mr. Willingham will not be coming back to Denver with me. Will you, Aiden?"

The doctor's confused face swung to the patient. "Wait. I thought you were leaving together."

Aiden's jaw firmed and his eyes chilled as he looked over at them. "No."

The doctor's pretty mouth fell open. "Why the hell not?"

Duncan looked at Aiden. "Because he doesn't want to take a chance on living life. He thinks if he's an ass he can cut himself off from people and they won't expect anything from him."

Aiden could only hold his gaze for a few seconds before he turned away. "I appreciate what you've done for me, but Denver is not the place for me."

Sighing, Duncan pulled his wallet from his back pocket. "I stopped and got this on my way in this morning, because I had a gut feeling you would get spooked." He selected a packaged Visa. "This has five hundred bucks on it. It should be enough to get you where you want to go. If by chance you change your mind, a flight from KC to Denver is a hundred and forty-one dollars. I checked this morning. A bus ticket is cheaper. Either way I'm helping out a veteran and I can look at myself in the mirror in the morning."

Crossing to the bed, Duncan placed the card on the rolling table. Aiden didn't even look at it, just continued to stare at the bathroom doorway. "I'm not going to worry about you anymore. If you decide to live, I'll have a job for you. You have my card. But I'm not going to force you."

He moved to stand in front of Aiden and held out his hand. "It's been a pleasure."

Aiden made him wait for several seconds before he reached out and took his hand. He shook once, then released.

Glancing at Dr. Hartfield, Duncan gave her a little bow. "It's been a pleasure, Doctor. Thank you for caring enough to contact me."

As he walked out of the room, he hoped that Aiden would call out and change his mind, but he didn't. Duncan turned down the hallway.

"Wait a minute, damn it."

Ah, yes. The doctor. He knew she would come after him.

"What the hell was that?" she demanded. Anger made her eyes shine and he wanted to bask in her vitality. She propped her hands on her hips.

"It was a man making a choice," he told her carefully. "Maybe not necessarily the right choice, but that's his prerogative. I can't make him come with me."

"So, what the hell has the last week been? Why did we waste our time?"

Duncan smiled at her and grabbed her flailing hand. "Why is it wasted time to let a person know that they matter? I don't consider a moment of this week wasted."

Some of her anger dissipated, but her eyes filled with tears. "What if he goes out and does the same thing over again and nobody finds him? He'll die."

Duncan nodded. "He will. But it's his choice." He gave her a chiding smile. "As a doctor, you know you can't save everybody."

A tear slipped down her cheek and she dashed it away with her hand. Reaching forward, he tugged her into a hug. "Watch him for as long as you can but don't push. He has to decide to change what he knows."

She nodded against his neck. Duncan took the barest instant and inhaled her scent, fascinated at the response his body gave. Letting her go, he stepped back. "It's been a pleasure, Dr. Hartfield. Take care."

Planting his cane, he pushed off toward the elevator. His last glance of her was the sight of her staring at *him.*

THE WEEK PASSED fairly uneventfully. Exactly the way she liked it. Lora ran the soapy rag over the pan, washing away the last of breakfast. They'd all settled into a schedule.

Chad stayed with them for the most part. Or at least close by. Rachel stayed with Mercy throughout the afternoon and took part of the night guard duty. Flynn took the graveyard shift, he called it. And the elusive Mr. Harper stayed up on the hill most of the time. She'd started packing sandwiches for Chad to take up to him when he rode out to check on him. The few times Harper had come down the mountain, Mercy always managed to find him to tag along with whatever he was doing. She'd developed a strange attachment to the scary soldier.

One morning she'd opened the front door to walk outside and had to slam to a stop in surprise. Harper was sitting on the porch stairs and her daughter stood behind him, with her arms wrapped as far around his massive shoulders as she could reach. She looked ridiculously tiny compared to the former soldier with the shaved head, but the man didn't move for several long seconds. Finally, he patted her little hands and sent her running to the playground.

Lora thought she'd escaped his notice, but when he stood up he caught her eye in the doorway. "She's worth her weight in gold," he rumbled. "I will do everything in my power to keep her safe."

Lora nodded and watched as he disappeared into the woods, huge gun held in his arms like a baby.

When she'd asked Mercy about the incident later, her daughter had shrugged. "He seemed sad so I gave him a hug."

Those words had humbled her.

But Chad seemed to be on a mission to drive her crazy. Where before he'd given her plenty of room to do everything, her personal space cushion had slowly started to shrink. Now he walked by her close enough that she could feel the heat of his body. Sometimes he lingered behind her until she had to turn. When he handed her things, he made sure to brush her fingers. Twice now he'd rested a broad hand on her shoulder for a few seconds.

Slowly but surely he was getting her used to him.

And it was killing her.

Lora found herself waiting for those tiny touches, and worse, *needing* them. When he walked up behind her she quivered, praying he would close the distance between them. But she felt like a hypocrite. Other men put her on edge, but Chad made her *aware.*

No less than a hundred times she imagined turning to him and simply walking into his open arms. The visual was haunting because she hadn't felt that way in years. If ever.

And somehow, he always had a supply of the spearmint Starlight mints she loved in his never-ending pocket.

Lora began to wonder if she could be in a relationship again. Derek had done a number on her in every way he'd been able, but physically, she was responding to Chad. When he walked into the room a shudder of need went up her spine. At first, she'd thought it was fear because it was so visceral, but then her body had tingled with awareness. It was incredibly confusing to her.

Chad wanted more of her and that fed her need. She'd seen the erection when he'd gotten out of the hot tub nights earlier and a couple of times since then he'd shifted uncomfortably, his hand going to his groin. Lora ached to place her hand there without inciting a traumatic event that would haunt her nightmares.

Would Chad understand that?

Lora walked to the living room window and looked out at the perfect spring day. Mercy was on Taco, trotting around the pen. Chad sat on his own big horse, elbow braced on the saddle horn as he called something out to her. Mercy looked up with a grin and tugged the reins lightly, guiding the pony into the opposite direction. As she trotted around him she giggled, showing more confidence than Lora had seen in a long time.

Chad was good for both of them, but he would be getting the short end of the stick with them.

"Do you have that list, Lora?"

She turned to Rachel, forcing a smile. "I do. It's on the counter. Thank you for going down."

The guard shrugged, her muscular shoulders shifting easily. "No problem. It's nice to see new scenery every once in a while."

Lora sighed and looked back out the window, but looked up as Rachel stepped beside her and peered out the window. She laughed, turning to give Lora a wink. "Ah, I see you're happy with the scenery here."

Lora flushed. "I don't…I can't."

"Why not?"

She blinked and crossed her arms over her chest, not sure she could articulate it. "My ex…" Her voice trailed away and she just shook her head.

Rachel sighed and rubbed a hand across Lora's back. "Okay. I get it. I'll be back in a bit."

Lora watched Rachel jog down the steps, tall and beautiful and very confident in her skin. She'd been like that a long time ago, but she didn't know if she'd ever be able to get back to being that woman.

Rachel returned a few hours later, Chad's red truck laden with shopping bags. Flynn waved them away and gathered all of the bag handles in two big hands, carrying them inside the house easily. Rachel tossed her one bag specifically.

"I got you something while I was in there."

Lora peeked into the bag and drew out a pile of nylon. "A bathing suit?"

Rachel nodded and stepped close. "You were the most relaxed I've ever seen you the night of the dinner. Why don't you see if Chad will take you down again?"

She held up the one piece by a strap. Rachel knew she wouldn't go for flashy, but this one seemed very pretty, a mix of blues and greens. She *had* been relaxed then.

"Maybe I will."

Nerves attacked her when the chance came to ask at dinner that night, but Chad beat her to the subject. "Rachel said you might like to use the bathhouse again."

She nodded, incredibly appreciative of the other woman.

Chad's eyes darkened, but he nodded his head. "We can wait till Mercy is in bed if you'd like."

Lora nodded again, feeling like a dimwit, but her throat was tight with emotion.

But as the time neared, anxiety began to get the better of her. She hadn't been separated from Mercy since they'd run from Denver. She sat on the bed reading to her at bedtime, but she didn't know if she could leave her behind.

Mercy seemed to pick up on her concern. "Don't worry, Mommy. Harper said he would stay right outside my door when you went down to Chad's mom's house."

Lora cocked an eyebrow at that but when she glanced up, the former SEAL hovered in the shadows of the hallway. He gave her a single nod, then went back to running his thumb over the massive knife in his hand.

Two weeks ago the image would probably have freaked her out, but instead it made her completely secure in her daughter's safety. With a final kiss on Mercy's forehead, she turned off the light and left the room. As she passed Harper, she smiled up at him. "Thank you," she whispered.

He gave her a wink and leaned against the wall. "No problem."

They rattled down the drive in Chad's truck. Harper, Flynn and Rachel were staying with Mercy. Anticipation was building in her belly, more because she was alone with Chad than anything.

They pulled up into the drive and parked, but he guided her around the side of the house. "My parents are probably in bed. But it's okay. I told them we'd be out here tonight."

There was enough of a moon to see where they walked and they were soon standing under the pale lights of the gazebo. Chad tossed a couple of fresh towels onto the bench from the cupboard then returned to the front of the building. "Enjoy."

Lora frowned. "Aren't you going to join me?"

He glanced at her. "Only if you want me to."

"I do."

The words themselves were innocuous enough, but she felt them resonate through her.

Giving her a single nod, he waved a hand. "I'll wait until you get in."

Turning back around to face the house, he gave her privacy to strip down to her suit. Lora appreciated the consideration and skimmed her pants down her legs, then her shirt. The late evening breeze was cool, making the hot water in the tub feel all that hotter. She gasped as she lowered herself into the water.

"You can come in now."

Chad stepped inside the building. Lora turned her head away but tried to watch him out of her peripheral vision. Would he strip down in front of her or would he turn around?

Oh, hell. He wasn't turning.

One handed, he unfastened the button at the top of his pants and dragged his zipper down. The shirt slipped off after that. Then he did turn to sit on the bench beside the tub to take his prosthetic off. It only took a second before he was standing again, balancing on one leg as he hopped up the two steps, sat on the side and lifted his legs over the side.

Lora watched him by that time; she couldn't not. As he sank down into the water in his blue briefs, she thought he seemed a little relieved to be concealed. So maybe he wasn't as confident as he appeared.

That made Lora pause. Nothing would happen tonight that she didn't want to happen.

But the excitement of the possibilities made her heart race.

"The new suit looks nice."

She looked down. Literally, all he could see were the blue straps over her shoulders. "You can't see it."

He shrugged. "It's enough."

Daring made Lora tense. She wanted to stand up out of the water to let him see her. The memory of the bold erection he had last time they came in here spurred her. Staring at him without blinking, she stood up.

Water cascaded down her body and the cool of the air made her shiver, but the heat in Chad's eyes was enough to rewarm her. She stood in the middle of the tub for as long as she could. Then, courage depleted, she sank down into the water.

Chad gave her a lopsided smile. "I think I need to take back what I said before. You look gorgeous."

The heartfelt statement filled her with a glow like no other. "Thank you," she whispered. "You have no idea how much I appreciate hearing that."

"It's true. You're a beautiful woman, Lora. You have to know that."

She blinked at him and shook her head. "I haven't felt beautiful for a long time."

He seemed to understand that she wasn't talking about her fading bruises.

"If I could kick the shit out of him again, I promise you I would."

Lora nodded. "I know. And I would let you."

"Lora, I will take care of you for as long as you let me. And in any way you want me to."

Her throat tightened with emotion and she had to look away. "I know, Chad. It's just hard letting go of all the baggage, you know?"

He snorted and made a funny face. "I don't know anything about baggage."

She shook her head, smiling at him. "Yours is a lot more under control than mine. I don't know if I'll ever be able to be with a man again. Standing up in front of you in a bathing suit was about all the courage I have right now."

"Then that's all you need. I'm not pressuring you for anything. Would I like to be in a relationship with you? Hell yes, I would. Though it's unethical and unwise, I'm seriously attracted to you. But there's no time limit on it. I've been attracted to you for a long time and I'm willing to wait ten times that long if that's what it takes."

Lora swirled her arms through the water. "As much as I appreciate that, I don't think it's fair to you."

"Why?"

She made a motion with her hand. "Because. I don't know if I would ever be able to be with you."

He seemed to be digesting her words. "Well, let's take it one step at a time, okay? We'll do what you're comfortable with and build on that."

She leaned her head back against the rim of the tub. The hot water was nice but it wasn't easing her like it had before. Probably because she had too many thoughts swirling in her head. She replayed his words in her mind and she wondered what her limit was.

Lora lifted her head to look at Chad. He had his head back against the tub like she had, the long ridge of his throat arched back. The dark brown hair was still dry and had grown in a little bit over the past week and a half. She was on his left side and her eyes traced over the scarring that climbed his neck to his hairline behind his ear. They didn't seem as obvious to her as they used to. And now that she was this close, she could see that the tattoo was of a pair of combat boots and a rifle propped up in the middle, with a helmet hanging from the tip of the rifle. "Can you talk about what happened?"

He rolled his head to her voice and she realized she'd drifted closer to him, just a couple feet away. For a long minute he didn't say anything, his bright blue eyes darkened by the intimacy of the gazebo and pain from his memories.

She swallowed heavily, rethinking her request. "You don't have to. I shouldn't have asked."

Lora started to push away, but he lifted his left hand out of the water to her. Automatically, she took his fingers in her own and let him draw her down to the bench beside him. They weren't touching anywhere else, just at their fingers, but the connection between them leapt.

"We'd just been pinned down in a firefight. Duncan, the partner you talked to on the phone, arrived with backup just in time and we kicked serious ass. My guys were in a euphoric mood because a lot of them were newbies, wet behind the ears. It had been their first fight and we didn't lose anybody. One of the guys, Mike Dodd, came up and showed me a malfunctioning weapon. We worked it out and took off at a jog to catch up with the rest of the men. Dodd looped around a rock, rather than following the trail like everybody else had, and he stepped on an IED."

He went silent then and Lora found herself squeezing his misshapen hand under the water between both of hers. The pain in his eyes made her heart ache for him. She never should have asked.

"Mike Dodd was eighteen years old. A baby. Got blown in half by that damn bomb. The only good thing, if there is good in this, is that he didn't suffer. I was told he was dead before he hit the ground. My foot was obliterated and everything on that side got fried. I remember Duncan leaning over me and somebody saying the word tourniquet and everything went black."

"I was in hospitals for months. Walter Reed for a while, then they shipped me down to San Antonio."

"I can't imagine what you went through. The pain had to be excruciating."

He laughed, but it was without his usual humor. "You have no idea. Being burned is…" His voice drifted away and he ended by shaking his head. She didn't blame him.

Lora felt like she needed to share something equally as traumatic.

"Mercy wasn't my first baby."

Chad looked at her, brows raised.

"When Derek talked me into marrying him, we started trying for a baby. Within two weeks I had conceived. I rushed home to tell him our wonderful news and found him screwing the maid. Well, I let my mouth fly. Told him what an ass he was and how only small men cheated." She paused, swallowing convulsively. The memories from that night were as clear as if they had happened yesterday. "That was the first time he raped me. I spent that night in the emergency room miscarrying."

Chad's grip tightened on her hand painfully before releasing and she looked at him. Fury blazed in his eyes. "Why didn't somebody at the hospital say something? Did you report him?"

"I did," she sighed. "Several times. I only found out later that the sheriff was getting kickbacks from the family."

Chad was vibrating with tension. His jaw was clenched and his brows were furrowed, but he kept his touch gentle. The anger didn't scare Lora. She knew it wasn't directed at her.

"So how did you break away?"

She smiled, thinking of the most terrifying, most liberating day of her life. "I squirrelled away money here and there. Looked for a shelter out of state that would take us in. Once I had everything in line, I drove away. Sold the Mercedes he bought me and used the cash to start over."

He ran a finger down her cheek and turned her face to him. "That was incredibly brave."

Lora shook her head. "I had to. They were talking about Mercy as if she were a piece of furniture. What schools she would go to, families she could marry into. It was ridiculous. She was three, you know? Just a baby. And I knew it would only be a matter of time before she was physically in danger, too."

He nodded, lifting her hand to press a kiss to her fingers. "You did exactly what you were supposed to do to protect your child."

"The hard part was filing for divorce. Once he knew what state I was in, he hired people to find me. I think he would have eventually given up if it hadn't been for Rosalind driving him. Derek could have cared less about the divorce. He was able to screw whomever he wanted and not worry about backlash once I was gone. I didn't want money. But it looked bad for the family name. And the business."

She swirled her hand through the water. "Recently he's been pestering me more often. Sending Mercy gifts. I don't know what he's up to."

"We were supposed to find evidence that you were unfit," he told her quietly. "That was the gist of our assignment."

Lora knew the hurt was in her eyes when he went down to the floor of the tub in front of her.

"Listen to me. I knew within days that you were the perfect mother for Mercy. I watched you care for her and play with her. I sent in a report stating that the first week I was assigned your case, but the Malones insisted I continue with the surveillance. So I did. But even after several weeks I didn't find fault with anything you did. At all. I think you should be nominated for Mother of the Year after all the crap you've been through."

Lora gave a sobbing laugh and allowed herself to lean forward against his shoulder. He rubbed her arms and she thought he pressed a kiss to her temple.

"We're not doing very good on the relaxation front, are we?"

She shook her head against him. "We're not. Maybe we can try to start over?"

He pulled away enough to press a kiss to her forehead, then pushed back up onto the bench beside her. "Definitely. Put your head back and just let go."

Lora did as he suggested, trying to let some of the worry dissipate. For a few minutes she just let herself drift in the gently swirling water. Chad bumped into her a few times with the motion of the water, but she didn't mind it. It was enjoyable actually. She clasped his hand again and he gave her a little squeeze.

That tiny connection made her heart race, and she wondered again what her limit was.

"Chad," she said softly.

"Yeah."

"Do you think you can…" She paused to drag in a deep breath. "Do you think you can kiss me?"

Chad straightened in the water, his eyes latching onto hers. "Is that what you want?"

She forced her head up and down, but began to have second thoughts. Chad must have seen something in her expression because he shook his head. "As much as I want to, I'm not going to kiss you. You're going to kiss me. That way you will know when you need to stop. *If* you need to stop. Do you understand?"

She nodded her head, excitement singing through her blood again.

"I'm not going to touch you unless you tell me to. My hands will be on the rim of the tub the entire time. Are you sure you want to do this? If you're not ready I understand." His eyes narrowed on her face and he smiled suddenly, big and brilliant. "Do you believe I'm trying to talk you out of kissing me? Fuck that!"

Both of his strong hands went to the rim of the hot tub and he looked at Lora with a cute, expectant expression on his face. Unable to contain her own smile, Lora drifted forward, but stayed to his left kneeling on the bench. Resting one hand on his tense shoulder, she leaned in close enough to press her lips to his.

Chad tasted of sweetness and sex. And some dangerous spice that made her moan and search for more. Opening her lips, she teased across his, unable to believe how good he tasted. His lips opened slightly and his head tilted to seal with hers, nudging her to move in tiny touches. Lora thought she was in control of her own body, but she found herself drifting closer, until her breasts brushed against his solid chest. It didn't bother her, or repel her. Actually, she wanted more. Tightening her grip on him, she shifted her hands to his stubbled face. He groaned deep in his throat and she felt his slick abs contract. For the barest millisecond of time, she thought he was going to grab her, but he didn't. His hands were still on the edge of the tub, white knuckled from gripping so tight.

As he'd promised, he hadn't moved. Lora tore her lips away, panting in the steam. She rested her cheek against his and dragged in great draughts of air. Then slowly, regretfully, she pushed away to the other side of the tub.

Chad stared at her hard, his face flushed and his lips parted. His hands slipped down inside the water and she knew he was gripping his erection. The thought made her hotter than she already was.

"I had to quit, I'm sorry."

But he was already shaking his head. "Don't you dare apologize to me. You have nothing to apologize for. That was the best first kiss I've ever experienced."

Heat flushed through her and she searched his face, trying to decide if he was telling her the truth or not. It had rocked her like nothing she'd ever felt before. But she didn't have the experience he did, she was sure.

Lora shifted on the bench, very aware that she was wet and aroused beneath her suit. Her nipples were still hard, remembering how it felt to chafe against his chest.

"You're excited, aren't you?" he asked, grinning.

"I am," she admitted.

His eyes darkened. "I am too."

Three simple words completely wrecked her thinking.

"Promise me something."

She tilted her head. "What?"

"Any time you want to do that, you come to me. It doesn't matter what I'm doing at the time. If you need me, you come to me."

Unable to imagine doing what he said, but entranced nonetheless, she nodded her head.

They left just a few minutes after that. Lora watched Chad get out and sit on the towel, blatant erection straining his briefs. He shrugged and grinned when he noticed her looking.

Once again, Lora was plagued by dreams of incredible kisses and erections behind wet cotton. She woke up at four thirty and couldn't go to sleep again. It had been the same for two days now, this constant need and wonder plaguing her.

Wrapping her sweater around her, she padded out the bedroom door and down the hallway. She had almost passed Chad's doorway when she heard thrashing. Easing the door open, she peered inside.

Chad moved restlessly on the mattress, hands clutched in the sheet. A harsh frown contorted his face and he lifted an arm as though someone were about to hit him. Moving closer to the bed, Lora reached out and rested her hand on his forehead. It had calmed him before. And it did this time as well. He stilled beneath her touch, his breathing deepening.

She stood there, stroking her hand through his thick hair for precious minutes. It was still dark outside the bedroom window, but there was enough moonlight that she could see the relaxation settle across his face.

As the minutes dragged by, she continued to stand there, gently running her fingers across his scalp. She felt…indulgent. It had started out as a way to soothe him, but it was having the exact same effect on her. At one point she looked down and his eyes were slitted open. She jerked her hand away. He hadn't made a sound.

"I didn't want you to stop," he rumbled.

Hesitantly, she reached out to stroke him again, but he moved away. Shifting across the bed, he patted the corner of the mattress, up near the headboard. "You don't have to stand."

Lora looked at the spot he had cleared for her and wondered if she was making a mistake as she slid onto the mattress, back resting against the headboard. She could feel the heat of his body radiating to her, but he kept himself far enough away not to spook her. His head was the closest thing to her, resting near her thighs, face turned away. Lora reached out and began to stroke her fingers through his hair again.

She woke two hours later, curled on her side along the length of the cold headboard. Chad's head rested against her belly and her arm was over his shoulders. She held him as if she'd nestled into his warmth.

Chad shifted, sitting up in bed and turned to her, smiling sleepily. "Thank you."

Lora straightened her t-shirt and sleep pants as she stood, shocked that she'd let herself relax so. "I'm sorry I fell asleep on you."

He laughed as he rubbed his bare chest and swung his legs to the side. "You didn't fall asleep on me. You fell asleep with me. And I enjoyed every dreamless second of it. Thank you."

If his eyes hadn't been so sincere, she wasn't sure if she'd believe him or not. "It wasn't just for you. I enjoyed it too. Something about the repetitive stroking really calmed me."

"Well, you can come in and do it any time. Right about two my dreams usually start."

Lora looked away from the tempting play of his muscles in his back as he attached his prosthesis. "I should go…check on Mercy."

CHAPTER ELEVEN

CHAD FROWNED AS he watched her hustle out the door. It was probably best right now. He looked down at the morning wood tenting his boxers. Poor Lora was going to think he was always hard.

Which around her he usually was.

Checking his phone, he saw a 'call me when you wake up' text from Duncan. Well, he could wait a few more minutes. Chad grabbed a towel and headed to the bathroom for his shower.

Twenty minutes later he called his boss.

"Morning, Dunc."

"Hey, Chad. How goes it in the land of cow pies?"

He laughed, thinking of Mercy's observations. "It goes good. How did you know?"

His former First Sergeant sighed on the other end of the line. "It wasn't that great of a stretch to figure it out. It's the back of beyond down there. Great place to hide. Maybe you can bring back some of your mom's cookies."

"I can probably talk her into it, if she hasn't already thought of it herself."

"Hey." Duncan's voice turned serious. "We're still fishing with the trade commission, but something happened that may shake everything up."

"What's that?"

"Rosalind Malone was found dead in her pool two days ago. Right now they're ruling it accidental. She had a blood-alcohol level well over the legal limit."

"Oh, hell," he sighed. "Yeah, that may change things. Was she alone when they found her? Where was Derek?"

"Not sure. Still getting details. I'll call you as soon as I know anything else."

"Okay. Thanks, boss man."

"No problem."

After he hung up, Chad dressed and headed toward the front of the house. Lora stood on the front porch, watching the sunrise with a cup of coffee in her hand. Chad hated to disturb her moment, especially when she looked up at him with a smile on her face.

"You're so lucky to have grown up here."

"I was," he admitted. "But it's been kind of a love hate thing. When I was a kid, the chores were not fun. It's a lot of hard work running a ranch this size. But once I left home and went overseas, I realized how much I missed it. Where did you grow up?"

She looked off toward the east. "A little town outside of Baltimore. Pretty industrial. My dad worked on the railroad as an engineer. He was killed on the job when I was little. It was just Mom and I then. She died when I was in college, before I met Derek."

"Wow. I'm sorry." He touched her shoulder for just a second. "You've been on your own a long time."

Lora glanced at him and shrugged.

"I just talked to Duncan."

She looked at him, brows raised over her dark green eyes.

"I don't know how you're going to take this, but Rosalind was found in her pool two days ago, drowned. She appeared to be intoxicated when she died."

Lora's mouth dropped open in shock, but there were no tears. "Are you serious?"

He nodded. "Duncan isn't sure where Derek is."

She turned back to the sunrise, more pensive than when he'd arrived, but he didn't push her. It was hard losing people, even if they were enemies sometimes.

Mercy came out onto the porch then, rubbing her eyes and dragging Handsome by one leg. "I'm hungry, Mommy."

Lora turned to her with a bright smile. "Well, let's go get you something then."

Before she disappeared into the house, she looked over her shoulder and gave Chad a headshake. Message received. Don't tell the kid.

It was a strange day. Sometimes Lora seemed sad, her eyes tearing up as if the death had affected her, then at other times she seemed satisfied, joyous even. And he could understand both sides of the coin. If Rosalind had been pushing for custody as much as Lora thought, it would stand to reason that she would be hopeful Derek would drop the whole thing.

Their day went a little more to hell when Harper radioed down that there was a red truck, driver unidentified, coming up the hill. Rachel guided Lora and Mercy into the house while Chad waited in the drive for whomever was coming. When the red, jacked-up, chromed out Ford pulled into the drive and he caught sight of the driver, Chad cursed a blue streak. *What the fuck!*

Resigned, he opened the truck door, forcing a smile. "Tara Johnson! How the heck are you?"

The woman oozed out of the driver's side door, leading with her long slim thighs and enhanced breasts. "Chad," she drawled, "I can't believe you came home for a visit and didn't call me."

Chad forced himself not to cringe as her cloud of perfume wafted over him. "I'm not really here for pleasure, Tara. I brought a few buddies with me for kind of a guy thing, you know?"

Her bright blue, heavily lashed eyes widened. "Then who was the blond woman I saw driving your truck yesterday in town?"

Cursing internally, Chad shook his head. "She's one of the investigators that works at the company. She's brand new and we brought her out for some firearms training."

Eyes narrowing only slightly, Tara slipped her arm through his good one. "Then she won't mind if we get away then, hm? Let's go in and sit down for a little while."

Standing firm, he shook his head. "It's not convenient right now, Tara. I'm sorry."

Her pink-slicked lips pouted. "I drove all this way out here, honey, and I was hoping we could catch up. I have so much to talk to you about."

Tears filled her bright eyes, meant to make him capitulate, but he was unmoved.

"Mama told me about your divorce and I feel so bad for you, but I just can't spare the time right now."

Hell. If she made it into the house and saw him with Lora, there'd be no end to the acrimony.

Wait a minute. Why the hell was he being so polite to her? *Because she's a genuinely sweet person. She was just too much for me.*

Tara clutched at his arm as a tear slipped down her cheek. "It was terrible, Chad. I mean, not as bad as the incredible sacrifice you made for your country, losing your leg and all, but it was the worst thing I've ever experienced."

Another tear slipped down her cheek and when she walked into his arms, he softened enough to wrap them around her. Chad called himself a fool for giving in to her, but she'd been a friend for a long time. They'd gone out years ago and had fun. It was only when he came back from Iraq, missing his leg and scarred, that her solicitous behavior became too much. If she could have looked past the injuries and still been able to connect with him like they had before, everything would have been fine. Hell, maybe he would have married her rather than whatever his name was.

Her sobbing started to recede, so he relaxed his hold. Her gaze landed on his damaged arm and she shuddered.

Nice.

Chad let her go completely. "I'm sorry you wasted your time coming up here."

She tipped up her chin. "It wasn't a waste, dear. You'll come see me again."

The thought of having to deal with this all over again set his teeth on edge. "Well, Tara, I'm kind of involved with somebody now."

Her eyes narrowed and she scoffed. "You mean like, serious?"

He nodded.

"She knows about your leg and everything?"

Chad knew his expression cooled. "Yes, she does and it doesn't bother her. At all. I'm in love with her."

Tara's mouth dropped open in shock and she shook her head. "But we…"

"…used to be friends. But we've both moved on."

Fresh tears filled her eyes. This time he felt they were more sincere. But he wasn't going to retract his words.

The Texas beauty rallied, tipping up her chin and giving him a smile. "Well, then. I guess I'll be movin' on. It was nice seeing you, Chad."

He lifted a hand. "And it was nice seeing you again too, Tara. Take care."

The truck rattled down the dusty drive and he felt like he'd gotten a load off his shoulders. Her overblown, syrupy concern had driven him nuts for a long time.

Flynn came around the side of the barn, laughing. It struck Chad a little rough. "What?" he snapped.

Flynn shook his dark head, stopping beside him. "She wanted to save you, didn't she? Thought you needed fixed."

"Yeah," he sighed. "She didn't used to be like that before I went over. She used to be a nice girl."

"I'm sure she is a nice girl, just not for you. Lora's been watching the entire time. You should go talk to her."

Chad glanced up at the house but couldn't see anything behind the shine of the glass windows. "Yeah."

Flynn walked away without another word and Chad stared off after him. If he didn't know better, he'd think Flynn had been trying to be nice.

It took him a minute for his eyes to adjust to the dimness of the house. Mercy watched TV quietly, bouncing a little with the characters on the screen. Rachel gave him a nod when he relieved her and headed for her rest.

Crossing to the kitchen, Chad poured half a cup of coffee from the coffee maker and ladled in a couple tablespoons of sugar, then milk.

"Do you even taste the coffee?"

He grinned at Lora over his shoulder. "Course I do. Mama says the Easter Bunny left me in a basket when I was born. And that it's her fault I have such a sweet tooth, because when she was pregnant with me, she couldn't get enough of those jelly beans they put out at Easter time."

Lora laughed and sat at the kitchen table. Chad pulled another cup from the cupboard and poured her some coffee, with just a touch of sugar like she preferred. When he set it in front of her, she stared at it for a long minute before raising it to her mouth.

"Was that an old girlfriend?"

Chad sat down just to her left at the table. She didn't seem to mind the proximity.

"Not exactly. We grew up together. Her daddy's spread is to the north of us, so we've always helped each other out at roundup and hay time. We hung out." He shrugged, sipping his coffee.

"She seemed to think it was more."

Chad glanced at her, a little surprised and pleased to hear a bit of jealousy in her voice. "She would have made it more if I'd let her, but when I came back from Iraq, things changed between us. She wanted to take care of me. Which, in a certain context, I'm all for," he tossed her a grin, "but Tara made it sound like a sacrifice. It's hard to explain but when you come back injured, you're not the same man. Your perspective changes and things become more clear. I don't know, you kind of learn to wade through all the bullshit quicker or something."

Leaning back against the chair, he rested his coffee cup between his folded hands. "I was on the verge of taking off because of all the overblown concern. They had a parade for me when I got home and my name is on the stone in the square, but even after all that I couldn't walk down the sidewalk without somebody racing ahead to sweep it clean. More than once people opened my damn truck door for me. Usually women. I was wounded, yes, but not critically. They acted like I couldn't do anything for myself anymore."

Chad realized he'd begun to raise his voice. Lora watched him with a gentle smile.

"Sorry. Can you tell it bothered me?"

She held up her pinched thumb and forefinger. "Just a bit."

Laughing, he shook his head. "Anyway, I think the women in town took it upon themselves to get me married. Almost every day I had visitors. And at the time my mother was all for it. My parents were almost as bad as the townspeople. Their baby had been hurt. It took them a long time to be okay with me being out of their sight. I don't think they really realized how okay I was until Duncan offered me the job and I moved to Colorado."

"How long had you been home?"

"Hm, a few months. About six. I was on the verge of bolting, just going somewhere and getting lost. Then Duncan threw me that lifeline. I've been there ever since. But," he continued, "sometimes when I come home I have this to contend with." Again, he waved his hand toward the main ranch.

"Everybody is concerned about you."

"I know," he sighed. "And I really do appreciate it. But I feel like I can't breathe here."

"You need to set some limits." Lora laughed. "Although it's hard to tell if they'll abide by those limits."

Chad knew she referred to Derek.

"I'm sorry I'm bitching about my life. It's not that bad, really."

She shook her head. "Don't, please. I enjoy listening to you talk. I've learned a lot about you in the past ten minutes."

He snorted. "Good and bad, huh?"

"Nah. All good."

"Well, hopefully John and Duncan will figure something out to tie up this situation."

Not even three minutes later, Chad's cell phone rang. Glancing at the screen, he swiped his thumb to answer. "Hey, Palmer. How the fuck are you?"

Chad cringed and glanced guiltily at the living room, but Mercy was absorbed in her cartoons.

"I'm fine. Lora and the girl have problems coming their way, though."

Lora's gaze sharpened on him. She'd obviously heard.

"Why? What's up?"

"I have a feeling Mr. Malone is going to be out for blood. We sent Roger in as a flower delivery man and he chatted up one of the maids. Apparently things have been in a tizzy over the past couple of weeks. Lots of fighting."

"Since we've been gone?"

"Yeah, I think that's part of it. But there's a shake-up with the business too. The maid said it sounded like Derek's mother was changing her will to leave everything to the little girl because Derek's been such a fuck-up."

"Oh, hell," he breathed.

Lora had paled and was shaking her head. "We don't want it."

"Wait," Chad focused on the phone. "Has this actually been done legally, or is this just chatter right now?"

"It has not been confirmed," John told him. "But, if she were about to switch beneficiaries, that's a heck of a reason to off somebody before they actually do it."

"Yeah, it really is," Chad sighed. "Do you know where he is right now?"

"Nope. Haven't seen hide or hair of him for a week. I think you guys are secure, but stay tight. Duncan called in a favor and the FBI is checking things out. We found some interesting exchanges in their financial histories, so we're trying to run those down too. I think it's only a matter of time before reality catches up to Derek Malone."

"Okay. Thanks, Gunny. Keep us updated."

"Will do."

Lora looked shell-shocked. "Do you seriously think Derek would hurt his own mother?"

Chad frowned. "I don't know. Probably not. I have a feeling he wouldn't dirty his hands that way. He'd hire somebody to do it. That way he'd have a convenient alibi."

She gulped the rest of her coffee, blinking and suddenly pale. "So, if she has appointed Mercy her beneficiary, Derek is going to be after us even more. If he has custody of Mercy he has control of the money."

Chad reached out to rest his hand on hers. "Let's not borrow trouble. We just need to sit tight for a while till we have more details."

Tears filled Lora's eyes. Chad wanted to pull her into his arms, but didn't think she would accept that. But then she looked at him, and that need was there that he had seen in the gazebo. Opening his arms, Lora leaned into him and he cradled her gently. Lora sighed into his neck and relaxed, her arms creeping around his neck. He held her like that for several long moments.

"Do you like my mom?" Mercy's little voice chirped at his shoulder.

Chad forced himself to ease back slowly as he looked at the little girl. Her eyes were bright with curiosity. "I like your mother very much. Is that okay?"

She nodded her head up and down like a little bobble-head. "I told 'ansom you liked her."

Grinning, he tugged on a chunk of her hair. "You think you're a smarty-pants, huh?"

She took off at a run, giggling. Lora watched her with a smile, her cheeks a little pink, before she turned back to Chad. He felt the drag of her eyes over his face, coming to rest on his lips. Lifting his eyebrows expectantly, he waited to see what she would do.

Lora didn't disappoint him. Lifting her chin, she pressed her lush mouth to his, moving softly. At one point she pulled away, her lips a hairsbreadth from his, just breathing the same air. Chad felt his blood head south, unable to help himself. She was using her proximity against him. "Are you trying to get me excited?" he drawled.

Lora smiled against his mouth, nibbling. "Maybe."

"You don't have to. I've needed you for a long time."

She drew back and looked up into his eyes, frowning. "Really?"

"Of course. A very long time. I told you that."

"I know, but it just seems so strange to me."

"You need to get used to it," he told her softly.

CHAPTER TWELVE

CHAD UPDATED THE other guards. Harper gave no reaction, but Flynn cursed roundly. Rachel shook her head.

"This sounds like trouble," she murmured softly.

"We'll stick to our shifts, but be ready to be flexible. Harper, I like you up on that plateau. You can see more than anyone up there. Just watch your back. Flynn, I want you to stick around the house. Rachel, you are on Mercy. I want you to modify your shift so that you're up when she's up."

The former pilot gave him a salute, though they'd never been in service together.

"Stay sharp, people, and I want your side arms on."

So their schedule modified. Lora sat Mercy down to explain about her grandmother and she cried a little bit, but not a great deal. Mercy's bright little personality dimmed a bit afterwards. Lora tried to keep things as upbeat as possible, but when that kind of worry moved in it was bound to affect everything.

They went out for Mercy's morning ride on Taco, but even he seemed tense and uncooperative. Chad explained that was because of Mercy's emotions. They cut the ride short and headed back to the house.

Lora distracted herself by baking a cake. She'd left her bandage off today and her wrist was holding up well. The bruising was mostly gone from around her eye and cheek and Rachel had snipped out the stitches on her hairline the day before. Overall, she'd recovered. Just in time for the asshole to come back and harass them some more.

Chad did his best to keep them upbeat. They played board games, and at one point he attacked Mercy with tickles. Giggles rang through the house, making Lora smile at the sound, and she was struck with the perfection of the moment. She wanted this to last, more than just a few days or weeks, but forever. When she'd married the first time, this is what she'd expected, this contentment and satisfaction with life.

Chad had created this, she realized, just by being the man he was. He'd made her aware that she was more than a protector, that she was still a vibrant woman who needed to be recognized as such.

The thought of the kiss she had started warmed her from the inside out. Almost immediately, she had known she was in trouble. It didn't ease her need though. It had only made it worse.

And she felt like time was running out. Derek always managed to come out ahead of her. She wasn't sure that he wouldn't win this situation either.

No! I won't let him win. I won't let him have Mercy.

And I won't let him dictate my life anymore.

That night after she'd put Mercy to bed, Lora drew herself a hot bath. As she sank down into the water, she gasped, then moaned in delight. The sensual feel of the sloshing water against her skin tightened her nipples. Running her hands over them critically, she wondered if Chad would mind that she wasn't perfect. Or that she had stretch marks from pregnancy. Lora lathered her hair and tried to shove the worry aside.

As she walked down the hallway a half an hour later the nerves in her belly were almost enough to make her call everything off. Chad didn't know anything about her plans, so she could turn right around and he would be none the wiser. But in the end she felt like that was the coward's way out.

Forcing one foot in front of the other, she stopped in front of his bedroom door. Inhaling into her nose and out of her mouth, she tried to prop her flailing courage. Chad was an honorable man. He wouldn't turn her away. Even if she couldn't follow through with what she wanted to do.

Raising her fist, she knocked softly.

"Yeah."

Turning the knob, she leaned her head around the edge of the door. "May I come in?"

His eyes narrowed, but he nodded.

Lora stepped into the room, closing the door softly behind her. She pressed her back to the wood and crossed her arms beneath her breasts.

Chad had just gotten out of the shower. Dark curls stood out from his head where he'd run the towel over them. The expanse of his chest looked so warm and welcoming.

"What do you need, Lora?"

She choked out a laugh. "Well, since you ask…"

Brows lifted, he waited.

"I want to see what my limit is. I can't…guarantee we'll go all the way, but I want to explore and see. I know this is terribly unfair to you."

Chad shook his head and took a couple of steps toward her. "It's not unfair to me, but I think we better talk about this before we jump into bed and expect everything to be hunky-dory. I don't think I'd be able to live with myself if you looked at me like you did him. I was there, remember? Are you sure this is the right time?"

Lora cringed, just a bit. "I know it's not ideal, but I'm tired of living with him on my shoulder. I can't do anything without worrying. I'm ready to take back my life."

"Okay," he said softly, stroking her hair back behind her ears. "But let's start with baby steps." He took a step closer. "Will you let me give you a hug?"

Just the thought of his arms around her set off a war inside her stomach. Yes, she wanted to feel the security of not being alone. She wanted to burrow into his spicy scent and block out the world. But the absolute spike of terror the thought of being restrained set off was almost debilitating. Oxygen became sparse in her lungs and she gulped in air.

But wait. This is Chad, she told herself again. Sexy Chad that wanted her more than anyone else she'd ever seen.

Straightening her spine, she nodded.

Chad lifted his arms around her and pulled her in against his chest. Lora fought not to struggle and focused on his collarbone. Inhaling the scent of his skin, she tried to count down from one hundred. But as the weight of his arms settled around her neck, she tensed. Chad immediately eased the pressure and she was able to hold herself together.

Lora felt like she was dancing on the edge of a cliff, daring the wind to push her over, but she knew she needed to do this. She wanted to do this.

Chad pulled back and cupped her face, pressing a kiss to her lips. Lora frowned as he stepped away.

"What's wrong?" she asked.

Chad winked at her and crossed to the bed. He nodded his head to the other side. "I want you to lay down on the bed. I am going to lay down beside you and we're going to talk."

After the initial spike of fear, Lora could actually breathe, and just talking sounded like a good idea. She padded to the other side of the mattress as he removed his prosthetic, setting it to the side. Chad sat back and arranged the bedding so that they slid under the sheet. They were both still completely dressed as they laid down shoulder to shoulder, her left side to his right.

"I will never judge you," he whispered into the darkness, his words hitting her heart like a cannonball. "What was done to you should never happen to any woman. I know you feel like you need to make a stand against him, but I don't want you to rush this. I plan on being here for the long haul, no matter what. Okay?"

She nodded against the pillow, wiping the tears from her temples. She laced her fingers in his and turned on her side to reach her other arm across his chest. There was no fear as she squeezed him.

They lay there for a good while, and the steady thump of Chad's heart was almost enough to put her to sleep, but she wanted to relish the feel of his arms around her for as long as she could. "I miss this," she whispered.

"Hm?"

"This closeness. My parents were close like this, from what I remember. After Dad died it was just the two of us and we did good. Mom made sure we had a stable home. She was an accountant and she worked hard to keep a roof over our heads. I moved away to college, but I was close enough that I went home every weekend. Then one day, my mom didn't call like she normally did. So I called her. The phone rang and rang before the neighbor lady picked up and told me that my mother had had a heart attack."

His fingers tightened on hers and he rubbed her arm. "I'm so sorry."

"I think it was why I fell for Derek's line so hard. I just missed being close to people. And we had that for a while, but he ruined it."

"If he wasn't raised that way, maybe he didn't know how to deal with it."

"He called me clingy." The thought of the way he shrugged her off flashed through her mind.

"So, he didn't know how to deal with your *affection*," he stressed. "Had you been with anyone before him?"

"I had been with one other guy once, but it didn't develop into anything."

Chad stroked her arm again. "Then you found the exact opposite kind of guy you needed. Abusive, narcissistic and cruel."

Lora choked out a quiet laugh. "I realize that now. Where were you and Cheyenne to tell me this back then?"

Sighing, he rubbed his shoulder into hers.

They fell asleep that way and when Lora woke a few hours later, she was glad that he hadn't taken her up on her offer. It had been impetuous and could have ended in disaster. Chad had known that.

She listened to him snuffle slightly in his sleep. He didn't snore very much, but he didn't seem to actually hit a good relaxing, REM sleep. Though he didn't move from the bed, he moved a lot, turning his head, shifting his shoulders. Twice now he'd gasped and groaned, jerking as though he'd been hit. When Lora tightened her arm across his chest, his arm had tightened between them and he'd settled down.

But then toward morning, the mood of his dreams seemed to change. She thought he moaned her name and his hips flexed upwards. Lora's body heated. He was dreaming about her.

"Oh God," he moaned.

His hips surged up again as if searching and before she could talk herself out of it, she burrowed her hand beneath the sheets and under the waistband of his sweats.

They each cried out at the same time, for different reasons. Chad surged up into her hand and Lora was stunned at the need she felt in his hot body. His right hand covered hers and he surged up again. The delicate skin covering him glided over his rigid length and she pulled away enough to dance her fingers along him, amazed at his size. Chad growled and she wrapped her fingers around him again, moving her fist up and down. His hips surged and released in counterpoint to her movements, getting tighter and tighter to his body. Legs moving restlessly beneath the sheet, he started to pant. Lora looked up at his face in the light from the bedside lamp that they'd never turned off, and her heart contracted. The scrunched look on his face spoke of pain, but the sounds he was making were all pleasure.

She looked down at his hand covering hers and knew he was close. Milky fluid seeped from the end of his dick, giving her strokes a soft clicking sound now. His mouth opened in a wordless cry as his hips surged faster, and then he was there. Bucking, groaning, he ejaculated across his lower belly and their joined hands.

Lora's clit tingled and she almost came herself. Chad's hand that was covering hers fell away, but she continued to work her hand, making him flex and pant, till he pulled away. Lora looked up and found his eyes trying to focus on her. "I guess I should be embarrassed," he told her, "but I'm totally not."

He sat up and looked at the mess on his belly, grinning. "Damn."

Reaching over the side of the bed, he grabbed his discarded shower towel. He took her hand in his and cleaned every finger, smiling at her. Then he moved to the mess on his belly. "I can't believe you did that."

Lora couldn't contain her own grin. Getting him off like that had been empowering, and definitely more satisfying than any other sexual encounter she'd had in years.

She flexed the muscles of her lower core and could feel the lubrication her own arousal had created. Glancing at the alarm clock on the bedside table, she shifted. "I should probably go back to my room."

"Just wait," he told her.

Tossing the towel to the far corner of the room, he laid back down beside her, but kind of up on his elbow. His heated gaze glanced down her body and she knew for a fact he had to have seen the hardness of her nipples. She knew he had when he reached out and danced a fingertip at the very crest of her left breast. Lora jerked at the touch but prayed he would do it again. He did. Slowly circling her nipple, he leaned forward to press a kiss to her shoulder.

"I can feel your need, Lora. Will you let me ease you? Like you eased me? I'll go slow and we'll stop at any time, but I want to make you feel as good as I do right now."

Unable to do anything else, she nodded her head, her eyes sealed shut. "Can you just go slow please?"

Chad nodded immediately, the touch against her nipple retreating. "I won't move on until you tell me to." For several long minutes he glided his hands between her nipples, but didn't do any more than that. The entire time he did it though, he whispered to her. Gentle encouragements and compliments, things she'd never heard from anyone before.

"You are such a perfect handful and your nipples are so hard."

By the time he tugged at the hem of her T-shirt, Lora was ready for him. Levering up, she whipped it over her head, leaving herself bare. If the light had been any brighter, she probably wouldn't have been able to do it. But the bedside lamp had a low-wattage bulb in it, and she was on the shadowed side of the bed.

Chad groaned when he felt the heat of her skin and he leaned down to inhale. Lora shuddered at the feel of his head at her breast and she cupped him to her. As he moved to lave her nipple with his tongue, she cried out, her hips flexing. She felt the touch of his other hand at the waistband of her sleep pants, but he just moved a finger back and forth, tickling, arousing. If he had done anything other than that, she probably would have freaked. He was making it a point that she had to encourage everything he had done to her.

Lora closed her eyes for the briefest second, checking for fear, but there was none present. Not one little speck. Chad was not the kind of man to deliberately hurt a woman.

But he did know how to please them. She knew that even with as little as they'd done.

His gentle, chaste touches at her waist were beginning to drive her insane. Lora flexed her hips, needing his touch to move lower. Instead, he sat up and reached down the length of her legs. He danced his fingers across her ankle, up her shin, all around her knee, then slowly up her inner thigh. With a gentle nudge, he spread her knees.

The muscles of Lora's thighs quivered. His touch through the thin cotton of the sleep pants was maddeningly slow, but she didn't want to speed him up. This moment was too perfect.

Chad lay back down beside her, again taking her breast into his mouth. As he suctioned her deep, he cupped the heat of her pubic area with the width of his hand. Lora cried out at the touch she'd been hoping for and rocked against him. Goosebumps chased all across her body as sensation overwhelmed her. Covering his hand with her own, much as he had minutes before, she rocked against the pressure of his fingers through the cloth, chasing her pleasure. He was patient as she rocked against him for several long minutes, pressing kisses all along her side and across her belly. As her legs started to twitch and shift, he used the barest hint of teeth on her nipple. Lora moaned and arched as her body shattered into a million pieces. She panted for several minutes as her body flooded with joy.

It was the best orgasm she could ever remember having and as she closed her legs around his hand, holding him close, twitching, she knew she wanted another. Reaching up, she dragged his mouth down to hers, turning on her side toward him. Chad was more than willing to accommodate her, slipping his tongue inside to duel with hers. She flexed her hips again and he seemed to understand what she needed without her saying a thing. Removing his hand, he reached for the elastic of her pants, brushing his fingers beneath her waistband. Impatient, she grabbed his hand with her own and wedged it further down, through the wet curls at the juncture of her thighs to rest against her outer labia. Lora cried out as a single finger slid between her lips, and commenced to circling her clit. The aftershocks from the previous orgasm still had her body humming, so when he stroked her clit this time, directly and not through the fabric, it was cataclysmic.

Lora cried out, burrowing her face into his chest as Chad worked his finger high, then low, but he didn't penetrate her. In the crazy back corner of her mind, she made note of that, loving that he was still allowing her control.

He bumped over a particularly good spot and she clutched his hand. "Oh, right there."

Three, four, five times he stroked that same place and scalding heat poured through her as her second climax slammed into her. His touch eased to just the right pressure as she rode the wave then began to calm, until he stopped altogether.

Sighing, more relaxed than she could remember being in years, she reached her arms around him in a giant hug. He withdrew his hand and squeezed her back. His lips nuzzled her ear.

"You are so damn sexy."

Lora's throat tightened with appreciation. Accidently on purpose she brushed her hand down his front, not surprised to find him as hard as before. But he withdrew her hand gently. "I think we've done enough for tonight."

She agreed, but neither one rushed to leave.

"I should go back to my room before Mercy wakes up."

But she hated to move. Chad's arms were so warm. Then he dragged the sheet back over them and she couldn't move.

"Just a little bit longer," he whispered.

Since she was just as reluctant to part, she closed her eyes.

CHAD WOKE AS the sun began to creep through the window. Lora was snuggled in his arms and he hated to disturb the serenity of the morning, but they were going to be interrupted soon. His gaze tracing over her face, he debated leaning down to kiss her, but he didn't want to spook her. Instead, he squeezed her hand.

Lora blinked awake and when she saw him looking down at her, she smiled. It was the most beautiful awakening he had ever seen and he leaned down to press a kiss to her full lips. "We're going to shock some people if we don't get moving."

She stretched her arms over her head and her breasts popped out from beneath the sheet.

Chad groaned and leaned down to lip her nipple. "We are so going to be caught."

Lora giggled and rolled to the side of the bed, scrambling for her discarded t-shirt. Chad shifted to a sitting position, reaching for his leg. Rolling the sleeve over his stub, he positioned his leg over the cup and pressed down.

She stopped in front of him before she opened the door and tilted her chin up, as if waiting for a goodbye. Not wanting to disappoint her, he walked forward and dropped a kiss to her mouth. "Thank you for coming to me." He grinned. "And with me."

Lora gasped, her eyes shining before she shook her finger at him. But her eyes sobered. "I do want to thank you. You knew exactly what I needed last night. More than I did, actually."

He shook his head. "I can't take credit for your courage. If you hadn't come to me, I'd have left you alone until you were ready."

Her eyes watered at his words and she reached up to press a kiss to his lips before stepping out the door.

Chad ached with need, but that was a minor irritation. Lora's wellbeing was paramount, and if a set of blue balls was what it took, than he would do it many times over. That kind of trauma carried its own kind of PTSD. Hopefully she'd gotten counseling for the issue. He would have to ask her about it.

Gathering his jeans and shirt, he headed down the hallway for a quick shower. Yesterday had been surprisingly busy and he wanted to be ready for anything.

In spite of being on heightened alert, nothing happened. Chad knew from previous experience that it wouldn't come until they relaxed their guard. At least, that's how it usually happened.

It was a good thing nothing did happen, because his mind was shit. Thoughts of Lora the night before jogged through at totally inappropriate times, arousing him and leaving him wanting. Yeah, she'd jacked him off, but that just didn't satiate as well as a man and a woman being together.

When he went to bed that night after Lora and Mercy had turned in, he waited, unable to sleep. Every little noise in the house snapped his eyes open. Flynn and Harper were on duty, so he knew that the house was secure, but he wanted Lora to come to him again. She would be satisfied at least as much as last night.

When the alarm clock flipped two a.m., he conceded that she probably was not coming that night.

Then he started to wonder *why* she wasn't coming. Had the night before spooked her? She had come to him, so it wasn't as if he'd coerced her into it. She could have stopped him at any time.

By three a.m. he was tired of worrying and forced his mind blank. He needed to be sharp for the next day.

CHAPTER THIRTEEN

LORA LOOKED UP from the eggs she was beating to watch Chad appear from the hallway. Damn. So lean and tall, with his cowboy boots, he looked like he belonged out here on this wild place. Well, other than the ball cap. She wondered if he ever wore a traditional cowboy hat.

Chad grinned and she realized she was staring. Her cheeks flushed with embarrassment and she looked back at what she was doing. "Do you like scrambled eggs?"

"Of course," he murmured, appearing right beside her.

Lora shook her head. She hadn't even noticed him walk up.

After breakfast they walked outside. Storm clouds were building to the west and Chad frowned.

"What?" she asked.

Shrugging, he gave her a smile. "Nothing, really. Storms are just difficult."

Ah. Yes, they probably would be.

Pulling his cell phone from his pocket, he tapped out a message. "Asking Palmer if he's learned anything."

Then he removed the radio from his belt and keyed the mic, calling Harper back to the cabin. The big man arrived within just a few minutes, weapon cradled in his massive arms. "I'll take a short break and head back up."

Lora got the impression that storms gave perfect cover to the bad guys. Harper ate two plain turkey sandwiches and packed another in a sandwich bag for later. Then he went down the hallway and into the third bedroom, door closing softly behind him. Just a few hours later he came out of the room, stretching as if he'd slept all day. When she asked him if he would like coffee, he nodded his head. He drank it black, standing up and looking out the window, staring as if he could see things she could not.

Lora turned away from him. That cold silver stare of his gave her the shivers. And not in a good way.

When the storm moved in, it hit hard. Spring in Texas could mean blistering heat to snow storms, but most recently it had meant drought. Chad's father had said that they'd had the least amount of rain they'd ever had in the past ten years and that the ranch had suffered. Lora knew they had wells, but she didn't think they were unlimited. The entire family had been hoping for a better rain year.

As she stepped out onto the porch and looked up, she didn't think they meant this. Black clouds roiled across the sky, moving toward them fast. Dust and debris flew through the air and she prayed that the rain would come soon. The maelstrom that led the storm would then hopefully ease. Lightning flashed in the sky and looked too close for comfort.

"We should probably go inside."

Lora glanced up into Chad's worried blue eyes, not even realizing he'd stepped out beside her. Turning to look out over the land one last time, she nodded her head and shoved her whipping hair behind her ears. Just then the rain broke, coming down in pelting sheets to the parched ground. Lora reached her hand out to catch runoff from the roof, giggling as it splashed all over. When she turned back to Chad, he had a funny look on his face. "What?"

The corners of his mouth tipped up slightly. "Nothing. You're just beautiful."

Making a face at him, unwilling to believe he liked the wet, wind-blown look, she shook her head. "You're off your rocker."

Laughing, Chad leaned down enough to press a kiss to her lips. "Maybe."

The radio on his hip squawked to life. "We've got movement on the ranch. Looks like the little blond cowgirl is on her way up."

Chad cursed as the intimacy was broken. Lora could have cursed as well. With a regretful shake of her head, she headed for the front door. "Don't take too long."

Chad gave her a nod before stepping back out to the edge of the porch, just out of reach of the rain. He thought he'd been clear enough that Tara had gotten the message, but here she came.

As the big red truck her daddy bought her turned into the driveway, some twinge in his gut made him check the sidearm at his hip. When the radio squawked again, this time with a burst of sound and several clicks, the hairs stood up on the back of Chad's neck. He couldn't see inside the cab and when the male leg clad in alligator leather boots stepped down onto the muddy driveway, he took a hair too long to recognize the danger for what it was. When he did realize it wasn't Tara, he had a split second to key the emergency button on the mic before he felt the press of a muzzle to his head. A voice he didn't recognize ordered him to place his hands on top of his head.

Derek grinned at Chad as he ran toward the porch, shaking rain from his brand new black hat. Chad felt his sidearm being taken by the grunt behind him, but didn't dare glance back.

"Hey, there, Gimp. How the hell are you?"

Chad didn't respond. He prayed that Rachel had remembered the emergency tone sent through the radio and was even now racing away with Lora and Mercy. Maybe he could distract Derek.

"How's the nose there, buddy?"

Derek's pearly smile never changed. "Oh, great. Nothing a well-paid cosmetic surgeon can't take care of. Oh, wait," he looked pointedly at Chad's burned arm, clasped over his head. "Maybe not everything."

The insult didn't bother Chad, but he let his eyes flash with anger. "How did you find us, you bastard?"

Derek grinned even wider and tapped the brim of the felt hat he'd settled onto his head. "Well, that's a fun story. After Lora ran away with my daughter, we couldn't find her for a while. When she did finally turn up, well, Mother convinced me we had to find a way to keep tabs on her." He leaned against the porch railing. "They really do create some ingenious little tracking devices, you know? Like, tiny enough to fit in a teddy bear or something."

Chad felt a sinking sensation in the pit of his stomach. Damn.

Handsome. As conceited as Derek was, he had a feeling he could get him to talk about anything. He took a chance. "How is your mother, by the way?"

Derek's smile turned cunning. "Ah well, Mother met a sad end. I'm in mourning, can you tell?" He tapped the brim of the black hat. "But I'm excited to finally be back with my family. Where are they, Mr. Lowell?"

Chad looked out at the rain and shook his head. "I don't know, Mr. Malone."

Anger flashed in Derek's pale gray eyes. "We can play this game nicely or not so nicely. Which would you prefer? You may want to make your decision quickly because your lookout up on the hill needs medical attention, I'm told."

Chad went cold. That last burst of noise *had* been Harper. God, he hoped he was okay. "Lora and the girl aren't here. We're on a training mission."

With a skeptical look, Derek reached into his pockets to jingle the coins inside.

"Well, we have an issue, then. I can't leave without the girl, and as of a few hours ago, she was right here at this building. Just where did she go?"

Chad frowned at the shorter man, imagining wrapping his hands around his neck. He shrugged in response. The slam of a fist into his lower kidney bent him over for a long minute, but he straightened. "I don't know where she is."

A uniformed guard, hell, a mercenary in a black mask came out of the front door and shook his head at Derek. "They are not inside the building."

Running his gaze up and down the intruder, Chad realized he was sorely outgunned. These men were loaded for bear. The tall merc in front of him had an MP-6 submachine gun in his hands, a 9mm on his hip, and several canisters hanging from the nylon straps securing his black uniform. And he held the weapon as if it were an extension of his arm. But as competent as he was, the man had not found the girls.

Chad refused to smile, but it took all of his control. He could tell

Derek was livid by the way the blood suffused his face.

"I want this place scoured from top to bottom. She has to be here."

The faintest hint of panic laced his words and Chad wondered what he didn't know. "Why are you after them? They don't want you."

Derek flashed his teeth in a smile. "It doesn't matter if they want me or not, they're going to get me. It's time that I took a stronger interest in my daughter's life and if Lora doesn't want that…" He smiled and shrugged. "Well, she can just step out of the picture."

"She won't let you have Mercy. Ever."

"Then I'll take her. And Lora can take a leap off a cliff. Or maybe have a car accident. We'll have to see how she welcomes me back."

Chad's blood began to boil and it got harder to control himself. The guard behind him seemed to sense the building tension because he pressed the muzzle tighter to Chad's head and tightened his other hand on top of Chad's clasped ones. In spite of the warnings, though, Chad knew something was going to happen if Derek kept talking.

Thunder rumbled overhead and lightning flashed. Derek flinched and looked around him at the unrelenting weather. It was just easing into evening and the light was beginning to fade. The second masked guard had disappeared back into the house. Chad had no idea how many men were with Derek and he had no idea where Flynn was.

There were too many unknowns to try anything. The only good he could draw from the situation was that he was taller than the man standing behind him. He could feel the angle of the arm holding his hands and he didn't understand why the guy didn't secure him somehow. Inexperience?

He thought he heard one of the horses whicker, but couldn't be sure over the sound of the rain. If they had by chance made it to the barn, they could go out the back and into the scrub. There were trees on the mountainside, but it wasn't really forested. There were long open areas between each of the trees and little cover.

Chad watched Derek pace the deck and noted that he stayed close to the edge, as if he was worried about coming too close to Chad. That made him unaccountably happy.

He shifted a little, just to see what kind of play he had in his movement. Not much. The guy shifted behind him, as if readying himself.

There was a burst of sound from inside the house. Chad didn't wait to see what it was; he spun into action. Ducking straight down, he jacked his left arm up into the merc's gun hand. Though it went off when the merc flinched, Chad was well outside of range. He grabbed the gun hand and slammed it down over his knee. The weapon dropped to the ground, but the merc shifted into a ready stance, then charged. Chad let him come, wrapped his arms around his charging form and twisted, using his height to fling the merc away. As soon as the other man lost his balance, Chad lunged, landing several sharp punches to the guy's jaw and ribs.

A gun discharged behind him and pain blazed across the back of his right shoulder. Rolling away from the threat, he slammed into the front of the house, but got his legs under him quickly. The gun went off again, but he didn't have a chance to duck. Luckily, it seemed to go wide. When he turned to look at the source of the attack, he saw Flynn ripping the weapon from Derek's hand and slamming a fist into his face. The other man went down hard, senseless.

The merc lunged, but Chad had seen the movement from the corner of his eye. Twisting, he slammed his right hand down into the guy's jaw. It struck just right, because the guy fell to the porch, out cold.

Scrabbling sounds came from inside the house, then another blast of gunfire, muffled this time. Flynn rolled toward the house and when he raised up, the gun was in his hands, aimed at the door.

When Rachel lunged out of the doorway, gun raised to mirror Flynn's, they both jerked away at the same time. Chad was dismayed to see she had blood running down her head and even more blood running, sheeting against her shirt on the right hand side. Her eyes were clear and determined though as she met Chad's gaze. "I got them out the back, told them to head toward the barn, but I don't know if they made it."

Chad swung around and cursed out loud. Derek was gone. He

snatched up the 9mm the merc had tossed away. "Take care of her, Flynn."

Rachel shook her head. "I'm good. This is fine. Go get the bastards."

Leaping from the porch to the muddy driveway, he took off, running as fast as this leg would allow him to go. The rain was coming down in sheets, ending the terrible dry spell Texas had been suffering under, but making it incredibly hard on him to do his job. Derek was nowhere to be seen. He'd only had a few moments to get away, so he couldn't have gotten far, but the visibility could be measured in feet right now rather than miles. He pushed his boots as fast as he could pump them toward the barn. Flynn veered to the opposite corner to sneak around the back.

As he neared the open doorway, Chad checked his weapon and slipped inside. The relief from the pelting of the rain was significant, but the barn was even darker than outside. Daring to reach his hand out, he flipped the light switch.

The horses shifted a bit, and seemed aggravated, but that could be because of the storm. He debated grabbing his gelding and taking off into the rain, but he'd make an incredible target then. They still didn't know how many hostiles were outside.

Chad took the time to go stall to stall, checking for anybody hiding out. Flynn met him on the far side. "It's empty and nobody has come through here."

A flicker on movement caught their attention and a black-clad form ghosted through the trees about twenty-five yards away.

"Fuck," Chad breathed. He nodded Flynn after him and headed out into the rain again.

Tracking was useless. Intuition told him to head toward the rocky outcroppings that might offer some protection. Paralyzing fear tried to take over several times, but he forced it away. Lora and Mercy were out there alone with that jackass, and he needed taken out.

The slippery mud was giving him fits and he knew it would be even worse for Lora, because she would be towing, if not carrying Mercy.

Chad climbed, eyes searching, skin stinging from the pelting rain. Finally, finally, it began to ease, until suddenly it stopped as abruptly as it started. The lack of sound was deafening. It allowed him to hear the echo of a little girl's scream.

Adrenaline pounded through his veins and he turned in the direction he thought it had come from, further up the hill.

The mud had turned slimy and his boots were not the best for climbing, but he forced his body faster. Fear gave him propulsion and he prayed he could get there in time.

If Mercy was screaming, Derek had found them.

He almost ran over them when he did finally find them. Lora and Mercy were under the boughs of a pine tree, scrambling away from Derek, who was on the ground reaching for them. Chad holstered his gun, grabbed the man's legs and dragged him out. He tripped and landed on his ass with Derek's legs sprawled over top of him. The other man took the opportunity to swing a fist toward Chad, but he dodged the blow. Rolling away, he scrambled to his feet and then leapt on top of Derek, slamming his right fist into him as fast as he could. Bones crunched and the other man's head lolled on his shoulders. Letting him slump to the ground, Chad waited, but he seemed to be unconscious. Levering himself off the other man, Chad staggered back, aware that his body was throbbing with pain. Though he'd been on top, Derek had definitely gotten in some blows.

Chad turned to scan the area for other threats and heard Lora cry out, then there was a blast of sound. When he turned back around, he realized Derek hadn't been out cold as he'd pretended. Chad looked at the knife in the unconscious man's limp hand, and the huge tree limb hanging from Lora's. Blood coated the end of the wood, glistening in the evening light, and he was a little shocked at what she'd done. But appreciative. He moved to the man's side and without even checking for a pulse, knew that he was gone. There was a crater in his head the size of a softball. He pressed his fingers to the carotid artery and confirmed what he suspected. Derek was dead.

Chad looked up at Lora and saw the knowledge in her eyes, but he also saw the disbelief. With one blow, she'd ended years of torment and subjugation. As Mercy climbed out from underneath the tree and clutched her mother's legs, he saw the fear of what she had done change to fierce satisfaction. She had protected her daughter to the end.

When he heard the report of weapon fire, he lunged forward to wrap himself around the two of them and took the brunt of the fall on his side. Half a dozen more shots, sounding different than the first, echoed across the mountain before silence moved in. He peered over his shoulder.

Brock was just swinging down off his dark gelding and Flynn was moving in from the house side of the hill. Chad couldn't believe his eyes. What did Brock think he was doing?

"What the hell are you doing up here?"

Brock took off his dripping hat as he peered down dazedly at the black clad merc he'd just shot, then looked up. "Tara came up to the house. She'd been bound and gagged and her truck had been stolen, but she managed to get loose and make it to help. I knew something was going on so I came up the mountain."

Chad looked at the gelding again. It was breathing hard and lathered. He'd raced up the mountain it looked like.

Lora shifted and he moved, setting them away from him. "Did I hurt you?"

She shook her head, her bedraggled hair hanging down into her face. "We're fine. Is that all of them?"

He looked at the mercenary on the ground. Flynn was checking his pockets and unloading the weapon the man had carried, but even from here Chad could see the man's life had already leaked away. "We need to contact law enforcement. We've got a hell of a mess to explain."

LORA WATCHED YET another truck pull into the driveway and pull into the yard. They had been coming and going for hours. First it had been the local sheriff's department, and then it had been the FBI. The federal agency had had Derek under surveillance for the past several weeks. Months, actually. Duncan's quiet probes had spurred them to focus their attention.

After they'd come down off the mountain, she'd given Mercy a bath, but her little one didn't want to go to bed alone. Which was why she was curled up on the couch, even in the midst of the chaos around her, sound asleep. She stroked her hand over Mercy's feet, where they rested on the cushion beside her. At Chad's request, Garrett had brought up an old bear that had belonged to Chad years ago and she'd taken to it instantly. Handsome had been gutted, revealing the tiny black box GPS Derek had tracked them with, and placed into an evidence bag. Chad had explained that the receiver had had enough battery life to send a single ping every day. Just enough for Derek to keep tabs on them.

A black coroner's van had arrived to collect the dead. Ambulances had arrived to collect the living. Harper had had to be flown out by Careflight to Amarillo, and she prayed that the big former SEAL would be okay. He'd been struck in the chest with a round and from the look on the other's faces, it didn't look good. There'd been a lot of blood. She'd known that. Flynn had been the one to find him and his pale eyes were more haunted than normal.

Rachel had been grazed by a shot from the mercenary she'd been fighting with. Probably had a broken rib, but she would be sore more than anything. Lora wished she could have seen the woman kick the guy's ass, but she'd been a little busy then.

A cup of coffee appeared in front of her and she looked up at Chad's older brother, Brock. She gave him a tight smile as she took the cup. "Thank you very much."

He lowered himself to the chair catty-corner from the couch. "Are you doing okay?"

She nodded, cradling the cup to her. The coffee was scalding hot, but she was still chilled, even after the shower and bundling up. "Warming up. This will help."

Brock cradled his own mug, looking down into the liquid without seeing anything.

Lora frowned. "I'm curious why you came to help? I didn't think you liked your brother."

His dark navy eyes swung to hers. "Is that what you thought? That I didn't like my brother?" Frowning fiercely, he shook his head. "It's quite the opposite, actually. I just…never knew how to relate to him. He did everything I wanted to do, had a girl who loved him, did what he wanted."

"Didn't you have that option as well?"

Frowning at her, he shook his hand and ran a hand through his curls, darker than Chad's by a few shades. "I was always expected to be the one to take over, and don't get me wrong, I love my life here. But I never had the chance to live like he did."

Lora felt like she was wading through personal issues that the two brothers needed to hash out. Was this even her business?

"Honestly," he continued, "I think it's envy that has ruled us for so long. But how can I even say that when he returned wounded?"

Lora felt a presence move up beside her and looked up at Chad's quizzical expression. He looked at his brother as if he'd never met him before. "What the fuck are you saying?"

Brock winced and looked at his little brother. "Nothing, Chad."

"Why didn't you tell me any of this? Better yet, why didn't you join up to experience it yourself?"

"And leave Dad here alone? Who would have run the place?"

Chad gave him a disbelieving look. "Dad. Do you seriously think he couldn't do it?"

Brock just shook his head. "You don't understand."

"I think you put a lot of expectations on yourself and what you think people wanted for you but never bothered to talk to the people involved."

Frowning, his older brother sat back in the chair. "Maybe," he agreed softly.

The agreement obviously set Chad back. Brock had the typical older sibling personality, used to taking on responsibility.

Lora watched the two of them interact and wondered at it. She'd never had that understanding with anybody and marveled at the conversation she could see silently taking place between the two of them.

Chad held his hand out to his brother. "Don't waste your life wishing things had been different. Change the now."

Brock took his brother's hand with a nod. "I will. Hey, did you mean what you said to Tara? She told me she came up here the other day and you turned her away."

Chad's brows lifted in surprise. "I did." He glanced at Lora. "I'm in a long term relationship and off the market."

Sighing, Brock fingered the fabric of the chair he was sitting in. "I always thought the two of you would end up together."

Chad made a face and grinned. "I think that's what Tara thought too."

Brock stood up from the chair and held his hand out again to his kid brother, but Chad tugged him into one of those back-slapping man hugs. Lora couldn't help but smile as they stepped apart.

CHAPTER FOURTEEN

THE FBI AGENT in charge was a ball buster. Frank Calhoun, *Special Agent Calhoun*, Chad was reminded, didn't like that a private security company had messed with his investigation. No matter how good they were. After listening to hours of snide comments and fielding dirty looks, Chad asked him to step outside.

Calhoun, sorry, *Special Agent Calhoun*, had directed too many investigations to be circumvented. As Chad squared in front of the man on the front porch of the house, he forced himself not to try to wave away the smoke the man was blowing in his face or to crow about the collar. Yes, Derek, the focus of their investigation was dead, but they had two mercenaries in custody that were wanted by a dozen different agencies around the world.

"And you have enough evidence here," he waved a hand around the house, "to put them in lockup in this country for sixty years."

Special Agent Calhoun ran a hand through his thinning hair. "You should have contained him when you had the chance."

"You mean when I was fighting to get him away from Ms. O'Neil and her daughter on the mountainside? And I had a guy firing behind me?"

"Yes," the man snapped. "You lost a valuable target. He had a list of charges as long as my arm waiting for him, but you give us these penny-ante crooks instead. Malone had embezzled millions. Murdered his mother."

Chad leaned over the man, getting in his face. "And he beat the shit out of his ex. Where were you when he was trying to force himself on her three weeks ago? And where were you each time he violated that damn protection order she had against him?"

Calhoun's jaw clenched. "We would have blown the investigation if we had stepped in at that time."

Shaking his head in disbelief, Chad planted his hands on his hips. "So she was an acceptable casualty? And the daughter was an acceptable casualty."

Chad knew by the look in the other man's eyes that he was right. Bastards. "Get what evidence you can and get out of here. I need to get to the hospital to check on my man. Another casualty because you didn't step in sooner."

Turning, he headed inside the house. Calhoun tried to call him back but he ignored the man.

Duncan would have been proud of him. God, Duncan. Boss man had not been happy when he'd called hours ago, when all the crap went down. But he'd understood. Chad could hear it in his voice.

As soon as he could break away, he would be driving to Amarillo, where they'd flown Harper. The need to call the hospital again needled at Chad, but he knew he would get no more information than he had last time. He needed to be on site to get the info he needed. Flynn said that it looked like Harper had been shot twice. Close range. Luckily, the shooter hadn't been as good as Harper himself. If the man recovered it would be a hell of a story.

Chad's gut clenched, but he forced himself to walk inside fairly normally.

Lora was asleep on the couch. Most of the people had left, other than Flynn and a nameless agent at the kitchen table. Even as he watched the man received a text message, then gathered up the forms he was filling out. With a final nod, he left the house.

Through the front bay window, Chad watched the line of nondescript vehicles turn and head down the mountain. They'd tramped everything into the ground, collected all available evidence, and left a mess in their wake. Brock and his father had left long ago.

Rubbing his eyes, he looked up at the moon. It had to be creeping on toward three a.m., but he was restless as hell. Lora had curled up on the couch with Mercy and he took a minute to ease another blanket over the two of them. Now that the threat of Derek was gone, they needed to head back to Colorado.

Flynn sat at the kitchen table nursing a cup of black coffee. He was the only one who had escaped injury completely, lucky bastard. Bruises were developing all over Chad's body from the fights and his right kidney ached like a mother. Lora had patched up the scratch on his shoulder. And his leg was chafing. He just didn't have time to take care of it.

"Are you able to get them back? I have to head to Amarillo to check on Preston."

Flynn nodded. "Of course. I expected you to." He surveyed his boss up and down. "You may want to shower first. Harper's not moving for a while."

Chad looked down his body and realized he still had on the same clothes he'd started the morning with. He sighed. Another delay. "Yeah. I'll go clean up and gather my crap. I'll call Brock in the morning and send him up for the horses. Take your time heading back. We don't have to race anymore."

Flynn gave that single, somber nod and went back to staring into his coffee.

"Are you okay?" Chad asked.

For a moment, when Flynn looked at him, he felt like there were many things unsaid that he needed to let out, but then his eyes chilled. "I'm fine. Go get your shower, boss man."

Chad took his man's suggestion and went to clean up, even taking the time to scrub and care for his amputation. He rinsed the sleeve of rainwater and threw it into the dryer for a few minutes. Not the suggested practice, but he needed to get moving.

Half an hour later he stroked his hand down Lora's shoulder. She needed her sleep, but he wanted to reassure her before he left.

Her bright green eyes blinked up at him, puffy from sleep. "Is everything okay?"

Chad knelt on the floor beside the couch. "Yes, I just wanted to let you know what was going on. I have to head north to check on Harper. We are his family, as far as I know, and I need to be with him."

She nodded and reached out to rest her hand on his shoulder. "Of course you do. We'll be fine."

"Flynn and Rachel will drive you back to Colorado to your house. They will stay with you until you feel safe enough to let them go. There is no timeline," he stressed. "I want you to feel secure in your home."

She nodded her head against the pillow. "Thank you for that. I saw his dead body, but I know I'm going to be a little stressed going back."

"Which I'm sure is completely normal. I would too. Take your time going back to work. Hell, you may think about just having a few days fun with Mercy. Do things you've not allowed yourself before." He tipped his chin at the little girl curled in front of her. "She deserves to take some time too."

Tears filled Lora's eyes and rolled down her temples and he had to lean forward to press a kiss to her lips. "And as soon as I can, I will come to you. This separation is not the end of us, just so you know."

He winked at her and kissed her again harder, thrilled when she responded. She even looped her arm around his neck to pull him closer for a moment, before releasing him with a stroke down his cheek.

Mercy shifted and looked up at him. "You're gonna go see Harper?"

Chad nodded. "Then I'll meet you at your house in a few days."

Wiggling, the little girl dragged Chad's old classic teddy, the one he'd given her to replace Handsome when the FBI ripped him open, out from beneath the blanket. She pushed the bear at him. "You need to take this to him. He needs it more than I do right now."

Throat tightening because he knew how important the bear was to her, Chad took it from her. "Are you sure?"

Mercy nodded her head. "He'll need it until his family gets there. They live a long ways away."

Frowning, he shook his head. "I don't think he has family, Mercy. Did he tell you he did?"

She nodded again. "You need to find them."

Chad leaned over and pressed a kiss to Mercy's little blond head before pushing to his feet. Grabbing his bag, and with a chin nod to Flynn, he walked out the door.

As he drove north toward Amarillo, his heart thudded in his chest in protest. He hated leaving them behind.

"It's only for a little while," he whispered to himself.

DUNCAN SWIVELED HIS chair to look out the office window, eyes scanning the distant streets. Chad had just called him to let him know everything that had gone on. Worry hollowed out his stomach and he wondered how the hell Harper had left himself so open. The guy was a machine. That somebody had gotten the drop on him was truly something.

He rolled back to look at the whiteboard across the office. He didn't need to be anywhere important in the next few days.

When he called Shannon in, she had a slip of paper in her hand. "I knew you would want to be with Harper, so I've made your flight. You only have an hour and a half this time so you need to get your sexy butt moving."

Duncan knew his brows popped in surprise and he looked at her askance, feeling anything but sexy. Actually, he felt more tired than he could remember being in a long time.

With a heavy sigh, he pushed to his feet. He snapped his tablet closed and placed it in the case he carried for it. As he walked toward Shannon, he tried to look more awake than he felt, but she stopped him with a hand on his arm. "I know you've been down about something. If there's anything I can do to help, you just have to say something."

Smiling, he shook his head. "You already do more than you need to Shannon and I really appreciate it."

"Well," she told him softly. "If you need anything, just let us know."

He nodded, throat tight and walked past her. John met him at the elevator and took his hand. "Don't worry about anything, Dunc. Tell

Harper he needs to get his ass back to work."

Grinning, Duncan stepped onto the elevator. "I will. I'll call when I know something."

John nodded and tossed him a salute as the elevator closed.

Duncan walked through the doors of Northwest Hospital in Amarillo and seriously tried not to be swamped by a sense of futility. No matter where he went or what he did, he always ended up in hospitals. Even in the vestibule, the scent of disinfectant was enough to turn his stomach.

The volunteer desk directed him to a waiting room on the fourth floor. Harper was in surgery now and would be for many hours to come, assuming he survived. As soon as he walked into the room, Chad pushed to his feet and moved to meet him. If the handshake was a little tighter than normal, or the hug a little longer, neither of them said a word.

"Have you heard anything?"

Chad shook his head and sat back in the chair he had been in. There was a raggedy bear sitting in the seat beside him and he picked it up to rub the ears. "They took him into surgery before I got here."

They settled in to wait. A nurse came out at one point to update them on the non-news. As dawn came and went, they dozed, hands propped on fists.

Right around dawn, a doctor appeared. Tall and gray haired, he had the competent air of someone who had seen lives come and go. "Are you here with Mr. Harper?"

Duncan nodded and pushed to his feet. "We are."

The doctor propped his hands on his hips and went into the list of everything that was wrong with their buddy. By the time he was done, Chad felt no better for the knowing. After hours in the operating room, Dr. Reynolds gave him a very slim chance at life.

"Can we see him?" Duncan murmured.

The doctor led them down a hallway to the right and into a room. Even ass out cold, Preston Harper dwarfed the bed he laid upon. A respirator hissed rhythmically at the side of the bed. IV lines fed into both sides of his body. His entire head was swathed with bandages. "I can't candy coat this," the doctor said softly. "He is very seriously injured. The best news I can give you is that one of the bullets that entered his chest didn't do as much damage as we had initially thought. He still has…"

The room door swished open and a woman stepped inside. She was tall and lean, with short dark hair and a furious frown on her face. "Where is he?"

Chad looked at Duncan, hoping that he knew who the woman was, but boss man shrugged and lifted his hands. The woman didn't wait for them to respond. Dodging around them, she shoved her way deeper into the room.

"Oh…my…" she whispered. A hand lifted to cover her mouth as she moved closer to the figure on the bed. Then she reached out with both hands and leaned over to skim her fingers down his body.

"Ma'am," the doctor said. "I don't know who you are but you can't be in here."

The woman glared at him over her shoulder. "I most certainly can. I don't know what he's told you or not told you, but my name is Cat Harper. I'm his wife."

Chad looked at Duncan, hoping he had some insight, but he had the same dumbstruck expression on his face Chad knew was on his own.

Harper had a wife? What the fuck?

LORA WISHED FOR Chad's calming presence. It had been three days and they were beginning to get anxious, and this didn't help. She stared at the letter in her hand. It was from a law office in New York City that represented the Malone estate. They wanted to meet with her.

There were no other details, just that they would come to her in three day's time and if that was not convenient to let them know and they would reschedule.

Anxiety crept through her gut. She wondered what the hell they wanted with her.

Pulling her cell phone from her pocket, she pulled up the home screen in the hopes that she'd missed a text from Chad. No luck. Thumbing the screen, she debated sending him something, but didn't want to bother him if he was in with Harper.

The big man had survived several surgeries to repair damage to his lung, liver and bowel, but the other bullet had struck his weapon and sent metal fragments into his face and eyes. He was still under heavy sedation. But surprisingly a woman claiming to be Harper's wife had shown up.

As if in answer to her thoughts, her phone buzzed in her hand.

Heading home today. I'll say bye to my parents and be back 10ish.

Lora pursed her mouth, wondering if it would be too forward to invite him over.

I would like to see you, she typed. A little generic and understated, but true.

Ok!

As she moved through the day, she watched the clock like a mad woman. When she told Mercy Chad was coming, she squealed and raced through the house, as excited as Lora to see him.

"But he may not get here till after your bedtime."

Mercy scowled then clasped her hands together in front of her little chest. "Can I stay up late? Pleeeeeaase?"

With a resigned shake of her head, Lora agreed that she could, but the little girl was asleep on the floor in front of the TV by nine. When there was a knock on her door at ten, Lora crossed the room to look out of the security hole, then disabled the new alarm that the agency had installed while she'd been gone. As soon as Chad stepped in, she walked into his open arms, totally unable to help herself. Wrapping her arms around his waist, she finally let herself relax.

"I missed you," she whispered.

Chad stroked her back and she felt none of the anxiety she used to. "I missed you too, baby."

She pulled him into the house and re-engaged the alarm system. "Thank you for this, by the way."

Chad grinned at her. "Like that, do you? Palmer picked it out for you and the man is a genius with that kind of stuff. It'll work well for you. And give you peace of mind."

Lora was suddenly attacked by nerves. "Can I get you something to drink or eat?"

Shaking his head, Chad crossed the room to stand over Mercy. "She tried to stay up?"

Lora nodded. "She thought she could do it, but she fell asleep an hour ago."

"Can I carry her to bed?"

She nodded again and watched as he gathered her daughter into his strong arms. Mercy roused and smiled up at him. "Hi, Chad. I waited for you to get here. How's Mr. Harper?"

Chad glanced over her head to Lora, but she shook her head. She hadn't told Mercy anything about Harper, only that he'd been injured.

"He's a strong man. I think he'll be okay but it may take a while. And I'm sure the bear will help."

Mercy blinked at him and nuzzled her head into his chest as he carried her down the hallway. After tucking her into bed, he followed Lora back into the living room and sighed as he settled onto her couch. Lora sat in the corner opposite from him. "How is he really?"

Chad shook his head and scrubbed a hand over his face. "I think he'll be okay but it's going to take a while. One bullet went down through his body and caused a lot of damage. Recoverable but significant. The second bullet hit his gun and shattered the scope. Glass embedded in his face and a couple of pieces went into his eyes. They did one surgery but I think they're going to schedule another with a specialist. Something about his retina detaching. Not a good situation for a sniper."

Lora frowned. "And he doesn't have family?"

"Well, a woman showed up claiming to be his wife. And she seems really concerned about him. But it's very odd. I've worked with him for a couple years now and he's never said anything about any family."

"That's really sad. If he needs anything please let me know. I feel very guilty that he got hurt watching us."

Chad shrugged. "It's part of the job. He knew that."

He reached out to play with her fingers. "And how are you doing? Settling in?"

She nodded. "Flynn and Rachel were here for a day, but I sent them away once I got the hang of the security system. Rachel stopped by yesterday just to check on us. We have plans for lunch together next week. I think Mercy can tell a difference, too. We're going to be okay."

Scoffing, he tightened his fingers on her own. "Of course you are. I have no worries about that."

Lora pulled his hand into her lap. "I still want to see you, though."

He cocked a dark brow at her. "Well, you're not likely to get rid of me in the near future."

Warmth filled her chest at his words and she smiled, then dared to lean forward and press a kiss to his lips.

His bright eyes flashed and when she would have pulled away, he cupped her head and kissed her deeper. Lora didn't mind. Actually, she relished the contact and flirted with the idea of inviting him to her room.

When he didn't immediately release her from the kiss, the idea grew. She'd missed him a lot over the few days they'd been apart. Flashes of what they'd done lying in bed days ago flashed through her mind, ramping up her arousal. One of Chad's broad hands brushed her nipple and she froze, relishing the hot need that slammed into her.

Chad pulled back, thinking she'd stilled for another reason, but she grabbed his hand as he started to pull away. "No, don't stop, I just wanted to bask in what you stir in me. I can't believe I'm not freaking out at your touch. I love it."

He grinned, his eyes creasing with his laughter. "Glad I don't repulse you."

Cringing, she stroked his cheek again. "I don't mean it like that. You know that."

Chad stilled in front of her. "I know, Lora. And I don't mean to make light of the situation. It's just that I can hardly breathe for wanting you. And I'm nervous."

The thought of the tall, self-contained man in front of her being anxious about her, about them, made her pause. She'd never held that kind of power over a man before and she felt lacking. He needed a woman that could meet him step for step.

No, you need to be the woman he needs.

Lora didn't know where she got the strength to take his hand from her own, tug him up from the couch, then down the hallway behind her. Maybe it was the incredible anticipation that had built in her body as she'd waited for him to arrive. Maybe it was the simple desire to be looked at as a strong, vital woman again, rather than a female that needed taken care of. The thought of a future Mercy being in the same situation made her pray to know how to pass on this tenuous strength, so that her daughter would never find herself in the position of having to fight back from this somber place Lora found herself in.

Shoving as much of the crap she could behind the doors to her soul, she glanced over her shoulder. Chad was gorgeous. Though he seemed tired from driving and worry, his eyes were creased with that inner charm that had appealed to her at first. His hair was mussed and had grown in the month that she'd known him, but the curls looked good with his lean face. But what made him most spectacular was the way his expression lit up when he looked at her. He grinned as he followed her.

As they crossed the threshold to her pale blue bedroom, she had the slightest hesitation that the two of them together would bring back flashbacks, but she pushed through it. She had forced herself to sleep in the room for the past three nights, and she hadn't had any issues. If she dreamt of anything, it was Derek keeling over on that mountain-side, the bloody tree limb in her hands. She usually woke then, not because she was scared, but because she was amazed at what she'd done.

Chad glanced around the room. "Are you sure…"

Instead of answering him, Lora slipped her sweater from her shoulders and tossed it aside. Then, reaching for the buttons on her blouse, she popped them, one by one until the sides of her shirt draped her. As she moved to shrug it away as well, Chad stilled her.

"Please," he rumbled. "Let me."

Lora let her hands hang to her sides and let him do what he wanted.

Chad's lean fingers traced from her upper chest down, pushing the edges of the shirt wide as he went toward her breasts. They caught on the cups of her bra, then jumped over them to trace down her torso. Reaching back up to her shoulders, he lifted the yoke of the shirt and let it fall down her back.

Lora shivered, but not from fear. He looked at her as if she were his sun; as if he would die without her. His movements stilled and she looked up into his face, shocked to see his eyes glistening with tears.

"I don't want to hurt you, Lora. You've been through so much and I'm willing to wait. We don't have to do this tonight."

Daring to reach out and cup the erection she could see through his heavy jeans, she stepped closer. "You won't hurt me, Chad. I won't let you."

Grinning through his worry, he dropped a kiss to her mouth. "I love you, Lora. And your courageous heart."

Tears choked her then and she had to wrap herself around him. "You helped me find my courageous heart and I can't thank you enough for that. I want you to love me, Chad. And I want to love you back."

She reached out and brushed her hands over his broad shoulders, then down the front of his shirt. His buttons released easily. As she tugged the shirttails from the waistband of his jeans, he cupped her elbows in his hands. Gathering her hands in his, he held them clasped in his own and pressed a kiss to the knot of their fingers. "You're supposed to be letting me do this," he reminded her.

Lora grinned. "Then get to it."

Reaching around behind her, he found the hooks to her bra and released them, one at a time, slowly. Lora tipped up her chin and concentrated on not moving. Her hands came to rest on his sides and she tightened her fingers convulsively as the last hook released and he started to tug the straps down her shoulders. When her breasts felt the cool air, they puckered even more than they already were. Tossing the bra toward the corner, he reached out with both hands to cup her breasts, sweeping his thumbs over the nipples. Lora closed her eyes, savoring the rush of heat that swept through her. God, he felt good. Even the scars on his left hand provided a texture that caught on the tip of her breast, rasping.

Lora's knees wavered and she had to focus enough to stand firm. "You better hurry, Chad. I can't stand much longer."

The words had barely left her mouth when he was on his knees in front of her. Agile fingers reached for the waistband of her pants, tugging to unfasten the button and roll down the zipper. Lora shuddered as he swept her pants down over the swell of her hips. For the first time, anxiety crept in. She was not perfect, by any means. And if there was one area of her body she was self-conscious of, it was the area of her belly that had expanded with pregnancy. For the most part, it had retightened, but she'd been left with silver stretch marks. Unable to help herself, she rested her hand over her belly.

Chad looked up at her, blue eyes shining in the light of the bedside lamp. "Seriously? You think I'm going to begrudge you some marks? They gave you Mercy. How can you be ashamed of those?"

She blinked and realized he was completely right. They had given her an amazing little girl. Her hands fell to his head and she smoothed her fingers over the curls.

Chad urged her to step out of her pants and socks and when she stood bare before him, he reached up to tangle his fingers in the pale swirling hair at her sex. "You're so damn beautiful."

Pushing to his feet, he cupped her head in his hands and rested his mouth on hers, moving his lips slowly back and forth. When his tongue slipped out to nudge at the seam of her lips, she allowed him in, surging against him greedily. Her breasts were tight against his chest, but she didn't mind. Allowing her hands to wander down his body, she went after his jeans button again. "You are overdressed."

Grinning against her mouth, he pulled away and held his hands up innocently. "What are you going to do about it?"

She attacked the fastening with a vengeance, popping the button and dragging the zipper down forcefully enough that his body shifted with her movements. She made the same movement he had, sweeping her hands inside the waistband and down over his taut backside, pushing the pants down over his hips. "Sit down."

Turning, he dropped to the edge of the mattress. She worked his jeans down as far as they would go around his calves, revealing the prosthesis on his left leg. "Tell me how to take this off."

The fun and charm was suddenly gone from his expression, leaving only narrow-eyed watchfulness. He lifted his left leg to her. "Just pull on the boot. It will unseal, then you roll the sock down and off."

She did as he instructed and set the piece of equipment to the side, then tugged off his second boot. She tossed his jeans to the side then tugged on the tube sock of his right foot. Unable to help herself, she dragged her fingernails along the sole of his foot as she peeled it off. With a yelp, he jerked his foot away. "What the hell was that for?"

Lora grinned, thrilled to have found a chink in his put-together armor. "Just checking."

Chad laughed and lifted her up to kneel before him, dropping a kiss to her nose. "I give you fair warning. If you do that again, I'll have to retaliate."

She widened her eyes. "Oh, no. How would you do that?"

He frowned at her and lifted one brow dramatically. "Maybe I will eat you out until you scream maraschino cherry."

The play waned at the thought of him doing that to her, and the playfulness left his face as well. Her breathing accelerated.

"I want you to do that anyway."

The words had barely left her mouth when he switched their positions, carefully, gently. Kneeling in front of her, he wedged himself between her knees, then pressed carefully against her chest. Stretching out on the mattress, anticipation darted through her. She looked down the length of her body, trying to memorize every sensation.

Chad looked up at her with hooded eyes, his broad hands cupping her breasts. As she watched him, he plumped them together for a quick kiss, then swooped his hands into the hollow of her waist. He spanned them against her and brushed over the swell of her belly to the pale hair he'd teased earlier. With a single finger, he drew curlicues against the sensitive skin, moving closer and closer to her moist heat.

Lora shifted her hips, trying to get him to move there more quickly, but he apparently had a plan in mind. Snugging his nose into her pubic bone, he breathed the scent of her deep. If he hadn't glanced up at her just then, with pure sex in his eyes, she'd have freaked. But instead, she took a deep breath and held on.

Chad knew his way around a woman's body. Lora should have known he'd be wonderful at this. He was wonderful at everything he did. Her legs fell open and her body twitched as he ran his tongue from top to bottom of her slit, moaning against her. Lora felt her body loosen even more at his obvious enjoyment. Shifting beneath his mouth, she allowed her enjoyment free rein, not worried about anything other than the pleasure that was building in her.

"Oh, hell," she moaned, rolling her pelvis up.

Chad slid both hands beneath her ass and tilted her into his touch. Lora began to pant, because he was right there where she needed him. Yes, right there. *Right there.*

The orgasm that crashed into her was more visceral than any other she'd ever had. For a long, drawn out moment, time stilled, then slammed past her. She gasped and arched on the bed, tears trailing down her temples and into her hair as wave after swell of hedonistic joy shuddered through her. Chad eased his touch, but continued to press open kisses to her body as the pleasure plateaued then eased.

When he finally pulled away from her body, she continued to spasm deliciously, deep in the center of her body. Her eyes fluttered open.

Chad still knelt on the floor beside the bed, between her knees, but his shoulders moved up and down as if he had run a race. Lora sat up and leaned toward him, tilting his chin up with her hand. "I've never…"

Her voice trailed off and she shook her head, because there were no words to express what she was feeling. Or maybe there were just too many. She felt awed, appreciative, decadent, guilty, satisfied.

Loving.

As she looked down his body and realized how achingly hard he was, flexing with every harsh breath, she had a moment's worry. Men in this state could be rough. But as her eyes lifted and connected to his, the worry drifted away. Chad Lowell would never hurt her. That certainty settled into her bones.

"I want you to make love to me now," she whispered.

Chad's harshly restrained face crumpled into need as he allowed her to guide him into the bed. When he opened his mouth to protest, she pressed her fingers to his lips. "We'll go slow. And if anything doesn't feel right, I'll stop."

"And I will too," he promised. "No matter where we are or how close I am, I will stop."

She smiled through misty eyes. "I know you will. I have no doubts about that."

Lora laid down on the mattress and held her arms out to him, but he shook his head. Lying down beside her, he pressed a lingering kiss to her lips. "First time is all you baby. Show me your best cowgirl impression."

Laughing in delight, she pushed to her knees, then slipped one leg over his lean hips. She knew he was doing this for her comfort, not his, but she appreciated it. His cock flexed toward her, as if it knew that relief was near. Lora lowered her weight to Chad's thighs, below his groin and cupped his erection in her hands. Several nights ago she'd masturbated him to completion, and the knowledge that she could do that at any time pleased her greatly. If things did fall through and she freaked out, she could… *No. That wasn't going to happen.*

Lifting her foot to rest beside his hip, she opened herself for him, lifted, and sank down. For several long seconds, she stayed where she was, waiting for panic to shatter the moment. It never happened. Instead, her body shifted down against his tighter, closer, widening to accept him.

"Can I hold your hips?" he gasped.

Lora nodded, too caught up in the sensations to answer him any other way. Strong, lean fingers gripped her hips, with the thumbs teasing just above the cleft where they were joined. But he didn't make her move. He just held her and allowed her to make the next move.

Seated as deeply as he was inside her, Lora felt every heartbeat that quivered down his shaft. Lifting her hips, she paused at the tip, almost releasing him, then glided back down. Oh, god. She repeated the maneuver until she was riding him, with no pauses between. That felt…sublime. She sped up, losing focus of everything around her except the building need that had to be met. The first orgasm he'd given her had been amazing, but this one felt like it would be truly awe-inspiring.

Chad gasped beneath her and she felt his hands move up her body to cup her bouncing breasts. Lora moaned, curling her body tighter against his as that brilliant need flared brighter. The sound of their skin slapping together was as sexy as anything she'd ever heard before, but she needed something more. Chad lifted his hips and braced, his need as great as her own, and she had that extra little something she needed. A sensation unlike any other made her cry out, arching on top of him, the orgasm slamming through her till she thought she would splinter apart. Chad groaned beneath her. His hands left her breasts to grip her hips again, bowing up as if to seat himself as deeply as he could as his climax overtook him. Lora felt his ejaculation surge inside her and he cried out, every muscle straining across his chest as the orgasm played out.

Lora lost herself to the movement of their bodies, tears dripping down her cheeks as she reclaimed her sensuality. As Chad relaxed into a quivering heap beneath her, Lora felt some intangible chain fall away from her being.

Chad noticed her tears and sat up beneath her to cup her face. "What did I do? Did I hold your hips too tightly?"

She shook her head but he didn't seem to see.

"I shouldn't have pushed there at the end. I'm so sorry, Lora. I couldn't help myself."

"Chad, stop it. I'm not crying because you hurt me. I'm crying because it was more beautiful than I ever could have imagined. You need to not freak out every time I react to something. You're making me grow, and I appreciate that more than I can ever tell you."

Cupping his face in her shaking hands, she was overcome with such a sense of rightness it made fresh tears course down her cheeks as she leaned in to kiss him. Chad cradled her to his broad chest and fell over to the mattress, holding her hips to him so that he didn't slip out of her. As they curled up on the sheets, they fell asleep sharing breath and space, and it was the most content she'd ever been.

CHAPTER FIFTEEN

LORA STARED AT the man and woman sitting on her couch in the living room a few days later. They both wore blue suits, though the woman's was markedly more feminine. Even without being introduced, she had known these were the lawyers from New York. Very high-paid lawyers, judging by the way they carried themselves. But the shrewd look in their eyes as they looked around her house made her cautious. The looks had screamed disdain.

Chad stood just behind her chair, arms crossed, expression forbidding. He didn't like these people being in her house any more than she did.

"Ms. O'Neil, before Mrs. Malone died, she had modified her will. Her son, well," the man, Doug Sanders or something, trailed off. "In light of the series of events he has been involved with recently, Mrs. Malone had the foresight to change some things, effective weeks ago. The most important being that Derek Malone was no longer her heir."

Lora's eyebrows popped up in surprise. "She disowned him?"

The female lawyer, Nilson, *or was it Nelson?,* nodded her sleek blond head.

"Wow." Lora shook her head. "He was her only child. I never would have thought she'd do that."

"Well," Sanders sighed, "she did. Quite emphatically, I might add."

"Mrs. Malone did not plan to retire from her position at the company in the near future, though she gave directives in case something happened to her. She expected those directives to be used years from now."

Lora cocked her head. "What directives are you talking about?"

The two lawyers looked at each other. Sanders then turned his gaze to her. "She left the company to her only living, recognized heir… her granddaughter."

She stared at him for several long seconds, trying to figure out who that was. When it dawned on her, she could only shake her head. Chad and Palmer had said something about this days ago, but she never imagined it would actually happen. "She left the company to Mercy?"

The two of them nodded together.

"She's six. What the hell is she supposed to do with it?"

Mr. Sanders lifted a brow at her. "Well, the granddaughter is too young to run day to day operations, obviously, so that aspect would be left up to the child's legal guardian."

Lora's consciousness shifted for a moment and she could find no words for the shock pouring through her. Chad's hand on her shoulder grounded her and she looked up at him.

"That was why he was after her," he told her quietly.

All of the puzzle pieces began to fall together. Rosalind's attempt to reconnect with Mercy and Derek's interest in her. It was all because of the company.

"I thought the FBI had been investigating the company."

The lawyers shifted uncomfortably but Nilson dug into her briefcase. "This is a deposition by the company. I'll wade through all the convoluted talk and just tell you that basically, the illegal dealings and money issues stopped when Derek left the company. The FBI has released the Malone Corporation from all liability. I will say that restitution was paid to the affected account holders and the charges against the company itself have been dropped."

"Holy shit," Chad breathed.

Lora was thinking the same thing, just couldn't get her tongue moving to say it. "Um, I'm not a company CEO. I'm a high school secretary and mother. How on earth am I supposed to run this company?"

The lawyers looked at each other, and Sanders took the lead. "Well, Ms. O'Neil, you would have to appoint a proxy to do business in your stead. Or hire a reliable business manager."

Shaking her head, she leaned back against the chair. "I wouldn't even know where to hire one of those."

Mr. Sanders smiled at her kindly. Lora expected to see shark's teeth behind his lips, but no. "We've been the Malone lawyers for a long time Ms. O'Neil. We are here to help."

"I truly appreciate that, Mr. Sanders. Thank you."

His smile dimmed. "It's Samson, Ms. O'Neil. Doug Samson."

Lora cringed. "I'm so sorry, Mr. Samson. I have a lot on my mind right now."

The lawyer gave her a tight smile.

"I think," Chad interjected, "Ms. O'Neil is going to have to think about things and get back to you. In the meantime, why don't you look for a few options for her?"

The lawyers did their bobble-head nods and gathered their briefcases. Unfortunately they left stacks of information for her to read.

Chad ushered them out of the house and turned to lean against the door, one brow raised.

Walking across the room to him, she wrapped her arms around his waist. "The man is haunting me," she sighed.

Laughing, he squeezed her and pressed a kiss to the top of her head. "No, he just did what a lot of exes do when they die: leave a lot of crap for those left behind. We'll deal with it. Or appoint somebody else to deal with it."

She shook her head against the solid wall of his chest and leaned back enough to look at him. "You are amazing. Do you know that? They wouldn't have even made it in my door if you hadn't been here and you asked what I needed to know. Thank you."

"I'm always ready to help you. Always. I love you. How could I do otherwise?"

The words rolled over her and she couldn't believe them, not yet. "We've only known each other five weeks. Isn't it too soon to be professing love?"

Chad grinned down at her, shaking his head. "Maybe for you but not me. I started to fall in love with you before I even met you. I knew the kind of woman you were."

Laughing, she ducked her head and tightened her arms around his waist, running her hands down his back and tight butt cheeks. In response, his hips shifted toward her, excitement building between them.

They'd slept together all last night. And the night before. And the night before that. The sex had been cataclysmic, but the cuddling afterwards had been sublime. They suited each other so well. They were narrowing down what triggered negative reactions from her and they worked around them, and she felt more free than she ever had.

Chad took some time off from LNF and encouraged her not to go back to work. The school had promised to give her time to deal with what was going on and she was taking them up on it.

The first day they spent together lazing around the house. They took a walk around the block and Lora tried to change her hyper-attentive ways. The second day he showed up, he brought Mercy a bright blue bike with training wheels. When he lifted it over the side of the truck, Mercy had given a little scream. "I've always wanted a bike," she cried.

Lora gave her a look because this was news to her. "Why didn't you say something?"

Mercy blinked up at her. "I didn't want you to have to worry about me."

Tears came to her eyes at the amount of maturity in her child's expression. "Well, our life is changing. If you want something like that, you tell me."

Mercy grinned and nodded her head, then turned her attention to the bike.

The third day they'd spent together at the zoo, navigating screaming crowds of school children. Lora was truly frazzled by the time they made it all the way around the loop, and if it hadn't been for Chad's endless supply of Starlight spearmints and buffering hugs in the midst of the crowds she would have melted down.

Later on that night they ordered pizza to be delivered. Another first time event. Mercy hid behind Chad's legs as he paid for and took the boxes, shut the door and locked it. She let go when he walked the pizzas to the coffee table and set them down. As they pulled pieces from the box and munched happily, Mercy looked up at her. "Mom, I want something."

Lora grinned at her daughter, knowing that at some point she would have to curb the 'I-wants', but not just yet. "What's that, honey?"

"I want Chad to stay here with us. All the time."

Chad went still beside her, but when she looked up, he was grinning at Mercy. He glanced at her, brows raised, to check her response.

Lora sucked in a breath, knowing that she was on uncharted, sandy ground. In her deepest heart, she wanted the same thing, but did she dare say it? As she looked into the gentle reassurance in his expression, she knew it would just take a tiny leap of courage. "Chad, would you like to stay here with us?"

Lora forgot how to breathe as she waited for some kind of response. Chad seemed to be dragging out the anticipation though. After several long seconds, he nodded his head. But he held up a cautioning finger. "I would love to be a kept man, but it kind of goes three ways." Moving from the couch, he went down on one knee in front of Mercy, sitting on the floor. He reached into his pocket and pulled out a tiny gold ring. "Mercy O'Neil, will you marry me and be my awesome daughter? To have and to hold, in muddy times and clean? And help me keep your mother happy and safe?"

Mercy nodded her head as hard as she could, laughing and crying at the same time. She flung her arms around Chad's neck and sobbed.

Lora's eyes were leaking as well, so overcome with love that he had thought to include Mercy. But then he turned his damp eyes to her and she was rocked with the deep-in-her-heart knowledge of what was coming next. Levering to his feet, still holding Mercy against him, he circled the table to kneel in front of her. Then he reached into that pocket again and pulled out a shining white gold solitaire ring. His eyes incredibly kind, he held it out. "Lora O'Neil, would you do me the honor of wearing my ring? I promise to protect you and love you as long as I'm allowed, in whatever way I'm allowed, and I promise to always have Starlight mints at the ready."

Lora wept with fear and joy and laughter, knowing that she would never find another man like him. Nodding, she held her shaking hand out and allowed him to slip the ring onto her finger. Then she whipped her arms around his neck, and the three of them rocked back and forth. He pulled back enough to capture her lips with his own, sealing the love between them.

"No rush," he murmured in her ear. "We'll take it a day at a time. Just know that I love you with all my heart."

"And I love you," she whispered. "More than I ever dared dream I could."

Mercy wiggled to get free. "Can I eat my pizza now?"

Laughing, they all separated to finish their meal, but Lora and Chad sat hip to hip, basking in their adoration for each other.

THE END...

And now for a little taste of Embattled SEAL, Harper's story…

Five million thoughts raced through her head as Cat shoved her way into the hospital room. She had no idea who the men were, only that they were keeping her from her husband.

As she stepped to the side of the bed, she wanted to jerk him up and hold him against her, make him open his beautiful silver eyes and tell her he loved her.

But he hadn't done that for a long time.

Her eyes catalogued the machines. He was on a vent, saline dripped steadily into his arm along with another clear fluid she couldn't see the sticker of. Probably some kind of pain med.

There was a scuff on his heavy jaw and dark hair had already begun to darken his jaw. They'd left the johnny hanging, untied, merely draped over his massive chest. They probably couldn't have tied it even if he'd been vertical.

Lifting the edge of the fabric, she found several heavy-duty bandages high on his chest. She looked at the men. "Are one of you a doctor? Tell me what happened."

All three of them stood at the end of the bed, watching her. But the one with the cane spoke up. "I'm Harper's employer, Duncan Wilde. Would you explain who you are please?"

Cat looked the man up and down. Forties, salt and pepper hair, a little grayer on the sides. Kind, experienced brown eyes. "I'm his wife. Estranged for the past year and a half, but still his wife. Why didn't you call me if you're his employer?"

The man shifted against his black cane. "Honestly, there was no beneficiary contact in his employment file. Who did call you?"

Cat blinked. "I think the hospital. The VA I mean. Not this one."

The other gray haired man spoke up. "I called the VA to let them know he had been injured and to get his medical records. They must have called her." He stepped forward, hand outstretched. "Dr. Reynolds. I just operated on your…husband. He's had significant damage…"

Cat struggled to focus as the doctor went through the list of major and minor injuries, but her eyes kept drifting back to his form on the bed. He seemed bulkier to her, even lying the way he was. But his face seemed leaner. Deep grooves bracketed his mouth and her fingers itched to stroke them away. Damn, after eighteen months she should have been pissed, and in the back of her mind she knew she was, but she was more happy to see him right now. Thrilled, actually.

The doctor was still going on, cautioning her about getting her hopes up. She laughed and shook her head at the man. "You have no idea what you're talking about. Preston will be fine."

If you would like to read more about the disabled veterans of the Lost and Found Investigative Service, check out these books:

The Embattled Road (FREE prequel)
Embattled Hearts – Book 1
Embattled Minds – Book 2
SEALed with a Kiss Anthology
Her Forever Hero

Other books by J.M. Madden

Second Time Around
A Needful Heart
Wet Dream
Love On the Line – Book 1
Love On the Line – Book 2
The Awakening Society – FREE!
Tempt Me
Urban Moon Anthology

CONNECT WITH J.M. MADDEN

If you'd like to connect with me on social media and keep updated on my releases, try these links:

Newsletter

http://www.jmmadden.com/newsletter.htm

Website

http://www.jmmadden.com/

Facebook

https://www.facebook.com/jmmaddenauthor

Twitter

@authorjmmadden

And of course you can always email me at authorjmmadden@gmail.com

About the Author

I am a wife and mother of two. I am a stay at home writer, which I dearly love, and I recently added the title USA Today Bestselling author to my moniker.

I was a Deputy Sheriff in Ohio for nine years, and I found myself tapping that experience as I wrote Second Time Around, my very first book. No, I didn't tackle and cuff my husband, although there was that time in K-mart… Anyway, it was quite a change going from writing technical reports with diagrams, witness statements, inventories, etc., that would stand up in court to writing contemporary romance. I've always written, though, and it was always a dream to do something with that huge, leaning stack of spiral bound notebooks.

I've now published 15 books, with many more on the way. I thank you so much for taking an interest in my work!

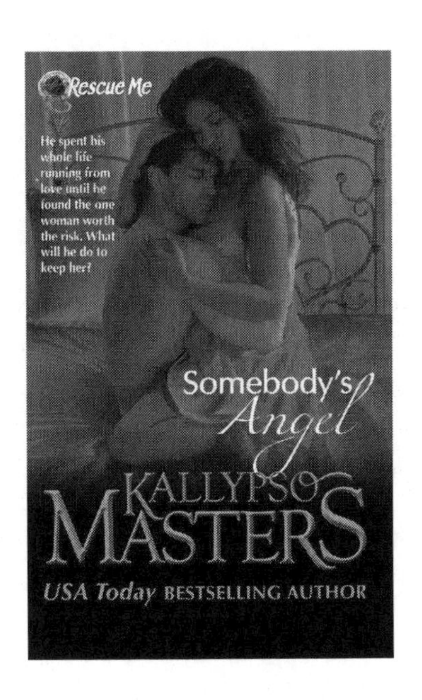

Excerpt from
***Somebody's Angel* (Rescue Me Saga #4)**
by Kallypso Masters

Available now in e-book and trade paperback

Description:

When Marc d'Alessio first rescued the curvaceous and spirited Italian Angelina Giardano at the Masters at Arms Club (in *Nobody's Angel*), he never expected her to turn his safe, controlled life upside down and pull at his long-broken heartstrings. Months later, the intense fire of their attraction still rages, but something holds him back from committing to her completely. Worse, secrets and memories from his past join forces to further complicate his relationships with family, friends, and his beautiful angel.

Angelina cannot give all of herself to someone who hides himself from her. She loves Marc, the BDSM world he brought her into, and the way their bodies respond to one another, but she needs more. Though she destroyed the wolf mask he once wore, only he can remove the mask he dons daily to hide his emotions. In a desperate attempt to break through his defenses and reclaim her connection to the man she loves, she attempts a full frontal assault that sends him into a fast retreat, leaving her nobody's angel once again.

Marc finds that running to the mountains no longer gives him solace but instead leaves him empty and alone. Angelina is the one woman worth the risk of opening his heart. Will he risk everything to become the man she deserves and the man he wants to be?

ABOUT THE RESCUE ME SAGA: These books are not stand-alone stories and should be read in order. Characters will recur in later books to deal with further issues in their lives as the saga continues and each book builds upon all previous ones. Sometimes main characters even need another book to help resolve major issues affecting their relationships.

CONTENT WARNING: These books are intended for mature adult readers who are not offended by profanity and graphic (but never gratuitous!) sex scenes. Due to the emotional way in which the author presents the subject matter in the characters' lives (past and present), the books might cause triggers while reading. Please click the preview to read the Author's Notes at the beginnings of each book before reading.

Excerpt from an interrogation scene in which Adam, his retired master sergeant, uses SERE School tactics from their Marine Corps training to get at what has Marc stuck in the present and unable to move forward.

Adam knew what had to be done to break him—humiliation and demoralization would play a part in it, for sure. Marc would gladly forego food and water if it would help him reach the breaking point faster, not that Adam had offered him anything to eat. Food he could live without, but he'd been given the bare minimum of water he'd need to survive without having his kidneys shut down.

No way did he see how this scene was going to accomplish anything Marc wanted to uncover. He trusted Adam too much to suspend belief and see him as a heartless inquisitor. Besides, how was he supposed to dig up answers if Adam asked so few questions? He'd spent a lifetime burying shit like that memory of Gino and their lair.

A lair? Who called their childhood hideout a lair? He wondered what it had looked like and regretted that Adam had disturbed the memory before he'd seen it again with his mind's eye.

Gone. Again.

Adam said nothing. Marc stood, waiting. What if the scene was over? Would Adam give up on him? No! They hadn't gotten anywhere! Disappointment flooded his senses that another attempt at getting to the root of his problems had failed.

"Arms in front."

Adrenaline pumped through his veins instantly. This scene wasn't over! Marc extended his arms in front of him, anxious to continue. His shoulders ached from having been in the same unnatural position for however long. He shook them out before presenting them to Adam. At least, he assumed Adam stood in front of him. That's where his voice had come from on the last command. The room was still pitch black, his hood firmly in place.

Adam wrapped something around Marc's left wrist and pulled tight. A cuff. Adam easily slipped his finger between Marc's skin and the padded leather. Not too tight. He then cuffed the right wrist. A raspy noise and jerking motion with his hands told him Adam was threading rope through the D-rings.

"Lift your arms."

Marc did so and soon found himself restrained from the ceiling, an eyebolt, he supposed. Adam adjusted the ropes until only Marc's toes made contact with the floor. The strain on his arms hurt more, because this was the opposite of how his arms had been restrained so far.

Silence. No more questions. No commands.

Tick-tock. Tick-tock.

Even the clock became white noise after a while. The quiet left Marc sinking slowly into his own dark thoughts. Only this time, memories of Gino with Melissa clouded his mind.

"She's not worth this, Marc. Why don't you think with your head for once, you asshole?"

Gino slammed him against the wall and restrained Marc's arms above his head.

Somehow, Marc managed to shake him off, or perhaps Gino released him. Marc surveyed the scene in the bedroom, his chest heaving as he gasped for air. Where had Melissa gone? After what he'd just seen, did he care? Marc grabbed his jacket and left Gino behind. If he wanted her so badly, then he could have her. Fuck them both!

Marc's head nodded, and he jerked back into his stance.

Slap!

The sting of the tawse across his bare ass stung momentarily, but he soon grew too tired to care. Definitely a tawse, though. He'd felt it before. When?

How long had he been hanging in this position? Sleep wasn't advisable if he wanted to keep from hanging by his wrists, so he fought to stay awake and try to keep his legs steady.

Adam made no sound at all. Was he even there? Surely, he was. Adam wouldn't abandon him, not like so many others had done in his life. His parents. Melissa. Gino.

Angelina.

His chest ached at the thought that she'd walked away like all the rest.

Marc tried to adjust his position but had very little wiggle room. Surely Adam would cut him down soon. How long would he have to remain in this position? He fought the urge to call out to his friend, not wanting to mess with the scene. Adam would interact with him when the time was right. He knew how to break a man in an interrogation.

Tick-tock. Tick-tock.

Crack!

The sting of something on his shoulder dissipated more slowly than that from the tawse. *Merda*, it stung. Marc fought his restraints, shifting on his toes again to relieve the strain on his shoulders.

Adam! It took a while, but Marc's mind registered he was no longer alone. The sense of relief washing over him made the sting in his shoulders more bearable for a moment. Adam hadn't left or, if he had, he'd returned. How long had Marc slept before Adam had woken him so abruptly? His arms ached from hanging.

"Enjoy your nap?"

He was told to answer truthfully. "Yes, Sir."

"Good, because that'll be the last one you'll have for a while. Time for some music."

Adam placed a headset over his ears. The padded headphones masked some of the ambient noise in the room. Marc waited, unsure what music his master sergeant had chosen. He expected loud and obnoxious if they were using sleep-deprivation tactics. Marc preferred Italian opera or…

The first chords of the "music" blasted forth. Way too loud. A demonic voice screamed into his ear. Who could possibly deem this music?

Tangled in a web of reversed lies
and my reflection is the one that's on my side.

Marc's nerves, already on edge from a lack of sleep and time/space disorientation, screamed, too. One cacophonous "song" bled into the next. Damián had to have done this. Did that mean Adam had told him about the scene? Was he one of the interrogators Adam referred to earlier? The man was into serious metal music. This crap made Marc's jaws ache. How could anyone call this shit music?

Marc couldn't always tell when one track ended and another began but needed to keep his focus. He guessed there had been eight or nine of them. If each lasted three or four minutes, he'd been listening for twenty-five to thirty-five minutes. Focusing on the number of songs could help him keep track of time. Not that he had any idea how much time had passed already. He needed to keep his mind occupied.

Focus.

Time—and the noise—droned on without a break. Eleven. Twelve. Thirteen tracks.

I am a dominant gene—live as I die

Was he a Dominant? He didn't have a clue.

Slap!

The tawse stung his thigh, jerking Marc awake. How the hell had he fallen asleep with that god-awful crap blaring in his ears? Marc couldn't think about the present, much less the past. Fuck. He'd lost count of the number of tracks. How long had he slept this time? Was Adam waking him immediately or letting him rest some to skew his ability to judge the passage of time?

I can bury the hatchet and let some shit go
But I got too many grudges to hold!

He'd never let go of one grudge. Awfully hard to bury the hatchet with someone who didn't exist anymore.

Gino, why did you betray me?

Slap!

Fuck, that hurt! Same spot on his thigh, still sore from the last slap. Did that mean he hadn't remained awake very long? He'd never played with a tawse and had no idea how long the sting lasted. Yet it was oddly familiar.

He needed to stay awake. He hadn't even been down here all that long—had he? Hell, he had no fucking clue what time—or day—it was anymore. Every time Marc's head nodded and he dozed off, Adam slapped his ass or thigh with the tawse and woke him. He also couldn't control his yawns, although moving his jaw was difficult under the tight hood.

Tired. Bone tired. After a hellacious week of very little sleep, being further deprived of rest while having his senses bombarded by this incessant noise left his body and mind screaming for escape.

No way out. He'd given Adam complete authority—no, control. Adam didn't remove the headphones to speak to him. Instead, he just kept waking him with the tawse. At least he assumed Adam was doing it. He needed to sleep, though, and if this went beyond eighteen hours or so, Adam would have to bring Damián or Grant from the club to wield the implement in order for Adam to take breaks.

Marc hadn't been smacked by the tawse for such a long time, he wondered if Adam was still here.

Sleep is overrated.

How many times had he heard Adam say that? So perhaps he hadn't taken a sleep break. As a Navy Corpsman, he'd seen Marines appear awake who no longer responded to wakeful stimuli. Micro-sleeps lasted mere seconds. Had he zoned out in one of those?

What if Adam had left him here alone, though? Marc didn't want to be left alone down here.

His mouth was dry, but no one had offered another drink since the first one however long ago. *Auuuggghhhhh.* A cramp in his right calf had him screaming in pain, but he couldn't put enough pressure on it to relieve it. Would Adam come to his aid or leave him dangling from the ceiling?

"Leg cramp, Sir!"

A tug on the rope above him and Marc felt himself start to fall before his back was slammed against the wall. He'd been cut down. Adam hadn't left him! Wrists still cuffed, arms aching at yet another change in position, he stood as Adam massaged the cramp in his calf away. He gritted his teeth as Adam's hands caused more pain than comfort at first, but slowly the cramp eased.

Adam, or whoever it was, broke contact, and Marc continued to lean against the wall, uncertain his legs would hold him without the crutch. The hood lifted off his lower face, and a cold, hard plastic bottle pressed against his lips. He opened wide to gulp down the precious water. When no more poured from the bottle, his tongue reached out to lick the lip of the bottle for any remaining drops. *Dio*, he wanted more!

Marc waited as the minutes—or hours?—ticked away.

The headset continued to blare into his ears. If Adam said anything, Marc couldn't hear. No one touched him any further.

Abandoned. Again.

Where did that thought come from? Adam wouldn't abandon him. Even if he had to leave, Marc was merely alone, not *abandoned.* He had spent time alone many times. Sometimes he preferred that to being with people.

Until Angelina.

Learn more about Kally and her books at http://kallypsomasters.com.

Made in the USA
Charleston, SC
14 October 2015